# THE
# SHAPE
# OF
# WHAT
# REMAINS

*The Shape of What Remains* is a work of fiction. Names, characters, places, and incidents are the product of the author's imagination or are used fictitiously. Any resemblance to actual events, locales, or persons, living or dead, is coincidental.

Copyright © 2025 Lisa C. Taylor

Between the Lines Publishing and its imprints support the right to free expression and the value of copyright. The scanning, uploading, and distribution of this book without permission is a theft of the author's intellectual property. If you would like permission to use material from the book (other than for review purposes), please contact info@btwnthelines.com.

Liminal Books
Between the Lines Publishing
1769 Lexington Ave North #286
Roseville MN 55113
btwnthelines.com

First Published: February 2025

Liminal Books is an imprint of Between the Lines Publishing. The Liminal Books name and logo are trademarks of Between the Lines Publishing.

ISBN: (paperback) 978-1-965059-20-3

ISBN: (eBook) 978-1-965059-21-0

The publisher is not responsible for websites (or their content) that are not owned by the publisher.

# THE
# SHAPE
# OF
# WHAT
# REMAINS

Lisa C. Taylor

*For Russ*
**Thanks for the soft landing.**

Brief Clearing

The world has left me scars of hail,
clotted snow, and the hanging
tongue of August. The brief clearing
is the same color
as your eyes and though
I implore it to stay blue,
it does not listen.

Lisa C. Taylor, from *Necessary Silence*, 2013, Arlen House

# Chapter 1

At first, there were pharmaceuticals, Prozac and Zoloft. Elevate those serotonin levels, chemicals to rearrange my brain after I retrieved a blood-spattered *Dora the Explorer* lunchbox from the road.

"I don't like how the drugs make me feel," I told Luke after I tapered off them.

His lips were a thin line. Wrong answer.

The problem was, I *wanted* the pain. It was my monument to Serena, better than the granite marker Luke put in our garden next to our yellow rose bush. *Serena Joy Calvano, beloved sister and daughter*. My grieving group said a physical marker would give me a place where I could sit and talk to her. I knew she wasn't there, her ashes scattered in the ocean off Cape Cod on the boat ride we took ten summers ago. We moved that marker twice, always planting a yellow rose bush next to it since Serena loved roses and the color yellow.

Each day, I would set up a list for myself and promise to accomplish two things even if one of them was getting out of bed. I was trying to finish my book, but I would have gladly abandoned my papers and sworn off research for one more walk in the woods with her. Once we uncovered a robin's nest with a cracked blue egg. When we picked it up, a little piece fell away. She carried that piece of eggshell in her pocket, wrapped in a Kleenex, and brought it to first grade.

For three months, I slept in her bed, clutched the stuffed monkey she held close every night. I inhaled her scent until it faded. One day, after returning home from a dental appointment, her bed was gone. The books on her white bookshelf, the lamp with cut out stars, and the purple curtains—all gone. The closet was empty of tiny dresses and shirts, and her white dresser that I had stenciled with stars, had disappeared.

"I took everything to Goodwill," Luke said. "I'm sorry I didn't tell you, but it's been months, Teresa. You need to sleep in our bed."

That never happened. I moved into the guest room, and when we relocated, I set up my own room that I pretended was like Serena's room, except it wasn't and never could be. The indentation that had remained in her bed sheets flattened and the sheets were washed before Luke donated everything. There was no way to keep any part of her alive.

It's been ten years and some days I still want to dive into the ocean that swallowed her ashes, the wind kicking up a gray cloud until the fine dust of my little girl dissipated in green waves. Luke, our son Wyatt, and I all held hands, swaying and slightly nauseous with the tide. Luke read an excerpt from *Winnie-the-Pooh*, a better thing than some religious drivel about Serena being too good for this world or becoming God's littlest angel. There will never be a reason for the pain that made a permanent home in my body, visiting me during a television commercial where a little girl is ecstatic that her mother is coping with seasonal allergies, or in the park when a child begs her father for ice cream, unaware that I am sitting on a nearby bench about to fall apart.

Luke never blamed me outright, but he asked *didn't you see the truck?* I see it in my dreams. It is behind me in the grocery store, in back of the classroom when I teach. The truck is parked outside when I'm at my damn book group. Yes, I see the fucking truck. It won't bring my baby back. The driver didn't even stop. A rabbit or a squirrel. I used to call her Bunny. Serena died on a perfect blue-sky morning in early November. Dried leaves and road dust. I'll never have another child, and I'll never love anyone as much as I loved Serena. Wyatt knows this. Luke does too, though I pretend it's my secret. He stopped brushing my hair, massaging my shoulders, and started staying late at the university. When I spotted him in Delarosa's Restaurant across from a glossy-haired woman, I kept on walking. Pretending is a game that younger couples play. I lost Serena on a day when fair weather clouds were bloated enough to block the sun. I will never be able to un-see the truck or her broken body in the road.

Two years after I lost Serena my mother-in-law, Bess, suggested a book group.

"Stories, Teresa. You, of all people, understand the power of stories."

Her book group met at the community center. The one I signed up for traveled to various bookstores, sometimes meeting up with a regional group.

"I'm no good with strangers," I told Bess.

"That's not true and you know it. You have a new group of students every semester. People who join book groups love to read. You'll have that in common."

# The Shape of What Remains

I never thought of literature as a topic of discussion outside of class but since staying in my bathrobe until midday wasn't working, I gave it a try. Eight years later, I'm still losing myself in tragedies I wish I'd written instead of lived.

Today the book group is huddled in a semi-circle in the front of the library meeting room, and I think *we're all just children wearing adult bodies*. When local members Susan, Kandi, and Tim decide to go out for dinner after the meeting I tell myself it's better than going home. I wait for them in my Honda with the defroster on which is kind of like being in a heated hamster cage. Finally, they pull up ahead of me, all three of them in the same car, smiling and laughing. Why wasn't I asked to carpool? I imagine their conversation.

*I tried to lose her, but you know how she is.*

*Just make the best of it.*

I pull alongside Kandi's red Mini Cooper. Tim is waving out the window in case that car wasn't enough of an emblem for me to notice. This is an opportunity to be included and I'm going with it. What else do I have to do? Check my messages to see if Luke called? My cell phone. I turned the ringer off during the meeting. I grope in my voluminous handbag on the passenger seat, turn it on just in case. No comforting chirp to indicate I missed a call, or he left a message. Clearly, I'm no fun to be around, just ask Susan, Kandi, and Tim. Shit. They're taking a right turn so fast I think for a minute they are going to hit the sidewalk. *Slow down.* Sharp left into the parking lot where Kandi pulls into the last space. I park, probably illegally, at the pizza parlor lot across the street.

They're waiting for me at the corner. The rain has picked up again, November rain, the worst kind, sharp and unforgiving.

"You know how to get back to the highway, don't you?" Tim looks concerned. I point to the right and he nods. There's a sign, jackass. A child could see the sign. Okay, lighten up. He's being nice, showing concern. I'm the one with no sense of direction. Before GPS, I got lost regularly.

Osaka is brightly lit with multi-colored Japanese lanterns lining the walls. Chrome and lacquer. I ordered sake though I have to drive home. I need the bright bite of alcohol.

"Good meeting, huh?" Kandi furrows her brow, pushes back a hank of gilded hair.

She's wearing a long coral sweater with a silk scarf over leggings with heeled boots. Even her nails are perfect coral ovals.

"I thought Pam did a great job moderating though I didn't enjoy the book. Phillip Roth needed to take a break once in a while," says Susan.

"Disagree." Tim is washing his hands with one of the warm washcloths they bring us on a little ceramic tray. "The end of *The Dying Animal* showed his range. That menstruation scene was amazing."

Tim is the lone male in our group, a late forties software engineer with a disabled wife. He is also the only one who thinks writing about menstruation is art.

"Range? Come on. A horny over-the-hill professor fucks a twenty-four-year-old and you call that literary range? I call it wishful thinking," Kandi says.

Susan puts her clump of a washcloth back on the tray, unwraps her chopsticks. She is the oldest, expecting her first grandchild in March. Still working as an English teacher in a private school, she lives in a condo. Her husband left her for his law partner ten years ago. At least they were the same age, also the same sex.

# The Shape of What Remains

"When Consuelo gets cancer, the game changes. Don't you think?" Tim says.

I nod vigorously. I'm a Roth fan even though I admit that anyone as prolific as he was produced a fair number of clunkers. I like his willingness to experiment with narrative voice, something I wish I could do, even in speaking.

"See, Teresa agrees with me."

Everyone looks at me. Fortunately, our waiter comes up and we're quickly perusing the menu to get him to go away. I pour tea for everyone.

"I think he confronts his own mortality throughout the book, but Consuelo's disease pushes him in a different direction. Suddenly it isn't just about sex. He finds his own humanity through her disease. I almost liked him by the end of the book," I say. I have to pee but I'm reluctant to ask Tim to move so I can get out.

"Remember what Pam said? How critics panned this book? They felt he was at his most neurotic, analyzing his alter ego, David Kapesh." Kandi sips her tea then pats her perfect bow mouth with the cloth napkin. A little kiss stain remains.

The waiter plunks down multiple enamel plates of food.

I stuff a peanut avocado maki in my mouth, wash it down with cheap sake. Once again, I'm invisible. They've moved on to Elizabeth Strout's book, a collection of linked stories. Phillip Roth was tall, good-looking for an elderly man when he died. Reportedly, he was ornery, didn't like to give interviews. I never minded his meanderings; in fact, I liked them. As base as David Kapesh was, he understood the fleeting quality of life.

Susan's Teriyaki Salmon looks like it is still alive, the tail attached and dark with sauce. She breaks into it enthusiastically. Eating is disgusting, piling food into these holes in our faces. Tim delicately picks up a shrimp, dips it into mustard sauce. I go back to stuffing cylindrical maki slices into my mouth. Dip, stuff, chew.

"Teresa will know." They turn to me and I wonder what it is I know.

"When is our next meeting?"

Kandi is right. I do know. It's the first Saturday in December. It's an hour drive for me but what else would I be doing on a Saturday night? My son Wyatt doesn't call. At college there are better things to do than call one's mother on a weekend. Luke will be pretending to be engrossed in his research while he's fucking someone. I know he's fucking someone. Does he give her back massages? Wash her hair in the shower? I close my eyes for a second, imagining his long fingers massaging my scalp. He used to hold out my terry robe and I'd step into it, feeling like royalty. Now I am the discarded wife. I hate the human race.

I throw down a twenty on the bill, knowing I've overpaid. I don't want them to think I'm cheap or that I care that Tim ordered the sashimi appetizer and Kandi had two glasses of wine. Someone is dying right now. Not Consuela or David Kapesh but someone real. A child, perhaps, or a young person with dreams of a future. People run over each other without realizing it. They don't stop to see anything because they think where they're going is so damn important.

Maybe Serena would have cured cancer or written a literary classic. Since we moved, no one knows about her except Wyatt and Luke and they're not talking. We don't discuss it anymore. For me, it's as if I've lost a limb or an organ. No surgery or therapy can fix it. I'll always be disabled.

We hug goodbye. Kandi promises to call. Tim's hug feels a little long, urgent even. I swear I feel him getting hard as he pushes his body against mine. Maybe I'm imagining it; it's been so long since I've been with a man. I know his wife isn't getting better; she's in a wheelchair most of the time now. He'd be interesting if I was interested. Maybe if I was divorced, we would go out occasionally, chat online about movies and books, spend civilized nights together in a clean hotel room.

When I close the door, a little bell tinkles. The rain has stopped, and the three-quarter moon has a rim of cloud around its surface. My cell phone rings and I can see that it's Luke. A tiny reserve of hope that I keep in my chest pops up, but I push it down. Serena would be sixteen this year. We'd probably be arguing about learner's permits and curfews. Maybe she'd be embarrassed by me, or I'd hate her clothing and wild boyfriend or girlfriend. There's no logic to love or death. How can you blame David Kapesh for grabbing onto every supple body he could find? I picture Luke's wire-rimmed glasses, intelligent eyes. We might have been something different. I put the phone to my ear, which I guess is what Kandi would call *wishful thinking*.

"Are you on your way?"

"Yeah, book group. What's up?"

"Nothing. Just want to talk. See you when you get home."

"Wyatt okay?"

"I'd assume. Nothing to worry about, Tess."

Talk? Have we spoken in complete sentences in the last ten years? Maybe he's going to ask me for a divorce. He's fallen in love with his graduate assistant and is planning to remarry a less damaged woman. I'll be completely alone.

Of course, I get lost. Google Maps isn't working properly on my old phone. Luke insisted that buying a newer phone would be wasteful, but

I might as well have a flip phone for all of its usefulness. Finally, I see a sign for the highway, not a large green one like the one I missed but a small one for panicked travelers like me. I park in the driveway, a silhouette of light behind the shade. My phone rings again: Wyatt.

"Hi."

"Everything okay?" I swallow hard.

"Yeah. I have, there's...uh...a girl I met. We're kinda seeing each other. Can I bring her home this weekend?"

"Sure, honey, sure." *Fuck me! Wyatt has a girlfriend*.

"Uh, Ma. Don't make a big deal."

"What do you mean?" We don't care about his sexual orientation or the ethnicity of any person he might choose. I thought we had made that clear.

"Dunno. Her name is Belle."

Belle, like *Beauty and the Beast*?

"Means 'beautiful' in French," he says, like I don't know this.

"Nice." I'm done with the conversation though I feel guilty for wanting to hang up. "Do you want me to pick you up on Friday?"

"Yeah. Can Belle stay over till Sunday?"

"Sure. Whatever you want," I say.

Is he sleeping with Belle? Wyatt? The boy who still has a collection of "Lord of the Rings" figurines in his room? Hallelujah.

## Chapter 2

Luke sits there like an ottoman or maybe a credenza. There's a glass of wine and a bottle next to him on the table.

"Want some?" For a minute I think he's offering himself but then I realize he has picked up an empty glass and is beginning to fill it, as if my answer was understood to be in the affirmative.

"I guess." I take a tentative sip.

"Wyatt has a girlfriend named Belle and he's bringing her home this weekend. I think he's worried about us accepting her," I say.

Luke smiles. "Us? The most open-minded parents in Northbrook. What's wrong with her? Is she in a cult?"

"Don't know. She's named after a Disney character. How bad can she be?"

"That only indicates ignorant parents," he says.

"Do you suppose anyone thinks he's named after Wyatt Earp?"

"You're the one who picked that name. As I remember, you thought it was masculine without too much machismo," he says.

"I talked like that?"

Luke laughs like old times. Our living room looks like the living room of couples in Westbrook or Middlebury, except for the pictures of Wyatt growing older and no pictures of Serena as a baby, toddler, six-year-old. She would always be six even when we are retired, infirm, dying. What will it be like to hold a grandchild who is Serena's age? I wish I believed in reincarnation; what a comfort that could be, but I think that we just rot in the earth and return only in the sense that everything takes on another form. That's why I had Serena cremated. I couldn't bear the thought of her underground. She hated dark, dank places. It was the last motherly thing I could do. I cried so much I felt as if I had no insides left. The thought of my empty arms was unbearable. The Compassionate Friends told me that was normal though it probably had an expiration date which I'm sure I've exceeded.

"The Compassionate Friends is about transforming the pain of grief into the elixir of hope."
– Rev. Simon Stephens, founder, The Compassionate Friends

What exactly is "the elixir of hope"? I don't think I've found it. There is no product that can mitigate the impact. Sure, there was talk of having another child, I was young enough. I couldn't bring myself to carry within me the vulnerability and possibility of loss. I'd hover over the child, never let them out of my sight and even then, tragedy might strike. It could be a disease or an act of violence like the horrible fate of the children at Sandy Hook or Uvalde. No, I'm done with loving that much.

When I met Luke, I fell hard. Those flecked hazel eyes of his and the habit he had of pulling books down from the shelves of his office to support whatever he was saying—that got to me. Then I started thinking about all the women he did that with — quoting Goethe and

Proust to students hoping to catch some of his brilliance. He'd pace back and forth, gesture for emphasis. How many women had he slept with? I didn't want to know. I just wanted to be the one he chose, but perhaps he decided, as I did after Serena died, that there really was no point in loving anyone.

After she died, I listened over and over to *Piece of My Heart* and *Cry, Baby* by Janis Joplin. Not my generation but loving her music was the one gift my father gave me before he left. I have a playlist on Spotify and still crank it up in the car when I'm alone. She sang of the kind of despair only a person who has experienced it can know. Her songs are another reason why I miss highway exits.

"Have you eaten?" Luke asks.

"Went out for Japanese with the book group."

Luke hates the book group, feels that books are private, okay for quoting but not for discussing endlessly. It devalues them, he told me. I joined the group because I needed another preoccupation besides death. I tried yoga, Tai Chi, and Qi Gong but the book group was the only thing that stuck. Whenever I tried to meditate, Serena's face would appear, begging me for pierced ears or a hip-hop class. Why wouldn't I let her get her ears pierced? How come I made random decisions to deny her things?

"How are your friends, Kandi, Susan, Tim?"

I'm surprised he remembers anyone's name. I didn't know that he retained anything on the rare occasions when we shared a meal.

"Fine, they're fine."

"I'm going on a trip." Luke smiles at me as if this is magnificent news.

"Oh?"

"You can come too. My sabbatical and funding was approved for the project in England."

"That's wonderful." I mean it. He had been trying for four years to spend a semester with Dr. Nigel Thompson at Oxford working on his new book about Shakespeare's antiheros. It was the culmination of years of study and considering that after graduate school he had only published two books— one about sentence structure and the other about the resurgence of the personal essay— it was about time. Once he wanted to write the next great American novel but after many tries he gave up. When Serena died he decided that becoming an authority on Shakespeare would secure his position at Northern State University. Leave the novels to someone else. I was disappointed. He used to get excited while he was writing; his entire face became animated when he talked about his characters.

Luke refills his glass and offers more. I sip tentatively at first and then with gusto.

"This is good. What is it?'

"Just a decent Petit Sirah."

"Mmmm." I sink into the green chair, the one we had reupholstered after Serena died so it wouldn't be her favorite color. We moved twice, each time packing up the ghost of Serena. She lives in photographs, the tiny plaster-of-Paris handprint she made in preschool, the paper star that I had laminated, and her calligraphy birth announcement in an embroidered frame. Our lives cling to vestiges of the past; they unpack themselves from boxes, find a secret place in each new home. We moved her photographs to the family room downstairs because of the questions.

*Your niece?*

*No, my dead daughter.*

# The Shape of What Remains

That kind of conversation isn't done in Northbrook. A person shouldn't offer information that might make others uncomfortable. Conversation is like garnish on an entrée at a restaurant; no one cares about it; no one eats it. I learned to keep my past close by, a wallet-sized photo in my purse. I also learned to keep it private.

Luke leans in close enough for me to smell his tangy aftershave.

"So, what do you say? Want to come to England? You could work on your book."

I had thought I'd finish my research book on Chaucer but abandoned the idea when I couldn't get through the first ten pages without crying. I was afraid I'd short out my laptop.

"What about Wyatt?"

"He can come with us, too. I'll have at least a two-bedroom flat in Oxford. Wyatt could take classes or attend a program, take the fall semester abroad. Nigel has a nineteen-year-old daughter," he says.

"Wyatt has a girlfriend. He won't like this idea," I say.

"He's eighteen. He'll get over it."

"He thinks he's in love."

I didn't know this to be true, but it shows Luke that I know more about Wyatt than he does, a game I play. And I remember my own passion at eighteen. Douglas Walsh. I was sure we'd marry and have six children since he came from a family of eight. His mother invited me for Easter dinner, honey-baked ham and sweet potatoes. I've always detested honey-baked ham, so I picked at it politely, praying I wouldn't gag. Then he dumped me for Tonya Bradstreet. She had big white teeth and drove a Jeep, which may have been more important than her perfect teeth. I locked myself in my room that summer and blasted U2's "I Still Haven't Found What I'm Looking For" and Fleetwood Mac's "Little

Lies" over and over. My mother would bang on the door. *Terri! Turn the damn music down. I've got a migraine!*

I got over it. Shawn Leibowicz. Sex on the beach in Chilmark. Old fashioned intercourse.

"You can talk to him when he comes home this weekend with Belle."

"Belle. Wyatt and Belle," Luke laughs.

I try to push down the pleasure I feel at seeing him laugh.

"Why don't we take them to The River Inn?"

"Are you trying to impress Belle? Remember, we need them to break up before May," Luke says.

"Six months is a long time when you're eighteen," I say.

"What do you think, Tessie? Will you come?"

Luke hasn't called me Tessie in years. A shiver runs through me. Tessie would go to England, get her hair cut short with streaks of gold in it, wear a flouncy mini skirt with leggings, maybe call bathrooms "loos." What is Luke up to?

"We could take side trips — Stratford-on-Avon, Liverpool."

Luke is trying to sell me on this idea like we're some damn couple in love. I take another sip of the now-full wine glass. It's not like anyone would miss me or I even have a job to return to. Adjuncts don't get tenure, and I barely finished my Ph.D. after Wyatt was born. When I couldn't get out of bed for my eight o'clock class, the administration gently suggested I cut back. I kept cutting back until I was teaching one class and not every semester. I gave up tutoring at the local high school. No pension, no recent publications except one book review and two short stories. I've done the math. If Luke leaves me, I'm entitled to half of his pension and my meager Social Security. I'd have to find a job and just what kind of job is there for an academic with no book and only part-time teaching and tutoring experience? *Raising children*, I imagine myself saying. I mean women do take time off to raise children, don't they? Wyatt is only eighteen.

Maybe I was a soccer mom, driving and cheering him on at games except Wyatt wasn't a soccer player. He quickly acquired a friend with an intact mother who could drive him places. I'm useless, which is why I'm curious as to Luke's motive in asking me to England. It's not like I'm good company.

"What will we do with the house?"

"We can close it up or rent it, get a neighbor to look in on things. We can throw out the plants; we kill them anyway." Luke is on his third glass of wine, but he still seems completely sober.

I can't make an argument for the book group because he knows I don't give a shit about it. Sure, it gives me direction, read the book, discuss the book, read the new book, discuss the new book. Sometimes I bake or set up meetings. What if he starts sleeping around in England? I'd be stuck in some tiny flat in a foreign country without any clue about public transportation.

"You can Zoom with your friends," he says.

That will enhance my life. I can Facetime or post pictures on Instagram. I don't keep in touch with friends from the past since most of them eventually became uncomfortable with my extended grieving period. I could follow Wyatt's friends. I'm sure he'd appreciate that. Maybe I'll meet someone on Bumble. My profile would be like my life. *Woman with personal tragedy and cheating husband looking for a reason to get dressed in the morning. No religious types or gun enthusiasts.*

I tell him I need to go to the bathroom, but I actually need to get away from him to think. I lean against the sink, peer at my reflection, pull out my phone and check my Instagram account. What would Janis do? I picture frizzy-haired Janis Joplin belting out *Me and Bobby McGee* and that line about freedom and nothing left to lose. What did I have to lose? When I was fourteen and unhappy with everything, I related to a woman who knew pain. I wish she had lived so I could have seen her in concert, go backstage and have a heart-to-heart with her about this shitty world, maybe talk her out of the drug cocktail she would take to do herself in. Years later, I'd drive around in my old Toyota, playing her music and I'd feel like Janis *knew*. She was twenty-seven and sixty at the same time, bitterness and wisdom and gut-wrenching love all rolled up in those lyrics. But she took to the road. I knew my answer. Thank you, Janis. I will go to England because there is no point in staying home. For what? The book group where my only asset is my ability to remember the date and location of our next meeting? Though I'd long ago given up hope of reinventing myself, there is something appealing about getting the hell out of here. I've always wanted to go to Italy, my great-grandmother's heritage. I wonder if there would be people there who look like her. I dab my lips with colored lip gloss, wash my hands. What would I leave behind? My mother-in-law. Luke's mother is the former Bessie Golden, the Jewish equivalent of a debutante. Her parents auditioned her before a series of suitable men; doctors, lawyers, and accountants. Instead, she fell for Dominic Calvano, son of an auto mechanic. To his credit, he went to college and became an engineer. I adored my father-in-law and his penchant for Italian opera and cannoli. He died at 74 of a heart attack, which is ironic since he had the biggest heart of anyone I know. Bess is a trim seventy-two-year-old with a seventy-eight-year-old second husband, Ira. They go on trips to the Greek Islands and the Caribbean. Her book group in Westport has been meeting for over twenty years. After Dom died, she spent about one year grieving and then pulled herself together. *I knew this would happen*

# The Shape of What Remains

*if he ate that rich food. But he wouldn't listen, told me his father lived to ninety eating gelato and cannoli every day. I couldn't get that man to eat a salad. I mean, he wouldn't touch a damn salad!* Now they subscribe to theater, go to independent films and eat at the local deli on Sunday mornings where they have lox and bagels and read the New York Times. When we visit Westport, we always share Sunday brunch with them. Luke calls it his Jewish immersion experience. Wyatt loves lox and bagels and he's happy to have two of them.

Bess was first on the scene when Serena died. I couldn't reach Luke right away and I still suspect he was with Tyra, a leggy graduate student who might get her Ph.D. in Comparative Literature or English if the right professor could convince her of her brilliance. Bess was there in one hour flat. She kept her mouth shut, dripped mascara-tinged tears all over her cream-colored silk blouse and gathered me in her arms as if I was the crumpled six-year-old lying in the road. She adored Serena, her only granddaughter. Luke's brother Ben lives in San Francisco with Cal, and they have a son, Raoul. They arrived late that night. My own mother arrived the next day from Martha's Vineyard. I understand the ferry schedule and its limitations, but she came in on the afternoon ferry, stopped for lunch and then showed up at about four o'clock when the house was already overflowing with people, casseroles, deli platters, and plates of homemade cookies and brownies. She slipped in and put a hand on my shoulder. Wyatt doesn't remember her being there at all. Luke found it unforgivable that she wouldn't be there for us during the greatest tragedy that can befall a family. But Bridget detests a crisis. Too messy.

When I return to the living room, Luke has put out cheddar, crackers, and my favorite olives.

"Maybe I'll go," I say.

"Maybe?" Luke downs the rest of the glass of wine, a purple film left on the crystal.

"I'll think about it."

"It will be good for you. I know I haven't been the most attentive husband."

No kidding. I could train a guinea pig to be more responsive. The refrigerator is better company. At least it provides me with nourishment. Why do I feel like we're having a tender moment? Luke pats my hand, condescending asshole that he is. I offer an enigmatic smile. He has no clue what I'm thinking which is a good thing. If he did, he might not consider me a suitable companion for his jaunt in the UK. I'm beginning to feel dehydrated, like the alcohol is sucking the moisture from my body, the reverse of what a peri-menopausal woman needs.

"I want us to try. I really do. It's been a long time," he says, popping a piece of cheese in his mouth.

"Ten years tomorrow," I say so he'll know that I carry this date inside me.

"Yeah, I know. We can't bring her back. We could have another child."

"Really bad timing," I say.

I'm forty-two years old and still menstruating. That's all it takes, isn't it? Extended childbearing years. Stars do it all the time. Once they hit fifty, they have a facelift so they can look thirty while they're raising children. It's all about fooling nature. Long ago I convinced myself that I couldn't bear to risk another loss. Then I lost Luke to Tyra and whoever came after her.

"I'm sorry." Luke finally sounds drunk, his speech slightly slurred, and his eyes tearing. Easy to be contrite when you have four glasses of wine in you.

I don't know why we made love. I led him up the stairs, a little wobbly myself. We tumbled into a bed we rarely share and he started kissing me, big sloppy tongue-in-the-mouth kind of kisses. I was thinking about Tim and his erection when Luke reached in back to unhook my bra. I thought he'd just fall asleep but he slid on top of me and inside me as if it was the most natural thing in the world. God, it had been so long. I was drunk enough to moan and arch my back. In the end, we're all animals whose bodies betray us.

"Tessie, I've missed you. I'm such a bad husband."

I didn't say a word.

# Chapter 3

When I awaken, he is gone. I never learn that lovemaking is the opening act for pain. Then he comes into the room with a little tray, coffee and a croissant. Not artistic but a nice gesture. He sits on the edge of the bed and kisses my forehead.

"Good morning. I have to teach in half an hour. Let's have dinner together tonight. I'll tell you more about England."

Shit, it's Thursday. My one class. I have to get up. I nibble an edge of the partially stale croissant.

I can't let him in only to have him spend the night with Brittany or Tamika. Luke's semen trickles out of me when I go to pee. How many sperm are swimming around inside of me? Does he have any kind of sperm count at forty-four? I've heard of men fathering children in their sixties and beyond. I peer in the mirror. I started growing my hair last year because I got sick of going to the hairdresser every six weeks to have it cut and styled. It's still brownish blonde and I wear it back in a ponytail most days. Serena had blonde hair and my eyes, blue with gray flecks. Wyatt looks more like Luke except he doesn't wear glasses.

Serena's hair had light in it, like permanent sunlight. What am I thinking? Nothing is permanent. I choose the opal earrings because in November, it is good to wear jewelry with fire. Ten years ago, we waited outside, Serena holding a lunchbox that contained a cheese sandwich, fruit, and homemade chocolate chip cookies. Was it an apple or a pear? Will I mark this date when I'm seventy? I hear Luke's car back out of the driveway. Then my phone rings.

"Hi, sweetheart. Just wanted you to know I'm thinking of you today. Ten years. I can't believe it myself. I hope you're not alone," Bess says.

"I have to teach in a little while. Luke will be home tonight. Did you hear about the project in England?"

"Yes. Good news. He told me he wants you and Wyatt to come with him."

"Yeah, we talked about it last night."

Bess has an uncanny instinct. She knows how much to reach out and when to pull back.

"How's Ira?"

Bess laughs her guttural laugh. "Playing pickleball. Fine. Just fine. Do you have time to meet for lunch later? I could drive in."

"You don't have to do that."

"I *want* to. She was my granddaughter. I *want* to."

We arrange to meet at Angelo's, one of Dominic's favorite restaurants about forty-five minutes away for each of us. It's close to the town we lived in before we tried to reinvent ourselves in Northbrook. Bess is the mother I wanted but didn't get, gutsy, no-nonsense but compassionate. She understands that life can be damn shitty but she doesn't dwell on that. There are no excuses in Bess' repertoire. Luke has a harder time with her. He was close to his father and doesn't understand what she sees in Ira.

I poke through my drawer until I find the blue glass bead Serena gave me for Mother's Day when she was five. She found it on a walk. I slip it into the pocket of my blazer. Serena thought it was the color of the sky. She started naming things that were the same color: robin's eggs, the sky, my eyes and her eyes, the blue part of the stained-glass windows at the Episcopal Church where her friend Lindsey went, Wyatt's blue matchbox car, the pillow Grandma Bridget bought for the couch. Perhaps that's why we have children, so we can see the world through their eyes.

It's raining again; cold rain. November is the worst month. I slip inside the Honda and crank up the heater and defroster. I hate this class, too many freshmen. Most of them are not English or Comparative Literature majors. It's also a general education class, Introduction to Women's Poetry. There are thirty students. They bring laptops and cell phones. I see them smiling at something under the desk and I know they are texting. Sometimes they are staring at the laptop screen and I figure they're looking at porn or reading their email. I don't care. I'm not the techno-police. This is college and if they want to waste Mommy and Daddy's money or whatever loans or scholarships are funding their experience, so be it. I grade the papers and tests and deliver the material. I can't make them love literature. I used to think I could change anyone's mind about poetry and literature. Students today don't seem to read as much except the two or three truly dedicated ones I get each semester. The rest of them seem more interested in getting laid or trying to score alcohol or drugs. Maybe I'm wrong but it just seems as if apathy has taken over a lot of college campuses. After shootings and racial and antisemitic incidents on campuses and in public places, I've lost my sense of safety. I don't understand hatred but I do know how quickly life can drain out of a person. I hope the government does something about gun control. But there is no law that will stop people from running over squirrels, frogs, or even children.

"Tess." Brett MacDonald flags me down. Assistant Professor, fiction. I bought his collection of short stories, <u>Hats and Raincoats</u>. The New York Times Book Review called it "a trivial collection of disconnected stories" but being written up in the Book Review at all can only help sell books. Brett's a good man. He invites me to readings and tries to make me feel as if I'm real faculty instead of temporary help.

"Did you hear that the visiting writer is Patricia Smith? We just got approval. She's coming in April. Do you want her to visit your class?"

"Sure."

There's one class I won't have to teach.

"Let me know if you have any students who can help with 'Impulse.' I'm kind of straight out with the editing."

Brett started the literary journal. It is a lot of work I'm sure, but I don't volunteer. When I am healthy enough to work that much, I would like a job with benefits.

"Got to run," I say.

I walk through the quad teeming with students. I used to love being on a college campus. The little pockets of students congregating in the quad or student union reminded me of my own college years. I think I feel most at home in an academic environment, which is why I stayed in school so long. I like dwelling in the world of imagination and ideas. Luke was like this, too. He spent hours in the coffee shop on campus, listening to snippets of conversations. People break up, fall in love, swear off sex, drugs, alcohol, discover Rilke or Shakespeare or learn quantum theory. It's much more interesting than the so-called real world.

Why did I sleep with Luke last night? Do body parts stop working if you don't use them? Something inside me that was dead came alive again. I don't want to love Luke. When he leaves me, it will be a lot harder.

After two and a half hours of Emily Dickinson, Sharon Olds, and Elizabeth Bishop, I'm ready for a break. Bess will regale me with gentle conversation and anecdotes about Ira. She'll ask about Luke; she always does. There's a kind of tolerant affection she has for him, like an errant schoolboy. She knows his foibles, I think. I touch the blue glass bead in my pocket. My arms are empty. There's no other loneliness that comes close to this.

When they found the driver a month later, it made no difference. Duane Anderson, III, a part-time truck driver, late to an interview for a security guard job. He had three children and no money. Negligent homicide and leaving the scene of an accident. Eight years, suspended after five. It's true what they say about revenge; you think you want it, that somehow it will make you feel better but it doesn't. He was pathetic, contrite, and frightened. He didn't see her, was thinking about the interview and how desperately he needed the job. His own daughter was one year younger than Serena, a sweet-faced little girl whose picture he showed to jurors. Now she would lose her Daddy for five years. Where was the justice in any of it? I wanted to hate him but I didn't. It just felt like the world was a shitty place and something terrible happened for no reason.

Bess is waiting at our favorite table, the one by the window where you can watch people walking by with groceries, bags, and strollers. We both like to people watch.

"Hi, sweetheart."

We kiss in the manner European women kiss, little dry kisses on the cheek. Her hair is rolled up, a royal blue silk scarf in a complicated twist around her neck.

"I ordered you a glass of Chablis."

Her hand briefly lingers on mine. It is as if she senses the emptiness but is too well-mannered to say anything and what could she say anyway? Duane Anderson, III has been out of prison for years now. I don't know where he lives, if he has a job. I like to think he will pause today, maybe gather one of his children close. I hope he became a better driver. I don't wish him ill. Had he been drunk, I would have wanted to tear him apart limb from limb. Truth is, he was sober and driving slowly when she darted into the road. That he didn't stop is unforgivable but he told the court that he thought he'd hit a deer and because he was running late, he figured there was nothing he could do anyway. He had no idea that a little girl's blood was staining the road. I don't know if I believe him though I want to think he wasn't cruel enough to keep driving when a child's life was ebbing away. I can't allow myself to think otherwise.

Bess takes better care of herself than I do, white teeth, lovely skin, and a recent manicure. My nails are ragged and worn down to little nubs. I tear them off. I need a haircut. Bess would never say anything critical nor will she lie and tell me I look wonderful when I don't. She just looks at me, asks if I'm okay.

"I don't know what to do about England. Seems preposterous," I say.

"You could take trips — see more of Europe while he is working."

"I don't know. Wyatt probably won't want to go. You know how it is with teenagers."

"Just do it. What do you have holding you here? You used to love to travel," she says.

There was a time when I would save my money to go on every trip possible. I climbed through Mayan ruins, hiked the Alps. When had I become so afraid of everything?

"I never told you this but I married Ira to pull myself out of depression. Dom was my one love. I think we only get one. Ira was the one my mother would have wanted me to marry. Dom was complex, brooding, handsome. I'll never get over him and you'll never get over Serena. You just have to immerse yourself in life because you're still alive and she's not. I know that sounds harsh but once you realize that, you do it for yourself, for her memory. Go to England, Tess. It will give you ideas for writing."

I have a ridiculous thought. Maybe I really married Bess and not Luke. She is the benefit of my relationship. Better than health insurance or a pension, Bess always has the right words. Is Luke my one love? If so, I am more of a loser than I thought. Easy for her to wax nostalgic about Dom. As far as I know, he kept it in his pants, always looking at her as if she was the most gorgeous woman in the world. Luke looks at me as if I'm pathetic — except last night and this morning. Guilt fuck? Last minute homage to his dead daughter? I feel a tingle between my legs and remember how much I like sex. Luke is a good lover, slow and tuned in. Before last night, he seemed creepy on the rare occasions when we made love. He'd try a move that I figured Tyra or some other woman had liked, or he'd rub me raw because some lover probably had a hard time coming. Keep your damn women straight, I'd think, pushing him away. After that, I'd go to bed early, read by the book lamp so he'd think I was asleep when he passed by the door.

"Do you think I'll have to get a collection of hats?" I ask.

Bess smiles. "I'm well on my way to hats with curlicues and ostrich feathers and maybe a touch of green eyeshadow and bright orange lipstick."

Truth is, Bess could pull it off. She looks comfortable in her skin and thus convinces people around her that she is put together. I feel disheveled next to her. She calls it my artistic look, which is Bess-speak for turning a liability into an asset. Messy becomes too smart to bother. It's not hard to see why I love her so much.

The salad is perfect — Buffalo mozzarella, fresh basil, mixed greens, tomato, and a drizzle of good olive oil. We should all bow to the basil god, fragrant, versatile, and like love, almost too good to be true. I nibble happily. I'm glad Serena tasted pesto that summer when my basil grew out of control and I made batches and batches of it. She said it tasted like a garden. I'd hate to think of her dying without ever having tasted my favorite herb.

"Sixteen. She would have been sixteen." Bess is going to make me think about this. The prom, the beginning of looking at colleges, a boyfriend or maybe she would have had a girlfriend. No way to know. I'd be starting the process of letting go, a process I still haven't perfected. Serena is forever six. Unfair, really. I'd like to be remembered in my late twenties, a wife and mother with a beautiful boy and girl and what looked like a doting husband. I had education, a promising career, and adorable kids. I wish I could tell the couples I see how all of that can disappear in a second. I see them walking, high-priced stroller and the older child dutifully holding a hand. They wear smart clothes and I know they think they've beat it — gained independence, money, a guaranteed future. I want to say, there are no guarantees. He may have a potbelly and an alcohol problem in five years. She could get breast cancer or the baby might turn out to have a progressive disease or die in her crib one February night and they'll spend the next ten years thinking about how they should have put her on her back not her stomach or whether or not a cell phone nearby was to blame. They'll think about soy formula versus breast milk and analyze everything she ate during pregnancy. And that's just because they can — they have the luxury of thinking that their behavior might have caused a different outcome. I don't ever think that. I'll never know why Serena ran out in the road that day. Did she see a kitten or a ball? She knew about traffic. We'd practiced so many times. I was right there, waiting for the bus with her as I did every morning. I turned to say hello to Diane, my neighbor to the left, and when I heard the truck, I turned back to see the dust kicking up and Serena flat on the road, her lunchbox upright next to her. There was no animal or ball that I could see. Six years old, not a toddler. It wasn't a busy road and trucks hardly ever came through. How many times have I wished she was sick that day or that I decided to drive her to school? I wished that Luke was the one waiting with her so the guilt didn't fall so heavily on my shoulders.

"Shit happens." Bess says, reading my mind. "I've always hated that expression, so crass. But I understand it. Sometimes random things happen and no amount of foresight will prevent them. I thought I could keep Dom alive by trying to control his diet and giving him lots of love. Turns out I couldn't. You couldn't know what Serena was thinking when she ran out in the road. Maybe she saw something on the other side of the road that you didn't see. The point is, you had six years with her."

It's true that we have to live in moments. Sitting in the book group, I try to concentrate on the words, the book, or the pretentiousness of a visiting member, anything to get me out of my own head. It's way better to dwell in fiction than reality. Bess understands that life isn't fair but she has decided to go with it because it would be in bad taste to fight it. If life fucks her over, she'll face it wearing her best linen suit, silk scarf, and jade earrings. She isn't afraid to show her feelings but she doesn't dwell on them, she moves on. Why can't I do the same?

"Too bad England isn't in the EU anymore. Ireland and France are beautiful. I like Spain, especially Barcelona and the coastal towns. Oh, Tess, it's going to be such an opportunity for both of you — and Wyatt, too, even though he doesn't yet know it. I'll talk Ira into a visit," she says.

Wyatt. I'd forgotten about him and the conversation we'll be having after we meet Belle. I tell her about Belle.

"I guess he isn't gay," she says. Wyatt is a late bloomer. We speculate on what is unusual about Belle.

"Maybe she has multiple piercings on her face like the woman who works at the Westport Big Y," Bess says.

"Fixated on Disney and wears pink tutus like Sarah Jessica Parker in *Sex in the City*," I say.

I shiver, thinking of those stiletto pumps and how those characters were supposed to be intelligent career women yet they seemed to spend all their time and money on clothing and shoes.

"Should I make a Disney themed meal like Mickey shaped pancakes?"

"Too obvious. Maybe you could just refer to Luke as 'The Beast.'"

"We were going to take them out to eat. I hope she's trained," I say.

"I learned long ago that you're not responsible for the behavior of the people your kids bring home," Bess says.

"Yeah, like you never could control me. Are you trying to say I've embarrassed you?"

I can say this because Bess understands. She's laughing and I know she's glad that the atmosphere has lightened up. It's true that I'm excited to meet Belle. I'm curious about what kind of girl Wyatt would find attractive. I also think it's funny that he's worried about my reaction. There isn't much I find shocking after teaching for twelve years. I've survived pants so low you could see their ass crack, thongs under sheer trousers, piercings, tattoos and even colored contacts that mimicked Martian eyes. If a student notices the mythological connections in the poetry of W.S. Merwin, I don't care if she is naked or wearing a spacesuit.

"Did he tell you that there's a job opening in Oxford?" Bess says nonchalantly.

"I thought this was just a sabbatical project."

"Well, he called to tell me that there's an opening and he might apply. He thinks a fresh start would be good for both of you. What do you really have here that matters — besides me, of course?"

It's true that my mother wouldn't be a reason to stay. I hardly ever see her and she's expressed no interest in Wyatt. She's made it clear that her bridge tournaments and theater group take precedence over family events. I never talk to my father. They divorced when I was in middle school and she "took him to the cleaners" as the saying goes. House on Martha's Vineyard, alimony, and half of his business. She didn't remarry but she has had a long relationship with Dr. Arnie Grayson, a gynecologist. My sister, Lena, lives in Chéticamp, near the Gulf of St. Lawrence and the foothills of the Cabot Trail in Nova Scotia. She has two children, Emilie and Mariah. I see them once a year, maybe. Her husband is a fisherman and they live close to off the grid. When Serena died, I got a card three months later. Her daughter, Emilie is a year older than Serena. My father moved to Vancouver years ago, remarried a

Canadian woman. I wasn't invited to the wedding and don't even have a current address for him.

"I'm not ready to think about a permanent decision," I say.

Truth is, I am trying to decide if I can stand being in a foreign country with Luke. If he continues his philandering, I would be another depressed faculty wife. At least here, I know the territory and can find things to do that are familiar.

"I'm sorry I told you. I know this has been a hard time for both of you."

I wonder how much Bess knows about Luke's screwing around. She's a smart lady and though she might be from the generation that looked the other way, there is no reason to believe that Dom or Ira ever did this to her. I get the feeling that she would have walked out and honestly, if it wasn't for what happened and how I feel like a shell most of the time, I would have left too.

"Maybe you'd find a job there," Bess says.

I almost snort at the thought. What skills do I have other than my passion for medieval literature? I know she's encouraging me to move on. She's been my steadfast supporter and I hate myself for thinking ill of her, even for a moment.

When we leave the restaurant, she embraces me— a rare gesture.

"Think about it, Tess. This will be good for both of you. And don't worry about Wyatt.

She tells me she's just finished reading *Thirteen Ways of Looking* by Colum McCann.

"It's a series of stories inspired by an incident that happened to him in New Haven. He was attacked after trying to help a woman who had been assaulted. Knocked unconscious. *Treaty* is one of the best short stories I've ever read. You should suggest this collection to your book group."

She goes on to tell me about the nun in the story who recognizes her former torturer on a television program, advocating for a peace organization. The stuff of nightmares.

"I don't want to spoil it but it's about pain, anger, and the fragile compromise of moving on. I think you'd like it."

England. Luke. Fragile compromises. Moving on.

I no longer read for answers but to lose myself in the tragedy of another, as if I might finally find something worse than kneeling beside the broken body of my six-year-old daughter.

# Chapter 4

When I applied for the one opening in my department last semester, I didn't even get an interview. They gave the position to Marissa Duval, barely out of graduate school. *She had experience teaching Composition and Rhetoric and we know you don't like teaching that*, my department head, Dr. Gerard Dillman, told me. Why didn't you ask me what I want to teach? She is maybe twenty-eight, with only a Master's Degree. I have a Ph.D. There was a time when I would have been a desirable candidate but my age, my long bout of depression, and the shitty economy make me a more suitable adjunct. The very word adjunct implies unnecessary. We augment the *real* faculty. Shore them up. Teach the classes they'd rather not teach because they're too busy being brilliant and published. In the meantime, we don't make a living wage. Most of the adjuncts I know have one or two other jobs, which is really like having two or three full-time jobs. Teaching two classes a semester is hard work, especially if you have thirty plus in your class. The *real* professors get graduate seminar classes or supervise a student or two on their thesis, which counts as a class. I get a tiny paycheck and a different assignment every semester but that and the book group are the only consistencies in my life.

I drive home, blasting Janis and wondering if Luke will show up for dinner. Most nights he doesn't. Sometimes he calls to tell me he's working late and sometimes he doesn't bother. I've taken to eating a salad or sandwich in front of the television or my computer, although it depresses me. Sometimes I go through the digitalized albums: Serena laughing, taking her first steps, eating pizza in a highchair, trying to give Wyatt a hug. Pathetic. I'm pathetic. Let it go, Teresa. At first, I thought her death was a bad dream. The Compassionate Friends said this is normal. You blame yourself (and I had good reason), then magical thinking. What is reality anyway? Who is to say that she isn't alive in an alternate universe? This is only one possibility. I expected to wake up one day and she'd be there, asking for mac and cheese or wanting a new bike. So much of my life was wrapped up in being her mother. I'm sorry, Wyatt. I must have been a terrible mother. I think Luke tried to pick up the slack, taking him camping (which Wyatt hated) and asking other fathers what they did with their kids. Wyatt never liked sports or camping. He prefers to play computer games and take things apart. Luke tried interesting him in Harry Potter but instead Wyatt taught himself computer code. To his credit, Luke did get Wyatt in a youth group where he met other kids who liked computers.

I tried to recoup my relationship with him when he was a teenager. Since Luke was fucking grad students by then, I was both mother and father. I think we get along okay now. I remind myself that I'm the one he called about Belle and he even demonstrated the normal level of anxiety that we, as hopelessly old people, might somehow screw it up.

When I pull in the driveway, it's barely four o'clock and Luke's car is there. He has a light schedule on Tuesdays but that never mattered in the past. He said something about dinner together when he rushed out the door this morning. He hasn't been home with any regularity in so long, I wonder if we even have groceries.

I smell the paella when I walk in the door; Luke's one culinary tour-de-force. He learned to make it in graduate school. Why the hell is he home in the afternoon making paella?

He has on an apron that says "Guinness is Good for You" and sure as its message, he is drinking one out of a tall glass.

"How's Mother?"

"Wonderful. Can we trade? I'll give you Bridget and throw in ferry tickets to the Vineyard."

"No deal." Luke smiles. "I felt like cooking so I came home. I figured you shouldn't be alone today. Want a drink?"

"It's four o'clock. Little early."

Luke shrugs and takes a long draw from his Guinness.

"Who makes those rules? Remember when we had champagne for breakfast in France? It wasn't even nine o'clock."

"That was vacation. It's different."

"Oh, I see. Vacation means you can drink anytime. Real life means you can only drink after five, preferably with hors d'oeuvres and guests. Cheese and crackers. Martinis. Bottle of good wine with dinner, fashionably served by seven-thirty."

"Okay. Can you make a mimosa?"

"That's my girl! Break the damn rules. Mimosas for dinner. Pretty soon you'll be pouring vodka on your breakfast cereal."

He finds an unopened bottle of champagne in the back of the refrigerator. He even cuts up an orange and puts a slice of it on the edge of the champagne flute, which he fills halfway with orange juice.

"To England."

"To England."

I sip tentatively. It's good but it occurs to me that like all good times with Luke, it has a shelf life. Just go with it, I tell myself. It's the anniversary of Serena's death and Luke is the one person who knows this despair. Even if we're playing at it, it's better than being alone.

## Chapter 5

A year after the accident, Duane Anderson III sent me a letter.

*Im sory. I wish I cud bring back yur little girl.*
*I think about it evry day.*
*Yurs Truly,*
*Duane Anderson III*

Thank you, Mr. Anderson. It comforted me to know that the barely literate man who ran over my daughter was repentant. He thought she was a deer.

"I didn't want you to get upset." Luke told me when I found the letter hidden under a magazine.

"Just brilliant," I said, crumpling up the letter. I was glad Duane was haunted.

I hope it followed him to his grave, poor bastard.

We're on day three of *let's be nice to Teresa*. Or should I call it, *playing at marriage?* I've already decided not to make love with him again. I don't wear my wedding ring anymore. It's in my jewelry box, which I suppose is stupid because it would be the first thing to be stolen if someone broke into the house. *Officer, it is a 14 K band of four diamonds.* I could sell it and go on a vacation — maybe a Mediterranean cruise.

Luke tries again with the speech about how he hasn't been a good husband.

Definition of a good husband according to a Google search:
*Someone who stays with you through the most difficult times.*
(Define "stays with you.")
*Someone who wants to grow old with you.*
(Define "old.")
*Someone who is generally happy alongside you no matter what happens.*
(Define "happy.")
*Someone who loves you for who you are, your unique personality and lifestyle.*
(Define "love.")

I like the last one because it is so inclusive. And #2---the growing old one. Ted Beemer, long married, seemingly loyal and contented until he took up with a twenty-something. Ted isn't an academic. He's our auto mechanic. He moved in with Veronica, Vanessa, Victoria…whatever the hell her name was…and they were blissful for maybe four months before she figured out that a fifty-nine-year-old wasn't as exciting as a twenty-something or thirty-something. What does he do? He talks Sybil into taking him back. Not me. I wouldn't take Luke back. I'd have sold the house by the time he asked.

And what about Duane Anderson III? Is he a faithful husband? What did his wife think when she learned he killed a little girl? I think of the sad-eyed woman who sat in the courtroom day after day. Did she lie next to him at night? Did they have another child? Some days when I'm driving in ice or during a torrential rain, I think of what I'd do. I pity new drivers who get into car accidents and kill a friend or boyfriend.

Duane Anderson III failed to be conscious of his environment—something I've been guilty of in the past.

Luke sidles up to me and hands me the phone I left on the counter. He's doing that sidestep thing that I used to think was sexy. One day, intensified by the worst heat wave in years, I turned to see him sidestep through the open back door of my rental house. I jumped when his hands encircled my waist, my hands submerged in soapy dishwater.

"Mine," he said, pulling me toward my bedroom, just a mattress on the floor. I smelled like Joy mixed with his shaving cream. No curtains on the windows, which were ground floor and open.

"Someone will see us," I protested as he unhooked my bra with one deft move. I could hear Mr. Van Dorsen's lawnmower down the street, wondered when the mailman would arrive.

"Shhhh." He pushed me down on the mattress in my college rental, tucked in neatly with the daisy-patterned sheets I had as a teenager. As we sank down, he twisted off his jeans and boxers and unzipped my denim skirt.

"I have to finish the dishes," I said weakly. If this were an apocalypse, I'd want to fall down on that bed again, with the green velvet pillow, Indian bedspread crumpled on the floor, vial of birth control pills in the bedside table drawer next to a pipe filled with weed. Midday, classes in an hour or so but we couldn't wait. In that moment, I was Joyce's Molly Bloom. *Yes, I will.* There, on the daisy sheets, he pushed his way in and I let him, as I would again, even knowing what I know. That is the great human tragedy: we're imbeciles groggy with lust, bitches mounted in the playground, the stallion pounding the mare. Desire churns and we go forward, as I did, my panties sticky through Statistics and Renaissance Literature.

My phone rings. Wyatt.

"Hi honey," I say. "How's school?"

"She's from Rwanda," he says. "Her family left before the genocide in 1994. She was actually born here."

Explains the "Belle."

"She speaks English, French, and Kinyarwanda, the language of Rwanda."

I reassure him, "It's fine."

"Don't ask her anything."

"Sure, honey. Whatever you want."

We're fine with Belle-from-another-place and her chocolate-colored skin. Wyatt's voice softens and he tells me he likes his Web Design class, doesn't like English Composition. Belle is teaching him some words in Kinyarwanda. She's vegetarian. Luke is watching me as if he's trying to memorize how to talk to our son.

"She's from Rwanda and a vegetarian," I tell him.

Luke looks relieved.

"Not bad to be vegetarian. Lots of people are vegetarian."

Wyatt, our son who spent every weekend in high school playing computer games, has a girlfriend. We smile.

## Chapter 6

The first meal I made for Luke was Coq-au-vin. Though most of my meals came out of a box, I'd searched for a recipe that sounded exotic but possible. I served it with a Caesar salad, green beans that I bought at a roadside stand, and brownies for dessert. I overcooked the beans and omitted the anchovies on the salad because they're disgusting salty little fish. We drank Robert Mondavi Cabernet Sauvignon. I remember the label. One candle lit in a brass candlestick I bought at the flea market, and I wore a shimmery blue peasant skirt that accented my hips and a low-cut top that showed off my breasts. Twenty-two, newly graduated and on my way to graduate school. He was nearly two years older, already working on his Ph.D.

"Good-looking and she cooks!" he exclaimed. Fussing over the napkins and trying to find matching plates felt grown-up and domestic; this is what it's like to be married, I thought. He would come home after a long day, kiss me long and hard. Maybe we couldn't wait until after dinner to make love. Some nights I would cook and some nights he would cook, though the only thing he'd cooked for me was pasta with

Ragu, embellished with sautéed onions and green peppers, until his Spanish roommate taught him to make paella.

I figured married people had sex all the time. It was so available to them. If they were trying for a baby, they could just fuck every free moment with impunity. Like when we tried for Serena. I wanted a girl, someone who would know how it felt to be a woman. How ecstatic I was to hold her, her fuzzy blonde head and that indescribable baby smell. I gave her a name that guaranteed peace, I thought. How could a Serena be bitchy? It sounded like flute music or water running over the rocks at the brook down the street from my childhood home. Serena, my bunny. But like the hysterectomy my classmate Bonnie had at twenty-five after being diagnosed with uterine cancer, Serena was excised, cut away from me.

I see the shadow of Luke's movements in the kitchen. He is fixing a drink, ice clinking in the glass from the icemaker, the soft thunk of the cabinet closing. The soothing music of Eric Satie wafts from the Bluetooth speakers. Meanwhile the muted afternoon sun paints a pattern outside the living room window. If not for the bare trees and beginning browning of the grass, it would seem like spring, not the start of another winter of shortened days and frigid nights. I wonder what the weather is like in the South-Central region of the United Kingdom. Will there be the endless banter of imported wives or academics? I remember our early dinner parties with Dr. and Mrs. So-and-So or Dr. and Dr. So-and-So discussing Chaucer and Rashi, Shakespeare and the beginning of his theories about tragic heroes like Macbeth with Lady Macbeth questioning his manliness to egg him on to commit murder.

*What beast wasn't then*
*That made you break this enterprise to me?*
*When you durst do it, then you were a man;*

# The Shape of What Remains

*And to be more than what you were, you would*
*Be so much more the man. Nor time nor place*
*Did then adhere, and yet you would make both* (I.vii.53-58)

Hamlet, Othello, Shylock—men with questionable morals. Lucas P. Calvano, tenured professor, part-time husband, and father. My own research on the secret and sacred texts, the bawdy writing of the ancients, rebellions and taboos now languishes in unopened files on my computer. *What hangs at a man's thigh and wants to poke at the hole it has often poked at before? Answer: A key.* I used to think that deciphering these texts would be a gift to the reading world. I know now that most people would rather have small tastes of literature like the sound bites on network news.

*Classical literature is slow,* Luke once told me and I understood exactly what he meant. I like to sit with a book for a while, have days of sadness when I finish because the characters have become part of my life. Sometimes I project what happens to them after the book is over like I wrote Serena's life story in my head after the accident. I think of Bess' book recommendation and wonder if Luke would be interested in reading it too. The thought drifts away as quickly as it comes. My reading life may be my last hold on something for me alone. I don't want to share it.

# Chapter 7

"Let's go out for dinner," Luke suggests in the middle of a work week. A date, I think. He's asking me on a date. It's not even a weekend.

I'm impressed at how long this charade is lasting. Dr. and Dr. Lucas Calvano, out on the town of Northbrook, home to six ethnic restaurants, a Starbucks and a Subway.

"Sure." I drag a comb through my hair, dab on some lipstick. The afternoon sun has gone the way of all November brightness, replaced by a copper sky that will give way to shadowy gray, then early darkness. It will soon be Thanksgiving, then Christmas, then the beginning of a new year with resolutions and hopefulness designed to get us through the dark days, blowing snow, and the drear of winter.

If I'm going to be stuck with him in a foreign country, I must perfect my public persona. Banter. We will chit and we will chat.

A light sleet is beginning and there's a sheen on the roads. He drives slowly, knowing that I am nervous about weather. Sometimes he ignores that and drives however he pleases and when I bring it up, he'll tell me he's perfectly capable of driving in sleet. There is only one other couple in Thai Garden, everyone else being smart enough to stay home when the roads are slippery. It's early in the season so sand trucks might be in short supply but I try not to think about it. It's just as likely to turn to rain in this month of change.

I order a Thai iced tea because I don't want to drink. If I must be married to this man, I would like to face it sober. Though I used to like the feeling of being out of control, the last ten years have soured its allure. Luke orders a Manhattan. I don't bring up the driving but think I could drive home, though I know he'll tell me he's fine. He hates being a passenger.

"I've applied for a tenure track position at Oxford. I don't know my chances but it's an incredible opportunity. These appointments are hard to come by, you know. Nigel said you can probably get an adjunct position there. That would give you time to work on your book. If I get the job, it comes with reasonably priced housing."

"We'd stay there forever?"

I imagine myself in England as an old woman, dipping biscuits into tea, eating cucumber sandwiches. What about my morning espresso?

"What about Wyatt?"

"He can go to school at Oxford Brookes University, maybe. It's nearby. We'll see what he wants to do after the spring semester. That won't be a problem."

"Wyatt has friends here."

"Tessie, you know he'll make new friends. He's eighteen and the friends of his childhood have moved on. They're all over the country. It's a great time to do this. Think of this as a chance for something new."

I can't discuss my fears in a public place.

"I know my way around here and I have friends."

This isn't true and he knows it. Most of my friends from my Serena life dropped away when the depression hit. They figured grieving should take a month, a year maybe — not ten years. They couldn't understand. When we moved, I didn't tell anyone but Rachel, a sometimes friend that Luke can't stand. I stuck to light friendships — book group, meet for coffee. Bess and Rachel are the only people who know it all. It was an awakening for me, the conditional nature of most friendships. Bridget, a.k.a. my mother, has always made it clear there were certain boundaries of bad taste that we were not to cross.

"You have me," he says.

I snort into my Thai tea.

He looks wounded, as if I've wrongly accused him of something. His absence from our house and marital bed has been entirely my fault. The depression. My lack of interest. Peri-menopausal fluctuations. My floundering career. Men have needs, my mother told me before I was married. Well, women have needs, too.

"Why don't you try medication again or therapy? It's been ten years. Tessie," his soft voice, cajoling. "It's time to move on." His hand snakes across the table and finds mine. I jerk my hand back. I'm not three. Even Serena at six was smarter than this.

"I have my life. You have yours," I say.

"Okay, what's your life like?"

Fucker. There's no right answer and I lose again. I teach one class a semester, get dressed each day, take a walk or go to the gym because my body is a fat, ugly worm. I force myself to sweat; it's salty, like tears.

"Not fair," I say, thinking he's put me on the defensive and I can play that game.

"What about you? How come you never come home?" I say.

# The Shape of What Remains

Luke takes another gulp of his amber drink with the unnaturally red cherry bobbing.

"There's nothing for me there," he says.

**Homemaker:** *A wife who manages the household while her husband earns the family income.*

If managing consists of putting dishes in the dishwasher and doing the laundry, then I'm a homemaker. I make $10,000 a year for my adjunct position. When I graduated, I had $25,000 in student loan debt. Although we paid it off—back in the good years when I had a full-time position and we were both pulling in decent salaries—I'm not making an adequate contribution right now. Fortunately, Wyatt is happy to go to University of Connecticut (UConn) where we get free tuition.

"What would you like there to be?" I ask.

I think of gauzy outfits, daytime television and Cosmopolitan Magazine with advice on keeping a man interested. How come men's magazines seem to be about sports, computers, investing? You never see a man's magazine with the headline, "Six Ways to Turn on Your Wife" or "The G-Spot: An Anatomical Map". No, it's enough that they bring their dick home each night. For that, we women should be grateful. Except that Luke doesn't.

"I'd like a wife," he says, and the gentleness in his voice is jarring.

I pretend it's the alcohol. He doesn't say he'd like his wife back, which is a little like asking for a new wife.

"Unless you've divorced me without my knowledge, I believe I am your wife."

I am the sober one.

"Tess, you know what I mean. You're seriously depressed." He draws out the first syllable so it sounds like seeer-ious-ly.

"I haven't killed myself," I say.

"I'm grateful but it's not enough," he says.

"Why are we going to England? If things aren't working out here, why would a transatlantic move improve our relationship?"

He fidgets with the cheerily pink napkin and takes another draw on the Manhattan.

"I can't stagnate waiting for you to heal. I had the crazy thought that maybe this would be good for you, a new start."

The server brings summer rolls with peanut sauce. They look like they're made with human skin.

"Heal? Losing my only daughter isn't an illness."

"Our daughter," he corrects.

"What am I supposed to do when you start sleeping around?"

He stares at me, the mole under his left eye suddenly looking like a little bug. He's handsome, though graying, and there are little stitched lines at the corners of his eyes. He needs a shave. When we were dating, he shaved two times a day so his face wouldn't abrade me when we kissed. I loved his soft lips and his tongue, imitating the act we were moving toward, the one I fell into two days ago, unconsciously. Now his eyes narrow to slits.

"Tyra was a long time ago. I was trying to fill the gap left when Serena died. She was my baby, my little girl, eenie beenie Serenie." Luke's eyes fill and I put my hand on his.

I think of the word try and trying. These are trying times. For the first couple of years, we were wounded together. We'd hold each other for hours sometimes. Poor Wyatt was kind of left out though Bess and Dom tried to fill the gap. Then Luke drifted away, literally and figuratively. We moved to Northbrook. Late meetings became research, which eventually became no explanation whatsoever.

49

"Nothing could have prepared me. Plus, I blamed you. God, I ran that scenario through my head hundreds of times. I know you would have done the same thing if I had been the one waiting with her that day. Then I realized I probably would have turned to say hello to Diane as well. It took about three years to come to that and maybe another two to forgive you and accept that horrible things sometimes happen. So many victims. Don't you see? And for the record, I never slept with anyone else after Tyra. I threw myself into my research, hoping you'd do the same."

"I guess I handle grief differently."

"I know that now, Tessie."

He knows I hate Northbrook. From the spider plants I kill to the tasteful draperies and groomed lawns, it has never felt like home. We don't entertain. It is a home for a family, which we haven't been in ten years. There is a family room downstairs. Luke had a bar put in and a couple of cocktail tables but Wyatt eventually begged us for a flat screen monitor so he could watch movies and play video games. He's the only one who goes down there unless I go to look at the photos of Serena, up on the wall.

I dip a roll in peanut sauce, take a bite and offer one to Luke. He licks off the sauce, then bites into it with gusto.

"I want you to see Dr. Bradford-Smith. She's an expert on grief."

"Isn't it a little late for that?" I ask.

He smiles in his pompous college professor way.

"No. Please. Try."

I nod, concentrate on the lime and peanut taste.

"I've made an appointment for you tomorrow at 2:00. Her office is in Northbrook Plaza."

"What if I don't want to go?"

"For God's sake, just give it a try," he says.

"Okay," I say as if saying it will make it real. I think of high tea and gray skies, crossing the same ocean that swallowed up Serena's ashes.

Luke smiles and raises his glass. We clink glasses and toast to the ocean we'll cross and flawed heroes. I cross and uncross my legs, press my solar plexus hard enough to feel a familiar twinge of pain.

## Chapter 8

*Dr. Regina Bradford-Smith, MD, Psychiatry* is what it says on the door of her office, which is next to Old Navy.

The waiting room is tastefully decorated with copies of Forbes, Time, and The Atlantic. There's a Japanese print on the wall. A large woman wearing a multi-colored caftan leaves the office. I push my insurance card though the window toward a pimply girl who looks about fifteen. Protective glass. I wonder if it is bulletproof. What the hell am I doing here? Luke has a way of making me think this is my fault, like I'm pushing him to have affairs.

"Teresa Calvano."

My name is called and the fifteen-year-old leads me down a short hallway to a room with a handsome leather chair, a fancy desk, and a loveseat. No couch.

"The doctor will be with you shortly," she says.

Regina Angela Bradford, Tufts Medical School. Then a residency at Brown, which says Regina Angela Bradford-Smith. Guess she met Mr. or Ms. Smith by then. There is a calligraphy plaque of a quote by

Friedrich Nietzsche "From Life's School of War: What Does Not Kill Me Makes Me Stronger."

A tall and non-descript woman with glasses and short, curly hair holds out her hand to me.

"Dr. Bradford-Smith. You must be Teresa."

"Tess," I say.

"Well, Tess. I'm glad to meet you. Why don't you take a seat?" She motions to the loveseat.

When the hour is up, I am surprised. She explained to me that the grieving process is entirely individual. She didn't say I was sick or crazy to be depressed after ten years. She also didn't pull out a prescription pad.

"It's too soon to know if medication will be helpful," she said. "I'd like us to meet once a week and I'd also like you to attend a group."

"What kind of group?" I asked, hoping it wasn't a Bereavement Group.

"It's a mix. Everyone is there for a different reason. You may find it helpful. It meets on Wednesday nights — right here, in the group room at the end of the hall."

Seven months to get my shit together. I have to go pick up Wyatt and the new girlfriend. He's texted me twice, reminding me that she's vegetarian, and please, Mom, don't ask her a lot of questions — especially about Tutsis and Hutus and the genocide.

When I pull up to the dorm, I text him. It's one of those chilly days with the wind kicking up. Wyatt prefers texts to calls. Embarrassing to be talking to your mother, I suppose.

It's about ten minutes before I spot him, and behind him is a stunning young woman. Her graceful neck and slender build remind me of dancers I saw in New York City — George Balanchine's company.

She has long hair, braided and hanging down nearly to her tiny waist. She's wearing a forest green sweater and jeans, and she's elegant. Gorgeous. My first thought, and I feel guilty thinking about it, how did Wyatt attract such a beauty? Clearly, she could have anyone she wished. Wyatt isn't bad looking and he is definitely bright but he didn't attend his senior prom, preferring instead to go on a camping trip with his computer friends. Some of them were girls but they were just friends, or so I thought at the time.

I extend my hand to Belle.

"Pleased to meet you, Dr. Calvano."

I notice she has five stud earrings in one ear and four in the other. She also has a tiny diamond stud in her nose.

Belle ducks down to get in the car, swan-like. Large almond shaped brown eyes look at me. She has a flawless complexion, full lips, and perfect teeth. How will Wyatt concentrate on his studies with this goddess of a girlfriend? There is such a thing as too much beauty, I think.

"Call me Tess," I say and Wyatt shoots me a look, "or whatever you like."

I pop the trunk and Wyatt loads their backpacks and bags inside, and I notice his arms looking bulkier in the form-fitting jacket he has on. He must be working out. He's also gotten taller, I swear. Three months and he's more manly than I remember. It looks like he's trying to grow a moustache.

Belle asks about the towns in Connecticut and how long we've lived here. She tells me her family lives in Rhode Island, near Brown, where her father is a research scientist. She doesn't mention a mother or siblings and I don't ask, taking my cue from Wyatt.

"How do you like UConn?"

"It's great. The people are friendly and the ice cream is good."

She turns to Wyatt, puts her dark hand on his light one. He fidgets but holds her hand.

"Do you know your major yet?" I figure anything about academics is in the "safe" category.

"Not sure. I'm thinking of Women's Studies or International Relations. I met Wyatt in my Women's Studies class."

A Women's Studies class? This is news to me.

"We talk about gender politics, queer literature, film, and history. It's an interdisciplinary class," Belle says. "Wyatt told me you teach writing and literature. I want to write a book someday."

Me too, honey, I think.

"I'm teaching Introduction to Women's Poetry this semester," I say.

"I love Sappho and Adrienne Rich," she says.

Wyatt, you've been holding out on us. While I thought you were perfecting your nerd-dom, you're out seducing the most gorgeous and literate woman on the UConn campus. I like this girl and suddenly I want them to marry and have beautiful biracial children. He's not going to be happy about England. If I was dating Orlando Bloom, I wouldn't want to leave him for a chilly country where they defer to a king and call soccer, football.

Wyatt is pointing out the high school, the local pizza place, and the Thai restaurant. Since he didn't grow up here, that's about all the nostalgia he can muster.

My phone rings. I pull into the driveway before I answer it.

"Tess. It's Tim." I pause to think before I realize it's Tim from the book group.

"Hi. What's up?"

"Chantal is gone. She's dead."

It takes me another moment to place this in context. Chantal. The long-suffering wife with MS. I didn't think MS killed anyone.

"I'm so sorry," I say after an awkward pause.

"She killed herself, Tess. I found her in the car with the garage door closed. I should have known she was depressed."

Well, buddy, the world doesn't always know. Some of us are pretty good at hiding it when we need to. Of course, she was depressed. She had a progressive disease that was sapping her ability to walk. That's one hell of a challenge.

"Hold on a sec." I give the keys to Wyatt who predictably has left his keys to the house at his dorm. I motion for them to go inside.

Why me? Are we connected in a bigger way?

When I felt his erection against me in that first perfunctory hug, I figured he just hadn't gotten any in a while. I know that feeling. I didn't take it as a sign of intimacy. I like Tim. He's one of the only members of the group who seems to welcome my presence, always asking my opinion about the book we're reading. Maybe he doesn't have a lot of friends. I know nothing about his life except his wife's disease, his job as an engineer, and the fact that he has two grown daughters who live in another state.

"What can I do?" I ask, hoping the answer is nothing because there is nothing anyone can do. Death leaves only logistics — cremation or burial, service in a church, synagogue or funeral home, flowers or no flowers, donations to a specific charity or a fund set up for the education of young children. It's good for a while because it gives you decisions to make, the comfort of being busy. I collapsed into efficiency for the days and weeks after Serena died, setting up a scholarship fund at the college in her name, planting a special garden for her. Then it hit me. She wasn't coming back and all these tasks were bullshit, a way of avoiding the truth. She was dead and I'd never get to see her grow up. We won't shop for maternity clothes together nor would I argue with her about the outfit I wear to her wedding or whether or not the despised aunt on his side had to be invited. When I'm old, she won't sit at my bedside, hold my hand, and tell me I'd been a good mother.

"Well, I thought we could meet for coffee. I know about your daughter. Read about it years ago but didn't think I should mention it because…well, you know, that group can be gossipy and I figured you wanted privacy."

He *knew*. Is there any place on earth I can go without someone knowing?

"Thank you," is all I can muster.

"The funeral is Tuesday. She wanted to be cremated so no rush. She left me a note. I'd like to share it with you. I can't really share it with our daughters or her parents. It's kind of personal."

Am I suddenly a therapist? If so, I would like to get $150 an hour, please. Still, I am curious as to what a woman about to commit suicide might write. After Serena died, I thought about suicide a lot — how I would do it? Guns seemed out of the question — where would I get one and would I have the courage to pull the trigger? I'm uncoordinated so I'd probably shoot the painting on the wall or a vase or something and my neighbors would call the police when they heard the shot. Carbon monoxide never occurred to me because we have a carport, not a garage. It seems complicated anyway. Pills would definitely be my choice but how many and what kind? After all, you can't just go to your doctor and ask for a lethal dose. There is a good chance that no doctor will write me a prescription for anything that could be deadly. I read somewhere that Tylenol can be lethal if you take enough of them. It would be awful to be on dialysis the rest of your life because you screwed up your kidneys but didn't die. No, you have to know what you're doing. About that time, I decided I didn't really want to die even though I wasn't convinced that I wanted to live. Since that time, I've existed in that middle place — kind of an earthly purgatory.

I leave it that we'll meet a week after the funeral. His daughters will only be home until next weekend. I know from experience that the critical time is a week to two weeks after the "event." All the casseroles are eaten, relatives have left, and you're left trying to decide what to do with the bed, the closet filled with little shirts and dresses, drawers overflowing with *Dora the Explorer* pajamas, socks, and miniature jeans. Compassionate Friends said to wait until you're ready. I never was so Luke did it. When we moved, it was easier because the reminders were gone. There was no room where Serena played, no toy I might find under the couch when I vacuumed.

When I go in the house, Wyatt and Belle are sitting on the couch, talking animatedly. I've never heard him talk so much.

"Buddhists believe that either you're reborn after you die or you enter Nirvana, which is a kind of nothingness," Belle says.

"I think they don't actually believe in reincarnation. It's like a loss of attachment to the physical world, and then our molecules dissipate or something," says Wyatt.

Their conversation reminds me of discussing the poetry of Rainer Maria Rilke with Luke, endless glasses of wine and later, our tumble into bed.

I offer drinks—cocoa or soft drinks— and put out some cheese and crackers and grapes. Luke should be home shortly, and we can go to dinner. Belle has put her bag in Wyatt's room. Luckily no memories linger in that space, just his bed and a chest of drawers. His room is right next to the guest room, and the master suite is downstairs. It is strange thinking of Wyatt with a girlfriend but we saw no point in putting them in separate rooms. We had plenty of talks about protection and hopefully he uses it.

"Can I cook tomorrow?" Belle asks, luminous face smiling. "I'd like to make Iosombe. It's a dish with eggplant, onions, spinach, peppers, and a little peanut butter. My grandmother taught me. I can also make honey bread."

I don't know whether to be grateful or insist we'll take care of the food but fortunately Wyatt rescues me.

"Belle loves to cook and she hardly ever gets the chance. We could go out after dinner and get ingredients and we'll make dinner tomorrow night."

Whose son is this? I was lucky if Wyatt would put his dish in the dishwasher after eating. He often had cereal for dinner in front of the computer. The only thing I remember him cooking was eggs or French toast on Sunday mornings. I was definitely the household cook until I stopped. I used to subscribe to epicurious.com and try out new recipes. Then Luke rarely came home and Wyatt didn't want to eat fancy meals. Most nights I eat alone, usually leftovers from something I make over the weekend. I've had cereal for dinner, too.

"Are you sure? I'd love to help. It would be great to learn a new recipe."

"Okay," Belle said, and her joy was palpable. How come she isn't miserable like the rest of us?

I go out to get the mail. If I had a dog, I'd walk it because I don't know what to do around so much exuberance. Fortunately, Luke pulls in, rolling down the window.

"Well? What's she like?"

# The Shape of What Remains

"You won't believe it. Think Kerry Washington and Beyoncé, only younger and more gorgeous. And she's nice. Moving to England will be harder than we thought."

"I made a reservation at Little India. They have lots of vegetarian options."

He's home on time. This faux family is operating like a well-tuned grandfather clock. I suffer through introductions all around and Luke's obvious surprise at Belle's vivaciousness and beauty. He's keeping his fatherly reserve, hug for Wyatt, handshake for Belle. When we duck into the bedroom, he says,

"She could be a model. I'm impressed."

Mr. Connoisseur of feminine beauty. You go near her and I'll kill you with my bare hands.

When he gets no reaction, he shifts topics.

"I sent my Curriculum Vitae and materials for that permanent position. It seemed foolish not to apply. There isn't anywhere else to go at Northern and change is good, don't you think?"

I thought we already had this conversation. Yeah, change is good for you. I'm not sure it's good for me. I've had enough change.

"How did you like the doctor?" Luke asks.

Shit. I don't want to tell him I liked her. That gives him a point in the *I'm more fucked up* category. I did like her though. She seemed competent and in agreement with my grief. I felt as if she understood.

"She was okay."

"I guess that means you'll stick it out?"

None of your damn business. Can't I have one area of my life that you aren't trying to control? If I get better, it will not be because of your intervention. I'm not dumb enough to sabotage my own progress.

"Maybe," I say.

The dinner is great. Turns out Belle loves Indian food and she raves about the Saag Paneer, saying it's the best she's had. She gets it hot which impresses me. I can barely stand medium. They share an order of garlic naan and we all drink mango lassis. Even Luke makes the smart decision not to order a drink. I can't remember enjoying Wyatt this much. He converses. It seemed as if he spent the last few years in front of a computer screen or with friends who didn't want to waste syllables on conversation. They hold hands.

"Thank you for taking me out," she said, at least twice.

I no longer dread the rest of the weekend. They will cook tomorrow. We can show them around Northbrook, or maybe go into Hartford for a movie or the museum. Then I remember Tim's phone call and Chantal. So young. They might have come up with alternative treatments. Medicine changes all the time. She's denied her daughters a mother, and their future children a grandmother. I don't know if she was in pain nor do I know if Tim was a devoted husband. I got the impression that he would have been happy to have an affair with me, and honestly, he's good-looking and smart.

What drives people to think there is no hope? We can put our animals out of misery, euphemistically called 'putting them to sleep' but we can't allay the suffering of people who are dying. Makes no sense to me. If Serena had lived but she had been critically injured or brain damaged, I don't know what I'd have done. Maybe I'd want to keep her alive because I couldn't bear the alternative or maybe I couldn't bear to see her like that and I'd want to end her suffering. I didn't have that choice. Suddenly I'm glad Wyatt is in love or in like with Belle. Grab the joy. It's all there is to carry any of us through.

## Chapter 9

The weekend was a diversion I needed. It helped me to remember love or at least that time of charged nerve endings. Wyatt seemed grown up which made me feel as if I didn't screw things up as badly as I thought.

I wish I had someone to call to ask what to wear to Chantal's funeral. I had never met Chantal, heard about her only from Tim and Kandi who once told me when Tim was in the bathroom that it was tragic how much she had declined. *He has to bathe her and everything*, she said. It's the part of "in sickness and in health" we all hope won't happen. We want to die in our sleep at eighty-five or ninety after dinner and a movie. A debilitating disease is a curse. I used to worry about having to take care of Bridget because I know Lena would never do it. Hopefully Dr. Arnie will take it on if she ever gets to that point.

I chose a black skirt and blazer. I'm not sure what I'll do after the funeral. I don't want to get stuck with a houseful of people like my book group or worse, all talking about the virtues of Chantal. Why did I say I'd do this? I can't even handle my own depression. Sometimes I even talk to Serena in the car. *Where should we go?* I pretend she wants to see the pond or the horses. It's crazy, I know. I dream about her and wake up feeling temporarily better, as if we've had a little visit. I wish I believed in something more than that but it's erratic. When I was driving to UConn to get Wyatt and Belle, I felt as if Serena was in the car, in the backseat where I made her ride because it's safer than the front seat, the death seat. Ironic. I could almost hear her breathe. I wonder what she would think of her big brother now. Would they be good friends or would she be a flouncy girly-girl who likes to hang out downtown and go shopping? I imagine her as strong-willed and intelligent. Maybe she'd be writing poetry or stories. Her grade school friend Bianca won the National Scholastic Art Award. They used to hold hands and sing together. They liked that both of their names ended in "a" and they both had middle names that began with "J". When you're six, I guess that makes you best friends. Serena would start out sentences with, "Bianca says...." *Bianca's mother let her get her ears pierced. Bianca's father took them to Disney World over winter vacation and she got a picture with Mickey Mouse and got to see Cinderella's castle. Bianca gets to stay up until 9:30 on weekends.* I'll probably regret the pierced ears the rest of my life but I don't care about the other ones, except maybe Disney World. We planned to go when Serena was eight and Wyatt was ten. It seemed like the best time since they would both have the stamina for all that stimulation. We never went. Wyatt asked at ten and again when he was twelve. Finally, he went with the school band when he was sixteen, said it was boring.

Tim lives in North Ainsville. I don't have a clue how to get there but he said it's about twenty minutes away. I haven't been to a funeral since Dom died. I don't know if Tim is religious and I hope he isn't Catholic since the Catholics condemn you if you commit suicide.

## The Shape of What Remains

There are lots of cars in the parking lot and I recognize Kandi's Mini Cooper. Shit. I check my lipstick in the rearview mirror. Tasteful and conservative is what Luke would call this outfit. I hope I'm not late.

There's a collage of Chantal in better times — dancing with Tim at their wedding, cradling one of their daughters, leaning on his shoulder on a plaid sofa while two little girls climb on them. She's Nordic looking, blonde hair, and square jaw. The photos at the bottom show her at her daughter's wedding using a walker.

I slip into a seat in the back next to a woman I don't recognize. Fortunately, I don't know anyone except Kandi and maybe Susan if she is here. There is no coffin. A woman in a robe steps up to the lectern. *Chantal Patterson was a courageous woman.*

She begins. I am stunned. Suicide is courageous? I always thought it was a cowardly act. Sticking it out amid pain is courageous. Getting up and dressed each day, knowing you have a progressive and debilitating disease is courageous. Maybe she wanted to save Tim from having to continue caring for her. If she really loved him, this might be the ultimate proof. Chantal used to be a science teacher. Some of the people attending are former students, I guess. It's clear from the little details the speaker offers that she knew Chantal. I hate it when a minister or Rabbi or priest delivers a eulogy on someone they never got to know. They deliver these generic lines about the mystery of God and how the person is now in a better place. How do they know that? Do they have a direct line to God, a kind of 1-800-GODLINE where they can find out what really happens after death? If they did, I'd be sending all my money to that church. This woman gets it right about the particulars of her life — from vacations in Gloucester to how she learned to drive a stick shift at thirty. There are two women in the front row, next to Tim. One is blonde like her mother and the other is dark-haired like Tim, and overweight. They both have men next to them, no kids. Maybe the heavy-set one is pregnant.

The blonde daughter, Nora, gets up and reads "The Summer Day" by Mary Oliver. She talks about her mother's involvement in her life, driving her to rehearsals when she was in *The Sound of Music*, baking brownies for her class. When she talks about how difficult it was when she got sick, how her mother tried so many alternative treatments, she stops, swallows hard, and gets so choked up, she can barely talk. The minister puts an arm around her shoulder and the choir sings *Amazing Grace*.

At Serena's memorial, we sang *'Tis a Gift to Be Simple* and *Somewhere Over the Rainbow*, which always makes me cry. I am suddenly pulled into another person's broken life. I wonder if he'll think that he should have been more attentive, should have seen the signs. Maybe a part of him is relieved and another part feels guilty for that. Death is complicated. We're forever replaying the last encounter we had with our loved one, thinking about how this script might have ended differently.

I slip out after the service, avoiding all the sniffling relatives. Kandi and Susan nod from across the room. I have no stomach for the buffet luncheon at the fellowship hall. Tim catches my eye, mouths a *thank you*. I feel depressed and uncertain about how helpful I can be. I've been grieving for over ten years. I'm no model for moving on.

The house is empty and I'm grateful. I don't want to hear about England, job opportunities, and hopefulness. I want to meditate on death and despair for a while so I put on Janis Joplin, make myself some soup, and take out the pile of student responses to "For the Anniversary of My Death" by W.S. Merwin.

# The Shape of What Remains

Some of them don't get it. He wasn't dead yet. Dead people can't write and publish poems. If I had known the day Serena would die, what would I have done differently? That is an impossible question. If I had known she was going to die, I would have done everything in my power to prevent it, holding her hand even though she felt she was too old for it, ignoring my neighbor, keeping my eyes on the road. How easy it is to think of what I should have done.

I wonder if Tim's daughters blame him. She must have been unhappy. How can anyone be happy losing control of their body? Some seem to rise above it like Stephen Hawking, whose progressive ALS left him paralyzed. He was considered one of the greatest scientists of my lifetime. Most of us don't have that kind of tenacity.

One of my students writes that it's a stupid poem because it's based on something no one can know. If I don't understand a piece of literature, does it make the literature stupid? Although opinion is fine in a response paper, I expect my students to cite the text or at least display some evidence of having interacted with the material.

Tonight is my first group session with Dr. Bradford-Smith. I'm not looking forward to it, wonder if I can feign a headache or sickness. The word "group" unnerves me, implies something touchy-feely. I've never been one to tell my life story in front of strangers. That is something my mother would call "airing your dirty laundry." The process of moving to Northbrook gave me the opportunity to be mostly anonymous, wife to Dr. Calvano, mother to Wyatt, and a writer working on a book while keeping herself linked professionally through an adjunct teaching appointment. Some of the newer colleagues thought I was lucky to have a husband who would support me so I could work on my writing.

I decide to just hang back and see what happens. Having the group comprised of people who have different experiences is somewhat reassuring. The Compassionate Friends tried to fill a need but even walking through the door reminded me that everyone in the room had a gaping wound. Some were festering and some nearly healed like the woman who had a stillbirth six years before. A non-person. Harsh, maybe but a stillbirth doesn't sing "Somewhere Over the Rainbow" to herself as she's skipping down the road. A stillbirth doesn't make you a birthday card with tiny pieces of mica glued to it because it sparkles.

There are so many memories: the last Christmas when Serena was so excited, she couldn't sleep and woke us up at five a.m. to see if Santa had come. She was five years old, a mere year away from extinction. It was her best Christmas and her last Christmas and I'm glad I sprang for the $100 doll, the Legos, an array of books and puzzles. I'm also glad she chose her favorite dish to have on Christmas Eve (baked mac and cheese). When she died, I had a little bag of stocking stuffers and books I had already ordered for her, hidden in my closet. Luke had to take them away when I wasn't home.

I don't plan dinner. When I get hungry, I eat some of the delicious honey bread that Belle made. Belle even helped clean up and left the room spotless, sheets stripped from the bed and neatly folded on the chair. Wyatt hugged me when they left, thanked me for letting him bring her home.

## Chapter 10

Dr. Bradford-Smith told me to write letters to Serena. At first that seemed ridiculous. How could I write letters to my dead daughter? What was the point?

*Dear Serena,*

*It's been ten years since we've talked and I have so much I want to say to you. We've moved twice and now we're in Northbrook in a house that you probably would like. There's a big playroom downstairs and you would have used it for your play stove and play food, made me meals. I had a stoneware tea set picked out for you for Christmas. You could serve real tea in it. I thought you and Bianca would have tea parties. Bianca is all grown up but I bet you still would have been friends. She's an artist and her mother said (the one time I ran into her) that she wants to go to art school. I wonder if you would have been an artist. I have all the cards you made for me for Mother's Day, my birthday, and even the little notes you left me in funny places. You told me once that you liked to write because it was a "secret code" — I guess that means that you were learning about the world of communication and now you knew its language. Your last teacher, Mrs. Grove, said you were the best reader and* writer in your class. You'd probably be reading Shakespeare and F. Scott Fitzgerald and Hemingway by now. We'd be looking at colleges.

I miss your smile; how your whole face would stretch and the two teeth missing in the front would show. I miss how you reached for me at night for hugs and how I would sometimes "fly" you into your bedroom and you'd beg for another flight. I remember how you named every one of your stuffed animals and I never knew where the names came from: Rocko, Cora, BB, Dime, and Mug. Your favorite was the dolphin, Mug. Grandpa Dom died and Grandma married another man, named Ira. She talks about you all the time.

I don't know where people go after they die but I hope you went to a place where they have everything you loved: pesto, mac and cheese, glittery rocks, mountains, low tide, porcelain dolls, tea sets, purple and yellow outfits, sneakers with colored laces, snuggles, stories, a fire in the fireplace, s'mores, chocolate cake with peanut butter frosting, wishes, tooth fairies, overalls, building sets, homemade chocolate chip cookies. I like to imagine you're feeling how much I love you.

I wish I hadn't turned to say hello to Diane that day. I didn't know you would run into the road. The man who hit you with his truck is very sorry. He didn't mean to do it. Maybe you saw something I didn't see. I looked for a clue but didn't find it. I hold your hand in my dreams at night because I always wanted to keep you safe so you could grow up and have a good life. I'm sorry, Serena.

I love you,

Mommy

"How did you feel after you wrote the letter?" Dr. Bradshaw-Smith is looking at me behind her round glasses.

"It felt purging to write it but it made me cry. I mean it was so preventable. Why wasn't I looking?"

"Tess, six-year-olds don't usually run into the road. It's normal to have some trust in that. She must have seen something. She probably looked first and saw that no traffic was coming. You said he turned onto your road so she wouldn't have seen him if she looked straight up the street. The truck came upon her fast."

"That's true. I don't know what she saw."

"Would it make a difference now?"

"Maybe not, but at least there would be a reason. The truth is I feel as if it was my fault and I think Luke believes this, too. Bess is probably the only one who doesn't blame me. She's said that she is sometimes amazed that her children grew to adulthood," I say.

"So, let's hypothesize. Imagine Serena saw a puppy in the road and was going to save it. How would you feel? Same outcome."

"I'd feel as if I should have yelled to her to get out of the road. She would go to rescue a puppy. Serena loved animals. It still comes down to the fact that she'd be alive today if I had been attentive."

"As parents, we guide our children. We cannot know everything that is going on in their minds. There was a seven-year-old in Houston who was hit by his school bus some years ago. The driver thought the child had safely crossed the street but he bent down to pick up a toy he dropped so he was out of the field of vision of the driver. Unfortunately, the driver didn't check to see him on the other side. You have to think about the many children he drops off each day and the trust he has that they will cross when the bus stops. His mother was right there, by their house waiting for him. She yelled, but it was too late. All of these people were responsible people and yet the child was killed."

I vaguely remember hearing about this on the news. All I could think of when I heard it is that I knew how that mother felt. She'd be running movies in her brain about how she should have taken him by the hand and dragged him out of the road or signaled to the driver that he was still there or *something*. When a random act of violence like a shooting happens, it is horrifying. Wyatt could go to a concert and get shot. I wouldn't let him go to Virginia Tech because of the shooting years ago but I know that is irrational. There could be a shooting at a basketball game at UConn or in the grocery store. Chances are he'll survive into adulthood but I can't protect him from everything. I think for me, it's the fact that this is my fault that haunts me.

I tell Dr. Bradford-Smith that I can't reconcile this. It's my fault and all the rationalization won't change that fact. She tells me to keep writing letters to Serena. *Serena will reveal the answer to you through these letters*, she says, which sounds a bit new-age-y but I go with it. I like writing the letters. There are many things I want to say.

# Chapter 11

I meet Tim at The Saucy Pot, a new restaurant just out of town. I have group tonight so I have a way to process this. Worried that I'm taking on too much, I set the timer on my cell phone to ping about an hour into our meeting. I figure I can claim a call or situation if I'm feeling overwhelmed. Since I started working with Dr. B-S, I have days where I feel as if my insides are sunburned. Everything is sensitive and raw. She says this is normal because I'm dealing with feelings I never dealt with before. Still, it exhausts me. In the past, I had the guilt but not the constant presence of Serena. The letters have brought her back in a sense. It's like I'm in regular dialogue with her.

Tim stands up when he sees me. He's lost weight, looks haggard. With his daughters gone, there must be no one around. I know the feeling of a full refrigerator of casseroles and deli platters and no one who wants to eat them.

"Hi Teresa. Thanks for coming."

"No problem." I put my hand on his.

The place is not crowded but it is overly cheery. Green gingham curtains on the windows. Bright paintings of farm scenes. Our server swoops in immediately with ice water and menus. *Is this your first time at the Saucy Pot?* I wonder why it matters but I suspect she'll tell me. *You choose your sauce and then you choose what to put it on — pasta, vegetables, chicken, fish. We even do desserts this way. You can have cake with chocolate sauce or Melba sauce, ice cream with various toppings, etc.*

I smile at Tim while we both ponder the absurdity of so many choices. I thought it was hard enough to pick one item on a menu. A tall server walks by with heaping plates of pasta and bowls of sauce. It's a place a child would love. Serena liked to make concoctions like mac and cheese with a dollop of pesto on top. What kid doesn't like ice cream with more than one topping?

"I'm so sorry, Tim." I know words are inadequate. What can one say? Does he blame himself as I did with Serena? Does he feel he should have been more alert to her mounting sense of hopelessness about her condition? It's as if he shrank since the funeral, his forehead more lined and his skin looser.

Tim lays an envelope on the table. I know it is Chantal's suicide note and I'm not sure I'm ready. Fortunately, the overbearing server saves me.

"Have you decided? Can I answer any questions?" She is decked out in green plaid and for a moment I think she is an extra on the set of some Disney movie. She's even wearing little white socks with lacy tops and saddle shoes. Saddle shoes. When I look around, they're all wearing them but the plaids are different colors. I feel like I'm time-traveling.

Once we've ordered and our server has moved off, presumably to indoctrinate someone else on the variety of sauces, he pushes the envelope toward me. I reluctantly open it.

# The Shape of What Remains

*Dearest Tim,*

*I am truly sorry. By the time you read this, I will be gone. My thought was to spare you the years and years of caretaking this illness will require. I also don't want to live this way any longer. Please don't blame yourself. I know how much of your life you gave up for me and I want you to love again. Remember how we went hiking in the Adirondacks, kayaking in Vermont, snorkeling in Hawaii? This was supposed to be the time in our lives for that kind of freedom but instead I became an invalid. Invalid. Strange word. I felt like a non-person. Asking for help with bathing, dressing, running errands is not the life I want. The girls will be okay. They are grown and I'd be of no use with grandchildren anyway. Some people can adapt to infirmity better than others. I tried but to me, life is about independence. I couldn't foresee this getting better and I knew it would probably get worse. Please try to understand. I didn't want to hurt you. You are a good man and we had some great years together. I remember what you said when the doctor told me it was progressing quickly. You said, we are in this together— but you were wrong. This was always my burden and I am unwilling to have it ruin two lives. I feel as if this is the last act of love I can offer. If there is life after death, I will meet you there.*

*Love always,*

*Chantal*

I wish I hadn't worn mascara because I'm sure it's all over my face. In a sense, her suicide was presented as a gift to him. What does one do with such a gift? I no longer think suicide is a coward's way out. She seemed like a brave woman who wanted to take charge while she still could. I understand that sentiment. I put my hand on Tim's before our server converges on us with platters and sauces. She is beaming and I want to slap her. Who gives a shit about marinara versus Alfredo when people are dying?

I'm not sure why I'm the one with whom he chose to share this.

"She really loved you," I manage, though my voice sounds like someone else's, husky and strained.

"Yes. The selflessness gets to me."

"I can understand how she wanted to define the terms of how she was willing to live, rather than let the disease define them for her," I say, and I really do believe this. I think I might have enjoyed being friends with a person like Chantal. In a sense, this was the only way she could take her power back.

"She told me that she felt out of control. The last doctor's visit, when he began to list all the services she would soon need, left her in tears. On the way home she said that she couldn't do it. I thought she was just grieving her loss of skills, not saying that she *really* couldn't do it."

I don't know what I'd do with the knowledge that Tim was handed. Dr. Bradford-Smith made me realize that knowing Serena was chasing after a puppy or a kitten wouldn't change the outcome or my feelings. I'd still feel responsible. I tell him about my therapist, careful not to reveal too much about the group. For someone as cynical as I am, it's amazing I'm sticking it out for now.

We agree to meet regularly until I leave for England.

"How do you feel about going to England?" he asks.

"Depends. Right now, I think it's a shitty idea. I'm beginning to make progress. My husband has, well, a bit of a wandering eye. You could say that I have some experience with Phillip Roth characters."

Shit, Tess, why did you tell him? Does he now think you're looking for company? I think of my mother's "airing the dirty laundry" saying. Then I think, why am I protecting Luke? If I am going to deal with my guilt and my grief, I have to deal with his sleeping around as well.

"If I was married to a woman as smart and attractive as you, I would honor my marriage vows," Tim says.

Yeah, well. You don't know what it's like to deal with crippling grief and a wife who barely got out of bed for a year. You never had to give little matched outfits to Goodwill or move family photos downstairs. I'm depressing.

"Thank you. It's complicated, Tim. He felt I should have moved on a long time ago. He was patient for a while," I say.

"That's kind of like me saying Chantal should have gotten over her illness. I still honored my vows, though I must admit it was challenging at times."

He looks at me and I remembered that prolonged hug and his erection poking me. Poor man. He probably hasn't gotten laid in years. I should haul him off to bed and put him out of his misery, I think, though I know I won't. I will meet him for lunch instead. Dr. Bradford-Smith told me to live more in the moment. I don't think she meant to be impulsive. Tim has a kindness that the rest of the book group lacks. It's nice to know I'm still able to feel something.

Driving home, I think about Chantal's letter. An act of love. How can death be an act of love? What would I do if I became incapacitated? What would Luke do? We're lucky that Bridget and Bess are still independent. I wonder if Bridget would ever want to depend on me. I was happy to extricate myself from her. Having daily contact would be oppressive. I always feel as if she's disapproving of me. I disappoint her because I don't have a tenure track job, haven't published a book, don't care about designer clothes and lavish vacations. As long as she gets to play bridge and go on three to four vacations a year with the gynecologist, all is good in her world.

Suddenly my stomach churns and I have to pull over. Damn that stupid Saucy Pot. A restaurant with a name like that is bound to be toxic. I vomit on the side of the road; something I haven't done since graduate school and that was for a different reason. Fortunately, there is no traffic. I feel lightheaded. What if I can't get home? Is there anyone I could call? Luke is in class at this hour.

I take it slowly. When I pull in the driveway, I'm relieved.

First, I call Tim.

"Did you get sick from our lunch?"

"No. You did?"

"I couldn't even make it home. I threw up on the side of the road off the I-84 exit. I felt like a college student," I say.

"Oh, Tess. I'm sorry. I feel fine. Maybe you're catching something. Why don't you lie down?"

I curl up on the bed and fall asleep. Serena is jumping rope. One, two, three. Her sneakers thump on the summer sidewalk. Iridescent beetles hover over my roses. I offer her lemonade and she asks me if she can have a lemonade stand. Some child had one in New Jersey, she says. She donated the money to charity. The summer sun is beating down and her hair is the color of daffodils. We drink lemonade on the front steps; plan the sign we'll make for the stand. *Let's give the money to the kids in another country. Maybe they don't have enough books to read.* Serena wanted everyone to have enough books. Sure. We'll do that. I'm smiling when I awaken. It's six o'clock and I have group at seven.

## Chapter 12

I tell everyone in the group about my dream, the first positive one I've had about Serena in quite a while. One person tells me that Serena is trying to communicate from the spirit world but that's a little too much like seeing auras for my sensibility. Dr. B-S says that our dreams are the most uninhibited part of our lives and there are lessons to be learned from them. Like maybe I wasn't a complete fuck-up of a mother. Even though Serena didn't get pierced ears, I drove her to another town for gymnastics and I never skimped on books. Both Wyatt and Serena could have any book they wanted. I start to think about the lemonade stand and that stupid saying, when life gives you lemons, make lemonade. Serena would do that. She'd see one of those nasty creatures like a silverfish or an ant and she'd rally for them to live, even if they needed to be relocated. I didn't listen to her because she was six and couldn't understand the impact of carpenter ants eating the studs or an infestation of silverfish. I just became discreet about my murders. Thoughtful even. I would relocate moths and leave the bees alone unless they got in the house. Worms were good for the garden.

Serena is still teaching me, except the lessons are now in my own head. We shared DNA. I wonder if that means that I still carry some of her within me. How does that apply to Wyatt? Sometimes he feels like a foreigner but then I'll catch him reading Mark Twain or volunteering at the soup kitchen. The relationship with Belle caught me off guard. Parents of Wyatt's friends would tell me that he was so polite, and would pitch in to help. My son? I would wait for him to clear his plate after dinner but most of the time he'd leave it on the table. I got tired of asking. I guess the true test of being a parent is how your children behave outside the house and he passed that test. I wonder if he will meet Belle's parents. Will they disapprove of him because of his race? I never got the chance to see how Serena would behave in the world. Her social life was limited to play dates. Luke's brother, Ben and his partner, Cal came in when Serena was two. Their son, Raoul is three years older than Wyatt. He goes to UC Berkeley. There was an occasional birthday party and she met her cousins Emilie and Mariah about once a year. I don't know much about my sister's kids because we aren't close. She chose a life I can't imagine, near poverty and next to no culture. She felt our mother represented the bourgeoisie. Can't argue with that. Bridget likes her spa dates, her hairdresser, being seen wearing the right clothes in the right places. I don't give a rat's ass about any of it but Lena still thinks we live an excessive lifestyle. My sister is the queen of self-sacrifice at the expense of feeling superior to others. Problem is, she wouldn't shut up about it until I programmed my phone to be silent when she calls. Maybe it was the calls about our suburban lifestyle being to blame for Serena's death that pushed me over the top. After all, Emilie and Mariah were homeschooled (unschooled) and thus never had to wait for buses in their remote little corner of the world. She also didn't worry about jobs with health insurance because they live in

Canada where they have national healthcare. Easy to judge the choices of others.

Instead of sisterly pride in my accomplishments, she chided me for wasting so much time and money on a frivolous intellectual pursuit. I don't consider anything intellectual frivolous though I'd agree that it hasn't exactly paid off. I don't want to pay her bills when her husband dies nor do I want to fish for my supper. This leaves only Bridget and the gynecologist. Not much in the category of family. Are all families this wacky? Judging from this group, it seems so.

When I get home, Luke isn't there. It's 9:30. I check my voicemail. *Had to meet with a grad student. Home around 9:30.* Leaving a message is progress. The next message is from Dr. Dillman. Something about wanting to meet with me. Did I screw something up? I always show up on time, get my grades in earlier than most. My book orders are submitted well in advance. He said it isn't urgent but to call him. I figure it's too late to call tonight. Shit. Now I will obsess about it.

I hear Luke's car. 9:37. Pretty good. He looks exhausted.

"Long day," he says, opening the fridge, grabbing the last Guinness.

"Did you eat?"

"Grabbed a sandwich at 5. You offering?"

I pull out some grapes and the good cheddar from Vermont.

"I have to fly to England next week. The committee wants to meet with me about the position. We're off anyway for Thanksgiving. Why don't we all go?"

Thanksgiving is an American holiday. The Brits don't care about pilgrims and neither do I. I always thought the Native Americans got the short end of that damn stick. Since I teach on Thursday, I'm off all week. Bess would invite us to dinner. She always did. I'd bring a pie.

"What about your mother?"

"She'll be fine. They may go out to California and have Thanksgiving with Ben and Cal. They haven't seen Raoul in quite a while. They see us all the time. We can be with them for Hanumas."

Bess has been creating a hybrid Hanukkah-Christmas combo for the past ten years or so, complete with a fully decorated tree, lit menorah, latkes, dreidels, and stockings. We have a brunch on Christmas morning that includes lox and bagels as well as sliced ham and pastries. We all like the quirkiness.

Strange but the next thought I had was that I'd have to miss group and my individual session with Dr. B-S. Those meetings framed my week. Still, it seemed like a good idea to see what could be our future living place.

"What will we do while you're interviewing?"

"Nigel's wife Lucy will take you around. Their daughter has some classes but will be home on Friday. I figure we could fly out on Monday night and come back on Saturday so we'd have time to get Wyatt back to school. We don't give a damn about turkey, do we? They offered to cover our flights. Nigel booked us two rooms at the Macdonald Randolph Hotel in Oxford. He said it's good and convenient to everything. It's walking distance to the center of town and the Covered Market."

"Okay."

"Great! I already told him we'd go because he had to book everything through the university travel department. I was counting on you," Luke says.

Like I can count on you? At least there would be five days where we'd pretend to be an ordinary couple.

"What's the daughter's name?"

"Abigail. They call her Abby," Luke says.

I know I'm elected to phone Wyatt. It's the division of labor in our relationship. He pays the bills, I deal with the son. I figure 10:00 is early for a college student but I get his voice mail. I hope he wasn't planning to go to Rhode Island with Belle. Okay, I'm excited. I haven't been out of town, never mind out of the country, since Serena died, except to Canada to visit Lena. I'm glad I renewed my passport for that trip to Nova Scotia. I write a note to call Dr. Dillman, Dr. Bradford-Smith, Tim, and Wyatt. Also make a hair appointment and buy a couple of new outfits. I Google the weather in Oxford. It looks similar to New England but a little warmer.

Luke kisses the back of my neck while I'm sitting at the computer. He has to lift my messy hair to do it. His hands stray to my breasts. I'm not going to do this again. I stand up and feign needing to use the bathroom.

Lines are beginning on my forehead. Still my colleagues think I'm in my thirties. I was only twenty-four when I had Wyatt, a careless moment. Terrible to say that but Wyatt is the result of a broken condom. I had taken a break from the pill because it was making me nauseous. I was two years into the Ph.D. program so it wasn't exactly good timing. Fortunately, the university had an excellent day-care program. When Serena was born two years later, I was done with the course work, and I'd mapped out my research for *Chaucerian Representation of Gender Roles and Human Behavior*. Bess helped with Wyatt a lot in those early years. I finished on time, age twenty-seven. I had a tenure-track appointment waiting for me, a one-year-old and a three-year-old. I was able to arrange my schedule and Luke arranged his so one of us was always home to handle the mornings. I hated the idea of rousing young children to haul them off to daycare early in the morning. We always gave them breakfast before taking them to the university-sponsored daycare. I taught one night a week and Luke taught a different night so a parent was always home for dinner and most times, it was both of us. It was a tight schedule but we were managing, buoyed up by Bess and various other friends who later faded out of my life.

Death makes people uncomfortable. Suddenly the foundation of their whole lives is in question. If something catastrophic could happen to someone like me, they couldn't help but think about the possibility of it happening in their lives. Coming home, locking their doors, and tucking their kids in at night gives them a false sense of security. I know. I used to feel that we'd finally landed safely in a town where the worst thing that happened was an occasional break-in or power failure. Children didn't die, though a few had to go to the Emergency Room for stitches or to have a bone set after falling off a bike or skiing. Even adults in our age group weren't dying.

After Serena's death, people started getting sick and dying everywhere. Maybe I just noticed it more. The obituaries became the first part of the newspaper I'd read. Women in their thirties and forties were getting breast cancer. Men were having heart attacks. Children were dying of leukemia. I'd check to see where contributions should be sent to find the clues. I know it seems morbid but it made me realize that all life is tenuous. We go along every day thinking we have all the time in the world but we don't. Today could be the day. Or tomorrow. I guess that's why so many dropped me as a friend. I wasn't exactly optimistic. If I wasn't obsessing about all the death around me, I was reading about war, nuclear accidents, or pollution. Sometimes I think it's amazing that any of us are still alive. My friend Rachel is a pessimist. *The fucking world is blowing up. If climate change doesn't screw us, these crazy politicians will start a war and take away more of our rights.* I kind of agree.

When I go into the bedroom, Luke is on the bed, *my* bed, naked, with a big erection. I guess all erections are big. We haven't slept in the same room in years except when we have sex, which is infrequent. Not exactly subtle. I'm speechless. What am I supposed to say? Get out of my room? He is my husband, for better or for worse and lately, it's mostly worse. Trouble is he's sexy. I get why coeds like him. He works out at the gym and he's got a great body. I don't think we even have condoms around (though I hope he's been using them with Tyra and anyone else) and I haven't been on the pill since the year after Serena died. I still haven't gotten my period but I've been late before so I'm not worried. What are the odds of getting pregnant from one lapse at age forty-two? I know, that is the same rationalization teenagers use. It only takes one time, though isn't a man's sperm count supposed to diminish with age?

Luke reaches out his hand and I know I'm going to do it. Might as well be getting along if we're going to England. We'll have to sleep in the same bed because Luke isn't going to tell Nigel to book three rooms instead of two since he doesn't sleep with his wife. I used to like sleeping with him, particularly in winter since I can never get warm. I'd curl up against his smooth warmth and think of the snowflakes blanketing our lawn, the hush of traffic, and his slightly spicy smell. I don't sleep as well without him. Luke's mouth is on mine and his hand is unbuttoning my shirt, while the other hand is unzipping my pants. He puts his hand down my panties and I know I'm already wet for him. He makes a little sound that I take as approval and even if I wanted to stop now, I don't think I could. Once he's inside me, it is like a tenor singing at the Met. I'm pathetic. I match his rhythm and I hear percussion, the deep bass of his moan. I feel like the luckiest and dumbest woman in Northbrook. In this moment, it's okay to leave behind Chaucer and the antiheros of Shakespeare and roll around on clean cotton sheets, listening to the rain.

## Chapter 13

Predictably Wyatt isn't happy about giving up Thanksgiving break to go to England. He had planned to meet Belle one day in Providence. Mostly he just wanted to eat and hang with his friends. What I've learned from being the parent of a teenager is when to give options and when to just present things as non-negotiable. This was non-negotiable since Nigel had booked the tickets and the rooms. Wyatt hasn't been out of the country except for Canada. You would think he'd be excited. I told him about Luke's summer opportunity but not about the long-term possibility.

"I don't want to go to England for the summer. I was supposed to work at Computer Town again. I need to save for a car. Can't I stay here? I'll be nineteen. I can be on my own."

I told him we'd deal with that one later and I will need Luke to actually log some father hours. For now, we were going to England over the break and that wasn't going to change. We'd still have our winter holiday with Bess and Ira. After all, he gets to see Belle presumably every day and every night. He can spare five days. I sweeten it by telling him I'd put some extra money in his account so he could buy a few things for the trip — like a good raincoat and maybe some shoes.

Mission accomplished. What do I tell Dr. B-S about the latest sex-capade with Luke? I told her we'd only slept together once in the last six months. I've now written five letters to Serena. She wanted me to bring in the latest one.

*Dear Serena,*

*We are getting ready for Thanksgiving. Ten years ago, I didn't think I'd ever have anything I could give thanks for but this year, I do. I'm thankful that I get to write these letters. I'm thankful your brother Wyatt is happy at college. He even has a girlfriend named Belle. She doesn't look like the Disney character. She is from Rwanda. I think you would have liked her. She's smart and strong like you. When she made us honey bread, I thought of you because you loved raisin bread with butter and cinnamon. You also loved homemade cinnamon rolls which I hardly ever made since they took so long. If I could, I'd make them for you every day. Honey bread has cinnamon and cardamom in it. It is sweet and slightly spicy. I think you would have loved it.*

*We're going to England for Thanksgiving. Daddy will be doing research there next semester and he's also applied for a job there. Though I hate to leave the state where you last lived, I also know that you're a part of me. I'll always keep you alive in my heart. Daddy said I could take the little stone with your name on it that he had made but I know you're everywhere. You're not fixed to a place and I no longer feel as if I need to be in one place. I will always love you.*

*Love, Mommy*

Truthfully, I was running out of things to say to her though I liked telling her the news. After I apologized, there wasn't a lot left to say. I can't bring her back. All the conjuring I tried to do didn't turn back the clock. Everything has to be aligned for a tragedy to occur — the combination of a parent looking away, a negligent truck driver, and a distracted child. The same can be true for fortuitous events. Luke had to impress Nigel, present a viable proposal, appear open to relocation. There is a random quality to all of this. There is a part of me that feels as if I didn't do anything bad enough to deserve this. I wasn't a perfect mother but I loved Serena completely and without condition. I wouldn't have abandoned her if she became obstinate and morose as a teenager or took up with a thug or even experimented with drugs and alcohol. I might have questioned my skills as a parent but I would have stood by her, tried to get her help. A damaged daughter is better than no daughter at all.

When I try Dr. Dillman, I get his voicemail. He calls back.

"Teresa?"

I wonder why people say your name when they are calling your cell phone. It isn't as if you have someone else answering it.

"Yes?"

"I know you were disappointed that you didn't get that temporary full-time appointment. You were certainly qualified for it. The candidate that took the spot, Marissa Duval, is pregnant. She wants to take next semester off. Would you like to teach full-time for the spring semester? I can't promise more than adjunct after that, though we'll see what we can do."

Shit! Does this mean the universe doesn't think I'm totally crippled? Could I handle full-time work for a semester?

"Can I think about it and call you back?"

"Certainly. I need a decision before the Thanksgiving break. We're already pushing the deadline for book orders for next semester," Dr. Dillman says.

I call Luke to see what he thinks. I mean, we're not supposed to go to England until the summer. I could save up some money and also make my curriculum vitae look a little stronger since I'd have some recent full-time work.

"Do you think you can handle it? You know what happened last time you tried."

"That was ten years ago. Yes, I think I can. I could prepare for it over the intercession," I say.

"If you're sure. I mean, it's your decision. Might be good for you."

Driving to therapy, I wonder if I really can handle it. I still have days when I have to push myself to get out of bed. The nightmares have stopped though and I've even had a couple of good dreams about Serena. I don't want to fail. Trying to do this and failing would be worse than turning it down. It could be career-suicide.

Dr. B-S never tells me what to do directly. Maybe therapists speak in code. She has this way of putting it back on me. I think it's called reflective listening. *What do you think?* I tell her that I feel as if I can handle it but I am afraid of the paralysis that has been a regular visitor since Serena died. Just because it hasn't visited in a while doesn't mean it won't show up. What if it shows up when I'm in the middle of a lecture?

"Who controls it?"

I don't know the answer though it's obviously me. It *feels* like something outside myself, like a force that descends upon me at random times. This isn't logical, I realize.

"What do you want to say to it?"

I hate questions like that. It's a fucking force, not a person. I want to scream. I can't talk to it. Then I realize that there's a part of me that likes the feeling of paralysis. It's my homage to Serena. *See, honey, I continue to be impacted by your death. It has rendered me helpless and will continue to do so for the rest of my life. That's how much I loved you.* I tell this to Dr. B-S. She nods vigorously.

"Yes. There is a definite payoff in helplessness. It allows you to continue to punish yourself for Serena's death. What will be left if you give it up?"

I think about this.

"Life," I say. It's true. Trips to England, classes to teach, books to write, friends to make. Ten years is a long time. Maybe I've repaid my debt.

"Enjoy England. Happy Thanksgiving," she says.

## Chapter 14

"Waiting in line is called queuing. The trunk of a car is a boot," I tell Wyatt. "In general, it's best to dress up, not down when going anywhere."

Wyatt sounds a little more enthusiastic about our Thanksgiving trip though he is still pleading his case to stay home during the summer. Leaving Belle indefinitely won't be an easy sell though Luke still hasn't been offered more than the fall semester of research. I tell Wyatt about my full-time teaching assignment next semester.

"Wow, Mom. Are you sure you can handle it?"

The classes won't be hard: two sections of Freshman Comp, Intro to Shakespeare, and Women's Poetry. I've taught all but the Comp classes recently. Bess added her voice to the cheerleading squad. She is sure I can handle it. It would be good for me to add more structure in my life, she says. Structure. I think of two-by-fours and footings. I lost my footing. This house of mine will be rebuilt. Still there is a little voice inside of me saying *What about Serena?* She didn't have this option. Rachel is all for it. *About damn time you used that fucking Ph.D.*

## The Shape of What Remains

There is a light snow falling outside. It is still November but an ash-like coating clings to the rhododendron. The days are shortening and bleak winter lurks. I need sunlight. Seasonal affective disorder is what they call it when people get depressed in the wintertime. Maybe I have all season affective disorder — like all-weather tires. It isn't worse in the winter though I detest endless gray days. We leave in a week. I can't remember the last time I flew but I remember the clouds, how we finally got above them and it was blue again. I imagine Serena in the clouds but sometimes I think of her floating in the ocean, on her back, smiling. She would have been a great swimmer. Her teacher said she had a strong kick and no fear. She was learning to hold her breath underwater and do the breaststroke. There would have been summers on Cape Cod or visits to Martha's Vineyard with the insufferable Bridget. Stop. I can't do this. Let her stay six.

We're reading *Blessings* by Anna Quindlen in the book group. It's about an ex-con who finds a baby dropped on the doorstep of the garage where he is living. He's working as a handyman for this old woman named Lydia Blessing. Of course, the infant is a female and of course he's a wonderful and nurturing father. It will be the event that will turn his life around, I am sure of it. Who would abandon a baby? I'm only halfway into the book and will bring it to finish on the plane. The plane that will take us to Heathrow where Nigel will send a car to pick us up. Suddenly there are people I don't know that we talk about regularly: Nigel, his wife, Lucy, their daughter Abigail. I don't know if they have other children.

Luke calls.

"I'm still working. Should be home by seven. How about a late dinner?"

It's a new behavior, the calling. I think it's my cue to make something but I've learned that he often doesn't keep his word. I've sat in the living room while Cornish hens dried up or clam sauce congealed. No. I start cooking when he walks in the door now. There used to be nights when he didn't come home at all although not lately. Now he comes home every night, usually no later than eight. He talks to me instead of going to turn on the television or the computer. We've had sex twice in the last month without protection and I still haven't gotten my period.

I think of the possibility of a pregnancy but talk myself out of it. It's near impossible with his age and my age and the infrequency of lovemaking. When Serena died, he wanted another child a year later but I wasn't ready. He asked about every six months for five years. Then he began to stay out late. I couldn't bear the idea that we were trying to replace her like adopting a new puppy when a family dog dies. There would only be one Serena Joy Calvano. Each child is individual. Wyatt is and was entirely different from Serena. It's like throwing all the possible combinations up in the air and seeing where they land. Will they have blue eyes, a facial tic, brown hair, freckles? Am I too old to raise a child? Maybe I would be unable to handle the responsibilities as an older person. Maybe the child would feel I was out of touch with his or her generation. I'd go to Parent-Teacher meetings and people would ask if I'm the grandmother. Shit. I'm not pregnant and here I am planning a future.

I pull down the stairs to the attic, get out luggage we haven't used in years. It is dusty, like my life. Underutilized. Teresa Calvano, Ph.D. Adjunct professor. Part-time mother of a college-age son. Part-time wife of part-time husband. We play at marriage. When a married couple is called for, we rise to the occasion, dressed in our suburban best. We bring a bottle of wine, drive up in the same car, fill out a card for a wedding, sign it Luke and Tess. We have a joint checking account but Luke pays our bills online and I don't know the password. My name is on the deed for the house and the titles of both cars. We share a name, a past, a house but not always a bed. How many relationships are appearance only?

I imagine showing up in England as a loving, cohesive family. One son. Nigel knows nothing about our unfortunate past, the incident that rearranged our family. I promise myself to start anew, at least for the five days of our visit.

Luke's car. He's early, only 6:30. I move to the kitchen to go through the motions of preparing dinner. I can do this. I will look as if I planned it all along. I put white wine in the freezer to chill just as Luke walks in, snow on his coat and a bouquet of roses and baby's breath in his gloved hands.

"What's the occasion?" My first thought is that the intended recipient of the flowers didn't show up and I'm the understudy.

"Do I need an occasion to bring my wife flowers?"

"But we're leaving in a week. They'll die."

"Enjoy them now. Better get them in water fast." Luke smiles, pecks me on the cheek and hangs up his raincoat.

"I didn't know you'd be home so early. It will take a little while to finish making dinner. I can let you know when it's ready."

"I'll make the salad," he says.

When we were first married, he swore he'd never become one of those husbands who read the paper while his wife (who also worked) made the meals. *We'll do it together*, he said. And we did, for the most part. Even after Wyatt was born, we split up courses. He would always make the salad or cook vegetables. I made the entrées since I had more of a repertoire. I was just teaching Serena to help with sauces and desserts.

Wyatt's job was to set the table and clear. He wasn't interested in cooking unless we were making pizza or grilling. After Serena's death, Luke retreated to his office on the rare nights when he came home for dinner. At first, he'd tell me he was just checking email and would help in a minute. After a while, he stopped pretending. He'd stay there until I called him in. I don't know what he was doing, looking at porn, emailing coeds, or just sitting and thinking. When he stopped coming home, it wasn't that much of a transition except I ate alone most nights. It was hard to rally to cook a meal for just me and I wasn't about to make him a meal that he could reheat when he got home. He had made the choice not to be there and he could damn well figure out his own meals.

My breasts feel tender. Either I'm getting my period or I'm pregnant. Same symptoms for both. At my last doctor's visit, Dr. Knowles asked about birth control, told me that perimenopausal women can have irregular cycles, which is why there are cases of unexpected pregnancies. I know I'm still ovulating because I can feel it some of the time, a little pang mid-month. I didn't want to tell her I wasn't having sex with my husband. I let her believe we used condoms. I wonder if Luke would be happy if I was pregnant.

"I'm a week and a half late on my period. Probably stress but we didn't use protection."

Luke fixes me with an expression that is hard to read — kind of a combination of disbelief and cynicism.

"How would you feel about it?" he asks, therapist-like. I know this line from Dr. B-S. How the hell do I feel about everything? Sometimes I get sick of being asked. I don't always know how I feel. Right now, I feel disappointed with his lukewarm reaction. Lukewarm. Ha!

"Not sure. Probably a hormonal glitch."

"Why don't we go to CVS and get a home pregnancy test? It would be easy enough to find out."

Why didn't I think of that? Because I don't really want to know. If I'm not, I'll feel a sense of loss, absurd because I don't even want to be pregnant.

"Do you have any symptoms?" Luke must remember how sick I was with Serena, throwing up every morning. I lost weight for the first few months.

"I threw up once but I think the food just didn't agree with me. I feel bloated and my breasts are tender but that's normal when I'm expecting my period."

Luke smiles. "Your breasts *are* tender. Nice visual — tender breasts."

"Apparently that term is more endearing to you than it is to me."

"How about I run out and get the test while you finish making dinner? I can throw together the salad when I get back," Luke says.

He grabs his raincoat and is out the door before I can answer. I was about to take a glass of wine myself when I thought to wait. Can I take the test tonight or should I wait until morning? It has been sixteen years since I took a pregnancy test. They used to tell you to take it first thing in the morning but maybe things have changed.

I want to hate Luke, have every right to hate him though it has occurred to me more than once that a divorce would make me lose Bess, one of the few constants in my life. Bess has perfect timing and she supports me wholeheartedly. I don't know how much she knows about Luke but she loves him unconditionally as well. It's just her nature. I thaw raspberries for dessert. I stop myself from pouring liquor on them when Luke walks in.

"I bought two of them, just in case, you know. It's supposed to be most accurate in the morning but I thought, I mean if you're okay with it, I thought you could try it now."

"Now?" As in stop what the hell you're doing, drop everything and find out if you're growing a baby, someone to break your heart and open up new wounds? Do I want to know? I think how disappointed we'll both be when I'm not pregnant and how terrified I'll be if I am. Luke seems animated, nervous. Like an expectant dad. Luke nods — hands me a pink box labeled "Lady Easy". For idiots. This test spells out the word, pregnant. That blue line can be so confusing. I guess it does assume you can read.

"Don't you want dinner?"

Luke shakes his head. "After."

I go into the bathroom. I'm one of those people who can pee on demand, a skill that is mostly inconvenient and only useful in times like this or when I go to the doctor's office and they hand me that little plastic cup. My hands are shaking when I open the cardboard box and the sanitized container. There's a picture of a happy woman. She's fucking ecstatic. They have been trying for years. This is the best thing to happen to her since she got married. She's thinking about how adorable she'll look in all those maternity clothes, the ones that say "baby" with an arrow pointing down. I want a shirt that says "brains" with an arrow pointing up.

My pee looks ordinary. I dip the little pregnancy stick into it. No fair peeking. I have to wait five minutes, kind of like an hour in real time. I don't want to leave the bathroom because then I'd have to talk to Luke. That is a conversation that can wait. There isn't much to do in a bathroom except the usual. We don't even have any reading material because I always considered that in poor taste. It doesn't stop Luke who brings in his own books and magazines, leaves them on the back of the toilet and then I move them to his home office, somewhat gingerly. I guess I'm a little germ phobic. I rearrange the shampoo bottles and refold some of the towels that were haphazardly put into the small linen closet.

I can hear Luke bustling around in the kitchen though I can't imagine what is left to do. He's making something, maybe a drink. Some people are able to anesthetize with alcohol. I won't even be able to do that, if the test is positive. The phone rings and I hear Luke's deep voice. He's laughing, conversing with someone.

Okay. Is it time? I carefully lift the plastic whatever-it-is and squint at the results. P-r-e-g-n-a-n-t. A chill goes through me. Then denial. Must be inaccurate. I'm forty-two and only had unprotected sex twice. A lapse in judgment and we made a life. Suddenly I have this thought that maybe that was Luke's intent. Get me pregnant so I wouldn't leave him. It doesn't look good for his career to be divorced. Now he's respectable. The eminent Dr. Lucas Calvano, family man and Shakespearean scholar. Virile. His little sperm retain their motility even at forty-four. He'd be proud of himself. I hate to give him that satisfaction but I don't know that I can lie about it. I sit on the edge of the bathtub and then the tears come.

Pretty soon I'm sobbing so loudly Luke hears me, knocks on the door

"Tessie? You okay?"

He opens the door (I forgot to lock it), and I fall into his arms, getting the front of his shirt wet. He strokes my hair like a child.

"Ah, Tessie. It's okay. Whatever it is, we can handle it."

I wish I believed that.

He can see the results on the side of the sink, I'm sure. He's still cooing to me, stroking my hair.

"Poor baby. I know it's frightening but we're in this together," he says, which is how I know that he saw.

"How could this happen?"

"I think we should move back into the same room," he says.

That seems a little beside the point.

## Chapter 15

It's drizzling when we arrive at Heathrow. Cold November rain. International Arrivals and Baggage Claim take way longer than I expect. Luke stops to buy The London Times. Finally, we see a balding man in a suit holding up a sign that says "Calbano." Close enough. Luke takes my arm and we make our way through the bleary-eyed queues and crying babies to Travis, our driver. After a hearty clipped British greeting, he immediately takes my bag. Wyatt has been sulking for the past few hours since he learned that his cell phone won't work here without incurring charges. Belle will have to wait a few days. I tell him he can use WhatsApp when we have wi-fi. He can also text her but I'm not saying anything.

Luke is hovering, asking me if I'm cold, locating my raincoat. We haven't told Wyatt anything though I did repeat the pregnancy test the next morning, half-hoping it had been a fluke. We have decided it's best to wait until January to make it public since the risk for miscarriage is high at my age. I will need tests to screen for birth defects. There are, I gather, a whole host of risks to having a baby at forty-two. When I

Googled it, I came up with lists of women who had babies into their fifties and even sixties. There are documented cases of women who acted as surrogates for their daughters, having IVF and their daughter's eggs implanted. Even with those unusual cases, there are a fair amount of naturally occurring pregnancies and high-profile cases like the Pulitzer Prize winning playwright Wendy Wasserstein who had a baby girl at age forty-eight and later died of lymphoma. She never revealed the father, even on her deathbed.

I did not acquiesce to the *share a room* proposal except in regard to this trip. I need my space for now and though I realize I can't get pregnant more than once, I'm saving the conversation about Luke's past infidelity for a time when I have the support of Dr. B-S. I didn't get to tell her the news and I'm fine with keeping it secret for now.

We're in the back of some limo type vehicle and Travis is pointing out the sites — we'll see Windsor Castle in the distance.

"It is about an hour and a half ride," Travis says in his lovely accent.

Mostly it looks dreary and rain-smeared through the window. Lots of gray. I left gray and apparently, it's following me, a shadow I can't shake.

I think of the children's song *Rain, rain, go away. Come again some other day. Little Tessie wants to play.* Do I want to play? When we boarded the plane in Hartford/Springfield, I was definitely excited. A change of scenery. Anonymity. That adventurer spirit I used to have kicked in and I was hungry for a new experience. I'm hoping Wyatt won't be crabby without his ladylove. Travis tells us that Nigel and Lucy will meet us at Chutneys Indian Brasserie for lunch, after we get settled in our rooms. Good choice. When I looked online for English specialties and turned up steak and kidney pie, I figured we'd try the ethnic restaurants. More variety of flavors; something all of us prefer. It's about 9:00 in the morning local time and though we barely slept on our overnight flight (except for Wyatt, plugged into his music, blissfully unaware of turbulence and clattering trays), I feel strangely awake. Travis tells us it's best to just stay up today and go to bed early tonight. Luke has his interview on Thursday but he will meet with Nigel tomorrow to discuss their research. Friday will be our day for sightseeing together before we leave on Saturday. That gives me two days to look around. Apparently, Lucy has cleared her schedule (what does she do?) to play hostess.

The MacDonald Randolph is known for its food, Travis tells us. *Do try the morning buffet and afternoon tea.* I think of *The Importance of Being Earnest* and cucumber sandwiches. I think we will break a record for meals together during this little interlude. The countryside looks a lot like New England now, grass and cows, bales of hay.

There is something civilized about the sound of a British accent. Then I think of all the countries the British tried to colonize or rule and the atrocities committed for land and power. We Americans have our own bloody history. Still there is a pomp and circumstance to the culture that I find oddly appealing. It's the antithesis of the direction in which the United States seems to be headed — a lack of concern about manners, short attention spans, and an obsession with social media and technology. My students come to class in an odd assortment of clothing — from pajama bottoms with fuzzy slippers to skimpy tank tops with no bra. One girl's top was translucent, and I could see her nipple rings. Too much information, as they say. It might be an illusion, but I think of the British as proper. I mean, they still have afternoon tea while we're dashing off to a drive-through for an iced latte.

It's nearly 11:00 when we get to MacDonald Randolph Hotel, a venerable looking establishment in this beautiful city of spires. We arrange to meet Nigel, Lucy and Abigail at 12:00. I'm starving. Planes have a way of serving meals at the most inopportune times. It felt like the middle of the night for me when breakfast rolled around so I only nibbled at a roll. I haven't had any nausea since that restaurant incident.

Wyatt is thrilled with the view of the city from his room, adjacent to ours. There is a fitness center and numerous meeting rooms. A distinguished looking place. I imagine dignitaries staying here. When Luke tries to kiss me in our room, I tell him I have to pee — which I do. There are all sorts of delightful looking toiletries in the bathroom, called simply the toilet in England. Nothing to eat though. I pull my hair back, dab on some lipstick. I need a shower. Flying for so long makes me feel grimy.

Would a man consider me attractive? Tim seems to find me so, or maybe he just feels as if we understand each other. It's been so long since I've noticed the reaction of men when I walk in a room. Mostly I feel invisible. I used to compare myself to other women my age and usually I compared favorably. I like to think I look intelligent though I'm not sure what that means. Once, about a year after Serena's death, I was in Starbucks and a man came up to me. *I hope your husband knows how attractive you are,* he said. I was still wearing a wedding ring at that time. Now I'm knocked up. Having Luke's baby. At least I know it's his. If the situation were reversed, he would be in deep shit.

When I came out of the bathroom, Luke had changed, hung up my blouses and coat. I want to lie on that king-sized bed, sink into the many pillows. How long can I stay awake? He moves around me, giving me space. On the elevator, I feel as if we've boarded a time machine and we're about to glimpse a possible future over lunch.

## Chapter 16

I can't help but wonder what Dr. B-S would think of my ability to make nicey-nice with the Thompsons. I can't get over the accent. For the first twenty minutes, I felt as if I was speaking in slang, my words sounded so coarse next to them. Then I focused on my papadum and vegetable curry. For probably the first time in my life, I was grateful that Bridget was rigid about table manners. I've never seen such skillful use of a knife. If the pieces got any smaller, they would be pre-digested. The daughter, Abigail, wasn't there which left Wyatt listening to the endless banter of adults. We really are boring. Once we had exhausted the conversation about our trip, the hotel room, dear Travis, and the lovely city of Oxford (did we catch a glimpse of Windsor Castle on the journey?), Luke and Nigel started talking about their research. This left Lucy, Wyatt, and me to chitchat. I should have good credentials in this department, having survived the book club. She mentions Oxford Brookes University as a place Wyatt might enjoy for classes. Bad topic. First of all, Wyatt isn't convinced he needs to come for the summer, never mind the semester or his entire college career. To his credit, he feigns interest, asks about their computer classes. The absent Abigail is going to be a teacher. Mrs. Thompson has many civic interests. Do they have other children? She doesn't mention anyone but Abigail and I know better than to ask. She looks like she is in her fifties but I think women in the U.K. age quicker. Maybe they don't have so many products at their disposal.

I really need a nap and a shower. I try to catch Luke's eye but he is engrossed in a conversation about Othello. Lucy looks sympathetic.

"Nigel, dear. They must be exhausted. We should let them rest and freshen up."

Turns out the Thompsons live walking distance from the MacDonald Randolph. The last thing I want tonight is drinks and I can't drink anyway. Refusing a drink makes me look like an alcoholic plus it may arouse Wyatt's suspicion since he knows I enjoy a glass of wine.

When we finally get out of there, we make arrangements to meet at the MacDonald Randolph pub at nine. Just for a nightcap. They understand that we need to get to bed early so we can adapt to the time change just before we go back to Eastern Standard Time. Wyatt wants to walk around on his own for a while. He's eighteen, I tell myself. I can't hover. We agree to meet at seven for dinner.

"Can you believe their graciousness?" Luke is bubbling over with enthusiasm about our newfound friends. "I'm so glad you like Lucy."

Who said I liked Lucy? She is upper crust and a little dowdy. I can't see myself having tea with her on Wednesday afternoons or aiding her on one of her philanthropic projects. They picked up the tab at the restaurant and seem to be footing the entire bill for this trip. What is it about Luke's credentials and research that makes him receive this kind of attention?

## The Shape of What Remains

The rain has stopped and there is an anemic sun poking through the clouds. It's definitely warmer here. The spires make it look a little like Disney World, or what I imagine Disney World to look like. There are throngs of people out and the young people look decidedly neater. I haven't seen a single face piercing or tattoo. Many of the students carry satchels instead of backpacks though some have packs, or rucksacks as Nigel calls them. It feels a little like America, circa 1955. I know that Oxford is like Harvard in terms of competition. Wyatt's GPA is decent but not Ivy League. We will need to look into Oxford Brookes University or another option.

I collapse on the bed, kicking off my shoes. Never make it to the shower. When Luke comes out of the bathroom, he slides next to me. We're breaking the rules by not forcing ourselves to stay up. He strokes my head for a second and then I hear him softly snoring. When we awaken, it's five o'clock and someone is knocking at the door.

"When's dinner?" Wyatt asks. He's carrying a bag and I think he's already spent the money we gave him. "This place is cool. You know, I can drink here."

I forgot about that. Europe is decidedly more relaxed about this and I do believe there is less alcoholism. Maybe not. Though I can't imagine a French alcoholic. Everyone drinks wine with meals in France and Italy. I don't know about England. Ireland seems to be more about Guinness and ales.

"Remember Dad is here for a job. You can drink when we go out but only one drink."

Wyatt is grinning. What stories he can tell when he returns to UConn, a school with the legendary Spring Weekend that used to result in arrests, much to the distress of parents paying the tuition for their kids. I figured we could always force him to come home on Spring

Weekend but the president of the university cleaned it up and recent years have been calm. Wyatt has had sips of wine and an occasional beer with Luke since he was sixteen. I'm sure he's had drinks with friends.

We shoo him out so we can shower and dress. I feel somewhat human again after the nap. I look at my belly in the shower. Still flat. I'll have to make a doctor's appointment as soon as we get home. My breasts hurt. I could stay in the shower for an hour, the pulsing of the hot water feels so good. Vacation. Okay, the change of scenery and lack of laundry and meal preparation is really great. I didn't realize how much of my life was taken up with mundane tasks. Some days the only thing I seem to accomplish is checking the mail or making the bed. Still, I feel as if I'm shirking. On vacation, I'm supposed to be waited on — that's the point. We stopped taking real vacations after Serena died because she wasn't there to get excited about the beach or beg us for ice cream.

Wyatt used to go away for a week with Dom and Bess over the summer — Cape Cod, Nantucket, Block Island, or Newport. Ira and Bess invite him now. He comes back tan and happy. Luke usually finds a convention of one sort or another and disappears for a couple of weeks. He used to invite me but I always refused. I use the time to kill the garden, watch movies, or occasionally teach a summer class.

I hear Dr. B-S's voice. Did I drive him away? I didn't ask him to have sex with Tyra. How could I think about sex when my daughter was dead? It seemed as if I didn't deserve any kind of pleasure. I'd feel guilty when we had a particularly delicious meal or when the weather was perfect. It was crazy. I'm living, though my life for the last ten years has been more like the skin a snake sheds. The shape of the snake remains but there's no substance. No essence. A shell of a woman, mother, professor. It looks real but I know it isn't. The life I lead is an imitation of the life I want. The lives any of us lead can be rearranged in an instant by a random tragedy. I hadn't thought about the possibility that good fortune could also change a life. All those firsts like getting my Ph.D., having children, a professional job, publication were life-changing. I am an academic, albeit an underpaid and under-recognized one. I will be full-time for one semester. Professor Calvano. How great it was to have my name on my office door. Now I use free offices when I need to meet with students. Adjunct professors don't get offices.

The elevator is wood and brass. Elegant like the rugs and chandeliers in the lobby. Luke is wearing a suit though Wyatt has chosen his new sport shirt and khaki pants. He looks taller, handsome.

"You look great, Mom," he says.

I guess I still clean up okay. From the outside, we are a model family out to dinner on holiday, snakeskin intact.

## Chapter 17

What defines life? Is it the moment we take a breath? Pro-lifers define life as the moment of conception but I disagree. Even though I am carrying a life, I don't recognize it as alive yet. After all, this gathering of cells can't survive on its own. Right now, it is just a vague feeling of fullness. Some life dies off and returns like the persistent rhododendron outside our house. How I wish Serena was a rose or a daffodil so she could blossom again in another season. Sometimes I think of abducted children and those posters from the National Center for Missing and Exploited Children. They have age-adjusted drawings. Child abducted at six and this is what she'd look like at sixteen. How can you know? Wyatt looks so different at eighteen than he did at eight. His face is thinner, nose longer, and his eyes not as large as they seemed when he was a child. No one knows if their girl child will be buxom or slight. My niece Mariah tends toward the plump while her sister Emilie is skinny like Lena. I've imagined Serena as a teenager, golden-haired and slender. Would she have been tall like Luke or medium height like me? I know parents who have petite teenagers even though they are both average heights. It is a great mystery how genetics combine in the creation of a person.

England is perfectly lovely. Brilliant, Lucy would say. From the tea to our walks around Oxford, it is a charmed time. Touring the different colleges, the gray stone and the spires speak to me, whispering of scholars like W.H. Auden, T.S. Eliot, Steven Hawking and even Bill Clinton. The only women I know of who went there are Rachel Maddow, Helen Fielding and Iris Murdoch, the writer and philosopher who died of Alzheimer's disease. I saw the movie *Iris* about her life and the devotion of her husband. Obviously an intellectually engaged life was not enough to stave off that dreaded disease.

During a side trip to Stratford-upon-Avon, about an hour away, we visit Shakespeare's birthplace and Anne Hathaway's house, which is different from what I remembered from a trip to England I took in college. I was distracted then and didn't notice details — the fireplace and baby minder (so many babies wandered into the fire). As Bess said, it is amazing that people make it to adulthood at all. In those days, it was truly miraculous. Women would cook in front of an open fire, wash the clothes, and tend to multiple children. One look away and you'd lose a crawling baby. And we think we're the generation that invented multitasking. The Royal Shakespeare Theater excited Luke as did the Shakespeare Institute and Shakespeare Birthplace Trust, which holds books and documents — an ideal place for a researcher. I suspect he'll be making many side trips here.

No decision about the job though Luke feels the interview went well. He met with the department and they arranged for him to deliver a lecture over Zoom in two weeks. If they make him an offer, he will have to return to discuss the details. At the very least, the research has been fully funded and we'll definitely be there from summer through the fall semester. We'll be there. I say that as if I believe it. Does that indicate I'm staying with him? Can I be assured that he won't find a female diversion in this venerable town?

We return to find the spider plant dead. I hated that plant and its little spiders. I could probably re-pot the ones that don't look completely brown but I throw the whole thing out, thus cementing our reputation as serial killers of houseplants. I didn't ask anyone to look in on our plants because it was only six days and they're only plants. Maybe I didn't ask anyone to look in on our plants because I secretly wanted them to die. Shall I discuss my murderous feelings toward the plant world with Dr. B-S?

Wyatt enjoyed his time with Abigail since she is about his age and was able to fill him in on trends. She definitely got the worse of both parents, skinny face and thin brown hair that fell over one eye. She could have used some orthodonture — a luxury that I've noticed many Brits don't seem to choose. Shit. I sound like Bridget. When did I get so judgmental?

Their home was all polished wood, rich-colored tapestries and artwork. Wyatt treated Abby like a buddy. She knew computers, and had an iPhone that he used to text Belle since we wouldn't get him an international plan for such a short time. Turns out she has a boyfriend. She took Wyatt to the pub and introduced him to her mates. He came back saying, *Bloody Hell, Gobsmacked,* and *Brilliant*. When we drove him back to UConn, he was sporting an Oxford sweatshirt that we bought for a ridiculous amount of money.

    Reasons to leave Northbrook:
    1. I kill all houseplants.
    2. The houses are boxy and look the same.
    3. I'm a failure as a suburban housewife.

4. My only social contacts are book group and therapy.

I don't know if I'll be a pariah in Oxford. Lucy hugged me goodbye which I gather isn't usual for the formal Brits. She grew on me. Turns out she studied English Literature and is somewhat of an expert on Keats. She has a Ph.D. but doesn't work though she's written a few books.

I'm meeting with Dr. B-S this afternoon and the topic du jour is Luke and whether he is keeping it in his pants. Time to take on that particular elephant in the room. I need some coaching as to how to approach it with him. I'm carrying his baby. Without those mercy fucks, there would be no baby.

When Tim called, once again I didn't know what to say.

"Hi Tess, it's Tim."

"Hi."

"How was Oxford?"

"Grand, as they say. Beautiful place."

"Want to meet on Friday?"

I go through my mental computer, which takes about five seconds since my weekly schedule is basically one class, two therapy appointments and book group once a month. None of those things happen on Friday.

"Okay. Where?"

"How about a hike in the park if the good weather holds?"

"A hike sounds good," I say, relieved not to go to another restaurant.

Tim hates phones and so do I. Phones delete facial expressions and gestures, like texting and email. I don't understand the popularity. It's so easy to be misunderstood when you are writing or talking on the phone. Think of all the times we communicate with expressions. I can tell when Luke is nervous or guilty because he picks up objects, then puts them down — fidgeting. If we're in a restaurant, he'll handle the silverware too much, play with the corner of the napkin or the salt shaker. Once he even took the little sugar packets out of their holder and then restacked them. He could be talking about the weather and I'd know he was nervous. How can you communicate that in a text? Tim stares at me. I don't know whether it's just his style or he's attracted to me. His eyes rarely waver and I find myself getting nervous in the wake of so much attention. Intention. He looks at my mouth when I'm speaking and then I start thinking about the shape of everyone's mouths when they're forming words. It is not a good thing to become conscious of speech when speaking any more than it's a good thing to become conscious of breathing. I know they teach breathing techniques in yoga but when I try to control my breathing, I end up hyperventilating. I don't think I'll ever be able to meditate. Letting thoughts cycle through my mind is like trying to will that truck away. I don't see it often but when it appears, it's going to stay until it is damn ready to go.

*Dear Serena,*

*I wish you could have seen Oxford. The pointy spires in the town looked a little like pictures of Cinderella's castle. I think you would have liked Shakespeare's house with a big cast iron pot for cooking that hung from the fireplace and a thatched roof. In the springtime, there are lots of public gardens, which is a good thing since you know I can't seem to grow flowers. We could have walked there, maybe had a picnic with peanut butter and honey sandwiches. I don't know if they eat peanut butter in England but if they don't, I'll have to bring some in honor of you. You would have liked their accents and the way the girls dress up. We saw a lot of skirts and fancy patent leather boots. Once, while we were walking, I saw a girl who was probably about ten years*

# The Shape of What Remains

old. She reminded me of what you might have looked like at ten — blonde hair tied back with a violet ribbon, a flouncy purple skirt and leggings. Her high forehead and big blue eyes were like yours. She had little freckles on her nose. She was eating ice cream and walking with her mother. I missed you so much right then.

We visited the different colleges at Oxford. It's very hard to get into this school — like Harvard or Yale in the states. Would you have been a scholar? I think of you as an artist but maybe you would have been a scientist or mathematician or psychologist. You would have come with us and gone to school in the town, maybe finishing your last two years of high school there. It's hard to leave your friends. I think your brother will have a hard time leaving Belle, his girlfriend.

When I visited Shakespeare's grave, I thought of you again. Final resting place. Your resting place is everywhere, but mostly inside of me. The memories will stay inside of me as long as I'm alive. Your daddy has his own memories and so does your brother and your grandmothers, Uncle Ben and Uncle Cal, Aunt Lena and your cousins Emilie and Mariah and Raoul. Some of those people were very young and their memories are small. My memories are big and I know your Grandma Bess and your daddy also have big memories. We remember five Christmases (or Hanumas), Halloween, your birthday, and just everyday things like bringing you soup when you had the flu and watching The Sound of Music on a snow day.

Each season brings a different memory — how you hated mosquitos, and the time you got poison ivy, the magic of jumping in leaves with that dried leaf smell, hot cocoa and sledding, and the awakening of everyone's garden after a long winter — how you used to name the flowers in Diane's garden. You called Tulips, Two-lips.

Miss you, bunny.

Love, Mommy

## Chapter 18

"What evidence do you have?"

Dr. B-S is asking me about Luke's philandering. If I am to come up with a reasonable way to confront him, I must have facts, she tells me.

"He works late nearly every night. He's often texting or emailing after dinner on the nights he does come home."

I remember about a year after Serena died, Luke got a call. He nearly tripped me trying to grab his phone from the table. Tyra, an undergraduate major who became a Ph.D. candidate in English. Suddenly Shakespeare became all-encompassing for her. The name became a household word because Luke didn't try to hide it in the beginning. He just told me he was working with her. Because she had just been admitted to the doctoral program, she needed special coaching, after hours. I knew they had sex because I could smell it on him. Once I visited his office to drop off a prescription he needed and there was an earring on the floor. She was five years getting her Ph.D. and then she moved to Norfolk, Virginia to accept a position at Old Dominion University. He slammed doors, swore at the slow-starting car, and poked at his breakfast, often just grabbing coffee and running out the door. About three months later, he started staying at the office late again and I figured he had taken on another graduate student. Amanda was closer to his age, thirty and divorced. She had a two-year-old daughter, was juggling parenthood, a contentious divorce, and a challenging Ph.D. program. Surely, I could understand how difficult that was since I had done all of this, except the divorce, I was sympathetic at first. When she knocked at our door one Saturday night, teary and apologetic, I figured it was a particularly challenging part of her research. There was a time when I actually trusted him most of the time. It was when he stepped outside in the freezing cold. I imagined something like this.

Luke: You can't come to my house, for God's sake. I mean this is my family, my *wife*. She's been through a lot, losing our daughter.

Amanda ended up dropping out before she completed her dissertation. I don't know what happened to her.

"Did you confront him?"

"Kind of. I told him not to bring his women around our home. Wyatt was still at home and teenagers are perceptive. Fortunately, he wasn't home when that particular drama unfolded."

"What did Luke say?"

"He did what Luke always does. He put it back on me. As I remember, he used his condescending tone of voice — *You know you haven't been yourself since Serena died. There is no need to become paranoid. My research is very important to me and I can't be around the house all the time. I wish you'd get some help.*

"So, he didn't admit to sleeping around?"

"No. He never admitted to sleeping with anyone except Tyra."

"Were you two still making love at that point?"

"We slept together occasionally — maybe once a month. I had my own bedroom because his late hours were keeping me up at night. About once a month we'd have dinner together and end up in bed. Usually, it was because I had a drink or two. It was weird sometimes. He'd touch me differently and I'd think he learned it from another woman. There was a creepiness to it."

"Tess, it is important you confront Luke. Is there any recent evidence that he is still sleeping around?"

I thought about this. He still works late sometimes though he's been calling me and making more of an effort to get home on time. We share a bedroom most of the time. The pregnancy has made him a lot more attentive. He even gave me a back massage last week, stopped and picked up some ginger candy at the health food store to help with the nausea.

"I can't think of anything recent except that he has talked about Cait, a graduate assistant from Ireland. She is helping him with the Shakespeare antihero stuff. When we were in the Thai restaurant back in November, he was texting someone. I don't know if they are sleeping together but they are certainly talking to each other. I don't know why all of his graduate assistants seem to be young attractive women. When I had graduate assistants, they were both male and female."

"I want you and Luke to see Dr. Scribner. His specialty is couple's therapy. Having support when you do this is paramount. I can call him and make the referral."

"Why can't you see us?"

"I am your therapist and my role is to support you. If I saw Luke's side of it and felt it was appropriate to be supportive of him, it would impact our trust and our relationship. It's best to have someone objective who can support both of you to work on the relationship."

# The Shape of What Remains

Dr. Scribner. I now have more therapy appointments than classes. Next semester I'll have four classes and three therapy appointments. I wonder how Luke will react to this but I don't have to wait long because I feel my cell phone vibrating.

"Luke?"

"Hi, Tess. Just got a call from Nigel. The committee loved me, Tess. They think it's a perfect fit. All those late nights have paid off. We're going to England, Tess. It's good money and they'll pay moving expenses after the fellowship is over. We won't do the big move until after that. I start next August but I'll move in July for the fellowship. Isn't it fantastic?"

"Congratulations," I say slowly. "I'm due in July, Luke. I can't exactly move then."

"Well, we can go as soon as you and the baby can travel. I'll make a few trips beforehand. I made a reservation at The River Inn. Dress up, sweetie."

*Sweetie?* Only Bess calls me that. Are we regressing? I feel like saying okay, sugar-pie.

"Dr. Bradford-Smith wants us to see Dr. Scribner for couple's therapy. She is going to make us an appointment."

"Couples therapy? Why? I thought we were doing a lot better."

"Can't we just try?"

"Whatever you want, baby. Okay. We can talk about it tonight."

*Baby. Sweetie.* I feel like I should be wearing a gauzy camisole and tap pants. Luke has this attitude. It's hard to describe but he kind of makes me feel as if everything is my fault. It's like he's feeling sorry for me and any compromise he is making because I'm damaged.

## Chapter 19

I am beginning to think I could start my own therapy practice. I know about the tasteful décor, the selection of magazines in the waiting room that won't reveal a particular leaning toward a liberal or conservative viewpoint. I know reflective listening. Dr. Abner Scribner. His parents should talk to Belle's parents. Didn't they practice his name out loud before they named him? I walked around saying Wyatt Dominic Calvano and Serena Joy Calvano. Both of those names work. Try saying Abner Scribner fast three times. Hopefully his classmates called him Abe. Do kids who are mercilessly picked on become psychiatrists? Actually, I think he is a psychologist, according to Dr. B-S. Ph.D. in Clinical Psychology with a specialty in marital therapy. Is he married?

I dress like a professional woman, venturing into my wardrobe to find a suitable blousy dress. Although I haven't yet gained much weight, my waist is quickly disappearing. It looks like I've been hitting the Guinness with fervor. Luke is meeting me at the suburban office where we will bare (or air) our sordid story. Dr. B-S said she would tell him about Serena's death if I signed a release.

Luke pulls up right on time. In fact, we are almost synchronized. Perfect couple. His slightly salt and pepper hair and trim physique makes him look professorial. I'm even wearing low heels and nylons on this cold day. I put my wedding ring on this morning so I could look suitably married. Besides, I don't relish the idea of looking like I'm unmarried and pregnant even though I know this generation doesn't care about such things.

We manage not to converse during the ten minutes or so in the waiting room. Luke is checking his messages and I'm, well, pretending to thumb through the magazines which are ones I'd never read like *Self* and *Woman's Day*. No *New Yorker* or even *Harpers*.

Dr. Scribner (do I have to call him doctor when he has the same level of education I do?) is older than I thought he'd be, probably in his sixties. He's tall, kind of Ernest Hemingway handsome with white hair, a beard, and glasses. He's wearing the uniform for therapists and professors — a tweed jacket with leather elbow patches. Do they even make those anymore? There must be a web site www.therapistattire.com — kind of like the web sites for priests or nuns to buy their outfits.

He ushers us into an office festooned with family photos of what must be grandchildren. There is a white-haired (equally well-preserved) smiling woman in the photo, taken on a sailboat. They are so happy to be able to charge money for listening to messed-up people. It probably funded the purchase of this lovely boat. Maybe she's a therapist too.

He has a file on us. A file. I know Luke hates this. He's a private person and the thought that anyone has notes about him or us is unnerving. I know all about the Health Insurance Portability and

Accountability Act (HIPAA) but still it seems like a violation to have our lives spelled out electronically or in hard copy. If our lives are made public, I want it to be on my terms, in a memoir with a big advance. That way I get to control the content.

Dr. Scribner offers a hand and a seat. I prefer the seat to the hand. Perfunctory, those handshakes. He invites me to tell my side of the story.

"After the death of our daughter, we seemed to pull together for about a year. It was like an agreed upon paralysis. We didn't socialize, just went through the motions of each day. There was kind of this net over everything, like it was unreal. Then Luke began to go back to his life. He started staying out late a lot of nights. Some nights he did not come home at all. I know he was working with graduate assistants, one in particular named Tyra."

Luke looks angry. Dr. Scribner turns to him.

"I couldn't deal with her depression. She was barely getting out of bed and didn't even shower some days. I understand how difficult this was for her — I mean she was the one who saw it happen. I'm sure she blamed herself and for a little while I blamed her, too. Then I realize that it just as easily could have happened on my watch. It was random. Yes, I stayed late and worked with Tyra."

"Were you having an affair with Tyra?" Dr. Scribner looks calm and professional.

Luke scratches his eyebrow, crosses his legs, and fidgets in the leather chair.

"Ummm. Kind of. Okay, yes. It wasn't intentional. It was hard — those late nights and the grief. Tess was so sad. I know it doesn't excuse what I did and as soon as I realized that I was just covering my own feelings, I went to a therapist myself and ended the relationship."

I look at him. When did he go to therapy? How is it possible to be married to someone for so many years and still have so many secrets?

Luke continues. "The affair lasted about eight months. After therapy, I broke it off with her and we managed to transition to a more professional relationship until she graduated and got a job out of state. After that, I decided to try to make a name for myself as a Shakespearean scholar. It has taken nine years for me to get the kind of recognition I wanted but now I'm getting it."

"What about Amanda?" I ask.

Luke shuffles again in the chair, scratching his leg and adjusting his glasses.

"I never slept with Amanda. She had an ugly break-up and a child to raise on her own. I think I was kind of a big brother figure to her. We talked a lot. It was hard to talk to you then so I enjoyed talking to other intelligent women. Amanda came to the house crying when her ex threatened to take her to court to win custody. He didn't like her being in a graduate program."

I almost expect him to say he didn't enjoy fucking Tyra so it didn't count.

Cheating is cheating, asshole.

"Did you and Tess have relations during these years?"

Relations. Yes, we have relations — mothers, brother, sister. What a stupid word to describe sex.

"Yes. Infrequently. Tess moved to her own room because she slept poorly and didn't want to keep me awake. We still got together about once or twice a month, usually if she had a drink or two. Tess has a low tolerance to alcohol." Luke looks at me and smiles.

"So basically, you went without?"

"I changed priorities. I decided that my penance was to immerse myself in research. There are no affairs without complications. My break-up with Tyra was messy and I didn't want to ruin anyone else's life. Plus, my mother gave me a talking to. She loves Tess and feels I should understand that everyone grieves differently. I tried to understand but I don't think I did a very good job. Mostly I avoided Tess and became a workaholic." Luke takes a Kleenex out of his pocket for no apparent reason, then crumples it and stuffs it back in.

Dr. Scribner turns to me.

"Do you believe him?"

I am running a video in my head — all the graduate assistants and their names, phone calls and texts.

"What about the texts you were getting when we went out to dinner?"

"Cait. She had questions about Othello and Ophelia. They always have questions. We're working on this research together. I told her it could wait."

"Having an affair is a serious violation of trust. How do you feel about it, Teresa?" Dr. Scribner says.

I don't know how I feel. Right now, I feel like telling him to cut the psychobabble. All that talk about feelings makes me want to hit someone. Tyra and Amanda were a long time ago. Although it felt like I was superfluous at the time, now it just feels like old news. I know they're gone. I just figured he replaced them with others. Now I'm not sure. I did wonder how a small-time professor could land a position at Oxford. That can't come without a lot of hard work. I just figured he was juggling it all — the work and the ladies. Is it possible that he's been mostly celibate for the last eight years or so? Hard to fathom.

"Surprised. Unsure that he's telling the truth. Mixed up, I guess."

# The Shape of What Remains

We agreed to meet again in a week. Luke notices that I'm wearing my wedding ring. He never took his off.

How many affairs are too many affairs? It seems to me that trust is something that shouldn't be broken. Did he deal with his grief by fucking around while I stayed in bed and denied myself pleasure? Dr. B-S has talked about the different ways people handle grief. There isn't a rulebook to navigate these things. I believe that Luke numbed himself with affairs. What is harder to believe is that no one moved him enough for it to last. He could have divorced me, made a life with someone less wounded. Why did he stay? Did he have his own demons about Serena's death? After all, he covered two mornings a week. It could have just as easily happened on his watch, as he said. Maybe he felt that he would have been more attentive. He's more of a morning person than I am, though I rally when I must. There are so many scenarios I run in my head; what might have happened instead of the awful truth.

Luke is bringing in the mail, including a large box. I pretend it's a present, something that will make me laugh or forget what I know and can't change.

## Chapter 20

I set the box on the kitchen table. Wrapped in brown paper, it is the size of a small instrument, a ukulele, maybe. No return address. My name is written in blue pen, lousy penmanship. like an afterthought.

"Well, open it already!" Luke is curious. Maybe it is a box filled with copies of a book I haven't written. What would it be like to receive my author copies, artistically rendered cover, blurbs on the back that talk about my talent, the emotional impact of my story? I would send a copy to Bess. Forget about Bridget. She might chip a nail opening the package. Does she even read anymore? Would Wyatt brag to his friends that I have a book published? No. He's in that dream place of nerve endings and intellectual pursuits. His life is his own now. Would it even make a difference if I finished and published the damn book? The tape is the kind you can't rip. Someone put a lot of effort into wrapping it. The box says L.L. Bean on it. Recycled. Letter on top.

*Dear Teresa,*

*We are moving to Florida. I found this stuff up in the attic and thought you might want it. I can't believe it has been ten years since that terrible day.*

# The Shape of What Remains

*Emma got into a car accident last year — a concussion and broken femur. I know how vulnerable being a parent can make you feel though I can't imagine your suffering. I hope you've been able to move on. I'm sorry I wasn't a better friend. I had nightmares about that day for years. I'm just coming off of ten years of anti-anxiety medication. Jake got a job working for Disney. Emma hates winter so she's excited. I'm happy she won't be doing any more winter driving. Buddy is fine. He will go to Florida International University next year and he's enthused about swimming and girls in bikinis and all that. How is Wyatt doing? He must be in college by now. I hope Luke is also doing well. I've included my new address and cell phone if you want to get in touch.*

*Love, Diane*

Damn right she can't imagine. What the hell gives her the right to need anti-anxiety medication? This wasn't her tragedy. I love how she co-opted my pain. What could she possibly send me that I would want?

Under the tissue paper, I spot it. The bird project that Emma and Serena worked on for a whole summer. There were twenty birds they colored and identified — just for fun. They brought it into school and showed it to the class. There were wrens, sparrows, a red-winged blackbird, mallards, a barred owl, a hummingbird (Serena called them beebirds), seagulls, crows, a bluebird, and a woodpecker. There were also photos that Diane must have printed. Serena in a tutu. Serena at the pool with swimmies on her arms. Serena splashing water at Wyatt and Emma. First day of school. All of them sporting new backpacks and lunchboxes including *the* lunchbox, hair combed neatly. Shit. Luke is moving to take the box from me. He has to pry my hands off of the bird project with little birds fluttering as they come unstuck from the ten-year-old glue. We photocopied those birds at the library and they colored them in. I helped them write fun facts about each bird. Woodpeckers eat insects, fruit, acorns and nuts.

*What's a predator?* Serena had asked. Now I don't even know how I would answer that question.

"I'll put it up in the attic," he spoke softly.

The attic is like heaven, right? A resting place, where all the handmade clothes are stored. Clothes it turns out I might use again. The toys went to Goodwill. I just couldn't part with the hand-knitted sweaters and the dress with sunflowers and a lace pinafore. She loved that dress at three. The tears are coming and I don't give a shit. Some friend, Diane. Now that she's moving, she comes back into my life just to unhinge me. Go ahead and move to relentlessly hot Florida, you asshole. They have huge mosquitoes and alligators, and the worst drivers in the country. You think you can escape danger by moving south? What about the Orlando Pulse nightclub shooting? It was a sunny day when Serena was killed. Not snow. Not ice. Just a few fair weather clouds. Go ahead. Look for a place without guns or careless drivers. Find me a guarantee so I can keep this baby safe. I want a fucking guarantee that no one ever again will take away my baby.

## Chapter 21

*Six Months Later*

I feel as big as a two-bedroom condominium. I feel empathy for overweight people. I can't imagine permanent swollen ankles, breasts the size of cantaloupes, and heartburn when I even smell something fried. We agreed that Luke would go to England after she's born and I'd follow when I'm up to it and she's ready to travel. Of course, it's a girl. Dr. Scribner says it will help me to heal. I think I'll want to put her in a bubble until she's twenty. Wyatt is embarrassed by all of it.

"Aren't you too old to have a kid?"

Yeah, it's icky to think of your parents having sex, especially when you've recently become involved in that particular activity and now you think you own the rights to it. To him, we must be ancient. Guess what, kid; people in their fifties, sixties, and seventies, and beyond have sex. We fuck because we're alive and it's like eating and breathing. We're animals, Wyatt.

"Apparently not," I say.

My female students were interested, asking me if I know the gender and if we've picked out names. The young women are, no doubt, imagining their own flat bellies swollen. Terribly romantic if you don't mind hemorrhoids and getting winded walking up stairs. There's pretty much nothing I like about pregnancy. All clothes make me look like I'm hiding a beach ball. Even sneakers bother my swollen feet. My doctor tells me I'm healthy and she's normal. Good weight and size, no genetic abnormalities or at least none of the ones they can test for.

I call her Peapod. I don't have a name and neither does Luke though I'm expecting Peapod won't make the final list.

Lucy was surprised when we told her. She's probably ten years older than I am and clearly childbearing isn't in her future. Still, she handled it like a champ, waxing poetic on the beauty of newborns and the superiority of English prams. She'd research nannies, something I can't even imagine wanting or needing.

Belle thinks it's wonderful.

"Ohhh Wyatt. You're going to have a little bitty sister."

As far as I know, he's never told anyone about Serena. He was only eight at the time and once we moved, he shed that history though I suspect this pregnancy is forcing him to remember Serena tugging on his arm, begging him to push her on the swings. He probably remembers the snow fort they built one winter, how they crawled inside and I was crazy with worry when I couldn't find them. They emerged triumphant and rosy-cheeked, chunks of snow melting to grayish puddles on the laminate floor.

Tim is beside himself that I'm leaving. We had been meeting regularly and there have been times when I've enjoyed his company more than Luke's. There's a kindness he radiates, full-on attention when we're together that helps me glimpse what can be the best part of a relationship. Sometimes I let myself pretend I'm having Tim's baby, an entirely new genetic mix. Why didn't I pull him to me that night in the restaurant? I could have let the others leave, checked into a motel with him. Luke wouldn't have even noticed if I failed to come home one night.

Now I'll be eating bland food and drinking tea when I'm not pushing a bloody pram in the rain. Our flat has three bedrooms and two baths. It's walking distance to the park. All I have to do is live there with Luke and call it a life.

Priscilla, Prudence, Wisteria, Rose, Ava, Briana, Monica. I don't like any of them. It's obvious to me that the best name was taken. Will Peapod always have to live up to the memory of a perfect six-year-old? Luke favors Laurel or Amelia. I hate them both equally.

When Wyatt comes home, he tells us he's decided to stay in Northbrook. It's his life, after all. He's not a child. It sounds like a conversation I might have had with my mother.

"I'm used to UConn. I made the Dean's List."

All true. The real agenda is Belle and we know it.

"I can get into a better dorm next year."

Translation: I can get into Belle's dorm next year, which is basically the same as living with Belle. Who am I to deny him? I'm just a knocked-up forty-something. It's not like I'm an advertisement for abstinence.

"Dad really wants the whole family there. And Peapod needs her big brother."

He hates when I call her that, reminds me that Peapod is a delivery service from Stop and Shop. Did I really want my daughter to call up thoughts of green trucks unloading groceries?

"C'mon Ma. She's not even born yet. She'll see me before you leave and again at Christmas and intercession."

I promise to discuss it with "your father." Actually, it makes some sense. Why should he have to change his life for Luke's work? Although I think it's great for kids to travel, I also think independence would be good for him.

"Absolutely not. We're finally a family again and I don't want us separated. Besides, we'll have a chance to see other European countries," Luke says.

I don't know how much country hopping I'm willing to do with an infant but I stay quiet. He's clearly imagined us as this modern, globetrotting family, pulling our wheelies behind us, dashing in and out of airports. The baby can fly for free until she's two, he reminds me. I think he's forgetting the accouterments a baby requires. I'll learn to make scones and proper tea. Peapod will sound aristocratic and call me Mum. I know I won't win this round, especially since I barely have the energy to move my swollen body across a room. I also think he overestimates the abilities of older mothers. I envision naps every afternoon. Maybe hiring a proper nanny to push the pram isn't such a bad idea.

## Chapter 22

It's my last session with Dr. B-S. I wonder if she knows I call her that. It's easier than leaving Tim. Our last meeting will be on Thursday. I've come to love his attentiveness and I'm not ashamed to say that I anticipate the hugs. In the marriage lottery, I might have ended up with the wrong man. Tim is excited about the baby, and has already given me a silver baby cup. I'm not at all sure why this is a thing. Have you ever seen a baby drink out of a silver cup? They end up on a mantle and get passed down to another generation. I suppose they could always be melted down for the silver.

I haven't written any letters to Serena in a while. Dr. B-S thinks it's because I'm finally beginning to move through the grief by saying what I needed to say. It may also be because I'm exhausted most of the time. It's enough to get through the day, moving a body that is forty pounds heavier up the stairs and behind the wheel of a car.

"Do you feel comfortable with Luke? It's important that you trust him if you're going to be living in a foreign country."

"I'm hoping not to care. I don't mean that the way it sounds. I'm just ready to put the whole sordid thing behind me. Having a baby at my age is consuming enough."

"The grief will always be there, in one form or another but you can manage it better. Write letters when you need them. I will be available by phone. After the baby comes, there may be new challenges."

I try not to think about more obstacles or the baby inside of me, her toes and fingers and the pink of her mouth. I hope she won't be blonde like Serena. I need her to look different. Dr. B-S hugs me, which is awkward. I'm not a woman who hugs other women regularly and I'm currently enormous. She's a therapist, not Bess. Our relationship is based on me giving her money in return for her expertise. Not a lot different from a hairdresser or gynecologist.

I tell Tim to choose a place to meet that isn't a restaurant since my stomach barely has any room left. He says I'm one of those women who looks radiant when she's pregnant. I think he'd find me radiant if I just got out of bed and hadn't washed my hair in weeks. Attraction makes us all into liars. We meet at the reservoir in the next town because it has flat easy paths and my balance is a little off these days.

"When are you due?" This is the kind of question complete strangers ask me every day. Can you imagine strangers asking you when you had your last period? Isn't this information private? Now that I'm nearly nine months pregnant, I'm tempted to pretend I don't know what they're talking about just to see their reaction.

"In two weeks, or right now." I smile even though he looks slightly panicked.

When I waddle on the paved path, my sensible shoes make a swishing noise, my enormous belly preceding me by several inches.

Tim is sympathetic and slows his pace to nearly a standstill. I'm halfway to the water when I feel a contraction.

"I'm having a contraction. Probably Braxton-Hicks."

"Does it hurt?"

It's a fucking contraction, buddy. Imagine someone tightening a vice grip around your abdomen. As soon as it's released and you can breathe, it tightens again. Then add in little stabs and you'll have some idea. If there is a God, I hope She'll save me from having this baby on the moss in front of the reservoir.

"I think you'd better get me to the hospital."

I text Luke: *Contractions. Peapod coming! Meet me at hospital.* I even managed a little baby emoji in case he doesn't get it. Sometimes Luke disregards my texts because he says I text too often. I'm hoping he didn't leave his phone in the pocket of his jacket or in the night table drawer.

Tim helps me walk awkwardly back to the car.

"I can drive Luke to get your car later," he says.

Honestly, I forgot that I drove here and I had a car that needed to be handled. Contractions are like turbulence on a plane. They have a way of making that novel or television show superfluous. Your hot tea spills in your lap, the flight attendants can't help because they've been told to sit down, and the luggage is slamming against the overhead bins. This is not the time to ask for a Coke or decide you have to pee.

Somehow, we get into his Nissan. He's shaking, barely finds the button to press to open the doors. He throws a blanket over the seat, maybe thinking I might break my water and stain the fabric.

He looks like one of those bobbing dolls, turning to look at me every second.

"You're making me nervous. Watch the road," I say.

"Should I call 911?"

"The contractions aren't that close. Let's just get there safely."

When he pulls up to the circular driveway, he runs to get a wheelchair.

I don't see Luke but maybe he is already in maternity.

"How far apart are your wife's contractions?" A male nurse in blue eases me into the chair.

"She's not my wife. I don't know. Maybe five or seven minutes. What would you say, Teresa?"

My face is scrunched up with a whopper contraction. Who the hell times their own contractions?

"Her husband is supposed to meet us here. Did a man arrive?"

The nurse looks at him as if he is crazy. A man. You know how many men are walking around the emergency entrance of any hospital?

"I'm staying until Luke gets here, okay? I don't want to leave you alone."

I nod. I really don't care what he does as long as this baby gets born.

When they whisk me to the birthing room, Tim tells me he'll be in the waiting area and will try Luke again. I am six centimeters dilated. No wonder it hurts.

"Do you want your husband to come in? You're pretty close. We can have him scrub up."

"He's here?"

"Yes, in the waiting area."

But it isn't Luke. Tim explains again that he's just a friend. It could have been a tad embarrassing to have him see me spread out like that, her little head crowning between my legs.

Luke rushes in just as she is being born, barely suiting up in time. She has dark hair and I silently thank the universe, and anyone's God for that.

"Healthy little girl," the doctor says, placing her on my breast. Luke leans over and kisses my forehead and the top of her head.

"I got here as fast as I could. There was a lot of traffic and I stopped to pick up your bag."

"Doesn't matter," I murmur. The baby is fluttering her eyes open and looking at me and I swear she looks like a wise old soul. Little Peapod. "Natalie," I say. "That's her name. Natalie Grace."

"Natalie Grace Calvano," Luke says. "I'll text Wyatt, Bridget, and Mom."

"Natalie Grace," I croon. The nurse lifts her gently off my chest so they can clean her up and put a little pink hat on her head.

"Tell Tim. Is he still out there?"

"You can have a visitor in about a half hour, once you're all cleaned up and we get you into your robe," the nurse said.

I don't care what anyone does from now on. An enormous peace comes over me and I smile. It's as if I hadn't used those face muscles in years. They pass Baby Girl Calvano to me, her little plastic bracelet proclaiming that she is whole and mine and at this moment in time, I can keep her safe.

## Chapter 23

I don't know when it became obvious to me that I'd made a huge mistake. It isn't just that Lucy turned dull, trying to absorb me into her routine of shopping and tea at the museum until she realized that a woman with a baby isn't as free as a fifty-something. I live around Natalie's schedule, trying not to be overprotective and failing. I hover, checking her bassinet, making sure she is in the proper position. I Google Sudden Infant Death Syndrome.

"Look, I know you're nervous but you're going to make her neurotic if you keep fussing with her every minute." Luke looks dapper in his regulation wool blazer with flecks of blue and green. His life is going swimmingly, a prestigious career surrounded by pretentious academics drinking tea while discussing the role of Polonius as a flat character in Hamlet, handily refuting the notion that Shakespeare was an early feminist. When I was invited to one of the early meetings, I couldn't bear all the pontification until Colleen spoke up. She is the only female Shakespearean scholar at Oxford, a broad-faced fortyish woman who stands nearly Luke's height. I liked her immediately because she disagreed with the men for sport. They looked at her over the tops of glasses or beyond her, as she dissected the theory about Ophelia's repressed sexuality ultimately leading to her madness. I brought Natalie in her carrier since she still slept most of the time and I was only there so they could appear welcoming.

"Why is it that men continually posit that a good orgasm will save women from madness? How is that different from the myth of the old maid? Remember the scene in *It's a Wonderful Life* where we're shown how the future would play out if Potter took over the town and Jimmy Stewart's character, George Bailey, didn't end up with Mary? Mary became a librarian and old maid, terrified of her own shadow. Maybe a librarian is one step away from madness. This was a Frank Capra wet dream — women needing men to complete themselves." Colleen was the lone coffee drinker, sipping espresso from a demitasse cup.

Because I am the wife and now a new mother, Colleen doesn't spend time with me. Like the others, she has a full academic life and she is working on new translations of Jacinto Passos, a Nicaraguan poet and essayist who died in 1947. As far as I know, she has no partner or children. She shows little interest in Natalie. Since I am nursing, I can get out of most of the faculty dinners which leaves me alone much of the time.

Wyatt won the argument to stay in Connecticut and he seems to be functioning well without us though it remains to be seen if his grades will suffer. He arranged to spend Thanksgiving with Bess and Ira. We Facetime once a week and he talks to Natalie, a bit like talking to a puppy. She responds to inflections but that is about it. I also talk to Tim every week, missing our walks and even that stupid book group.

"With all the shootings, nowhere seems safe anymore," Tim says. "Are the Brits this paranoid?"

"They've had their share of terrorist attacks but nothing like the U.S. And no one carries around assault weapons. America is alone with the literal interpretation of the Second Amendment. There are no gun stores or gun shows in Oxford or London that I know of."

"Yeah, like the Wild West here. You're lucky to be where you are."

"I miss being home. Never thought I'd say that since I hate Northbrook. I miss Wyatt, you, Serena's memorial place, and good restaurants. I'm sick of tea and scones and little sandwiches on white bread with the crusts cut off. Blood sausage smells like a bloody nose and kidney pie has the odor of a public restroom. I'm even sick of fish and chips."

"How is it going with Luke?"

"I don't see him much which might be good except it's lonely. Nat is great — adorable, easygoing but at my age I need more conversation than gurgles and coos."

When I hang up, I start thinking about that damn erection, how he had it again when he hugged me with a Natalie-sized beach ball inside me. We'd laughed because it's hard to hug a very pregnant woman. He ended up hugging me from the side, his erection poking at my hip. I hadn't known many men who have random erections after adolescence and early adulthood but I guess that implies I have a vast repertoire of men who press up against me regularly. I wish.

Luke writes me off. I mean I have a baby and that is, of course, the ultimate fulfillment for women. Some women may choose cats or dogs and plaster pictures and videos of the animals all over social media. I have a perfectly adorable infant who can reach, stare, smile, and drink a hell of a lot of breast milk. That is the whole thing. We haven't discussed Chaucer or the particular advantage of Brussels sprouts over cabbage.

## The Shape of What Remains

In October, Luke takes a trip to Trinity College with a few colleagues, including Colleen and a red-haired graduate student named Bronwyn, a name for which there doesn't seem to be any American equivalent. I'd never met Bronwyn Cooley but her name often came up paired with adjectives like *clever* and *accomplished*. I thought of Dr. B-S, how she urged me to forgive Luke, especially since his extramarital affair seemed to be limited to Tyra. It's easy to become paranoid when you live in a sterile walk-up with vast windows that overlook gardens and stone walkways, no friends to speak of, and a nonverbal companion. For the first month, I was in postpartum bliss, drunk on nursing and the flood of hormones. Now I'm over it. Natalie gives my life a sweetness but I need more.

When the email comes from Dr. Dillman telling me that Marissa had given her notice because they are relocating to Indiana, and he offers me a chance to reapply for the tenure track position, it seems like perfect timing. The renters could be out with a month's notice and I could move back in. Wyatt would have a place to go during the summer and on breaks and we could visit Luke in England. If Luke decides to stay long-term and becomes a citizen, well, I guess that's a conversation I can put off for a while. It's not as if he is any kind of companion these days. I get more out of talking baby talk to Natalie.

I email my curriculum vitae and contact old colleagues for references, including my friend, Brett McDonald. I know he'll tell them they'd be foolish not to hire me. I am familiar with the university, passable with their technology platform, and I have good ratings from students. I'm a low maintenance hire. I also don't care that it is an assistant professor position when I'd previously been an associate professor. That was over ten years ago. I am sure they can fast track me if it works out. I'd need to find outstanding care for Natalie. The person

I hire must be vigilant. Then I remind myself that Serena was school-aged when the accident happened. What are the odds of lightning striking twice? I don't want to find out. If I have to drive Natalie to school every day, I will. Maybe I'll enroll her in the Montessori School. It goes to eighth grade and then she'd be old enough where traffic accidents would be the least of it.

I don't tell any of this to Luke. He texts me from Dublin, gushing about the facilities and cutting-edge research. I am changing Nat's diaper while looking at the text, thinking there isn't a lot of difference between her shit and his shit. Nice that he's occupied. It gives me a thrill to think about his reaction when I tell him I'm going back. I know I'm getting ahead of myself. I don't yet have an offer but I feel confident. Luke's reaction will be as good as my first Mexican meal when I return to the U.S.— enchiladas molé with its hint of chocolate.

My Zoom interview is scheduled for Wednesday afternoon. Luke will still be away. I need to find a sitter for Natalie because I can't take a chance of her awakening and wailing during the interview. I call Lucy to see if Abby has any friends, careful not to reveal anything about the job.

"Good you're getting out. I was knackered for months when Abby was a wee one. My friend Tamsyn has a nanny, Anne. Tamsyn only uses her in the mornings so she can get in a walk and a dash to the shops. I'd be chuffed if you rang her."

Yeah, I'd be chuffed too if I wasn't peckish and damn sick of eggs peeking over the edge of a porcelain egg cup, and white toast.

When Luke calls again to tell me they are extending the trip by three days, I ask about James Joyce and the pubs so I can get him to admit that this isn't about the research.

"How's the work with Bronwyn going?"

"Brilliant. She's made a good contact at Trinity. Been a real asset to have her with us."

I'll bet. I've seen her assets and they aren't bad for a thirty-something. Ambition, brains, and that gorgeous red hair. Poor Luke. Postpartum nursing wife and she's older so she won't bounce back that fast, if you know what I mean. All that red hair begs the question that probably won't get answered. Do the Brits have Brazilian bikini waxing or is this an American thing like Botox? No way to know and good chance Luke isn't talking.

"You'd like the Writer's Museum and Temple Bar. We'll have to take a long weekend."

Not likely. He's off with the ginger, drinking Guinness under the protection of research. Fair play. I'll soon have my own travel budget. I've heard of academics bringing along a nanny when they attend conferences. Natalie will be portable for a while and I can tote her to the Modern Language Association Conference. Osmosis. Yeah, baby. She's going to start talking in metaphor and be bilingual before she can walk.

Suddenly I'm excited. I want to leave today, get home in time for Hanumas so I can see Wyatt, Ira, and Bess. Don't miss Bridget but she probably doesn't miss me either. She might not have even noticed that I left. When Natalie was born, she sent a gift certificate to an exclusive baby store called *Jennifer*. A baby store just for *girls*. That felt wrong on so many levels but I couldn't resist making the trip to Greenwich to spend the five-hundred-dollar gift certificate. There were French lace-edged dresses, tiny leggings in 100% organic cotton, precious Mary Jane style leather shoes for non-walkers, and several hundred thread-count Egyptian cotton crib sheets. It became clear that the five hundred dollars wouldn't go far but I did buy her a red velvet Christmas dress ($150), brightly colored organic cotton onesies ($50 each), and a couple of tiny sweaters. It took about forty-five minutes to empty that gift card. Thanks, Bridget. The first time Natalie soiled a $50 onesie, it washed out beautifully. I began to think maybe there was something about superior quality. Then she had diarrhea all over the Carter onesies I bought on Amazon (5/$25) and they cleaned up just as well. If you can't be a nice person, at least you can be an extravagant person.

Anne is older, a career nanny. It's a thing here, like Mary Poppins. She even wears a sensible hat and the kind of shoes that lace up and have a fat heel.

"Raised six of my own. Youngest one is in America, studying to be a doctor," she hands me a sheet of paper with references.

Natalie is wide-awake and stares at Anne.

"Look at the little miss. How're you doing, pet?" Anne takes her, cradling her with expertise. Natalie smiles and makes a little noise I call pre-talking.

"Isn't she a treasure? Look at that gorgeous dark hair. A beauty, she is."

I think of babies in the same category as puppies or kittens. Most are cute although occasionally I've seen a baby with the wrinkly face of an old man or a disproportionate nose. I'm not fond of cats who have smashed-in looking faces or dogs with protruding eye teeth. Other than that, they're all cute. She's a miniature human and diminutive features are pretty adorable. Okay, she does have a thicket of black hair and blue eyes. The best part about Natalie is that she doesn't look a bit like Serena. Her temperament is more intense and even her cry is lower pitched and more prolonged.

Am I a bad mother for wanting this interview? I can feel a small lump starting to grow in my chest. I'm a foreigner here, so I can't possibly know all the hazards. Anne is a stranger albeit one recommended by Lucy. What if Natalie chokes or pulls herself up and falls? Just because Anne's children survived their childhood doesn't mean all children will be as lucky.

I'm reluctant to leave my "treasure" with Anne. As a career nanny, she's adept with the unwieldy pram, happy to walk in cold drizzle. She even brought her *wellies*.

"Babies need fresh air. The flat can get stuffy. We'll explore the gardens."

I think it's too early for bees. What if she's allergic? C'mon Teresa. This is just for a couple of hours. The air is good for her. Once she settles a designer onesie clad Natalie in the pram, I go to my computer. It's still an hour before the call and I wonder if Tim is around. I text him to see if he can talk. I'm dressed up as if this were an in-person interview. No need to wear my mommy uniform of leggings and a long shirt (usually stained). Today I'm in a gray blazer and teal floral dress, pearls and gold hoop earrings. I even put on light makeup to cover the bags under my eyes.

"Sure. I'll take a break. Give me five minutes."

I peer at my reflection in the bathroom, add a little blush and some mascara. Then I apply *Summer Rose* lipstick. I rarely wear lipstick but Zoom makes everyone look anemic and blurry. I figure I should look alive and the opposite of depressed.

When I sign in, Tim is already online in his work uniform, blue shirt, tie, jacket draped over the back of a chair.

"You look great, Tess. Oxford must be agreeing with you."

"Not so much. I have an interview in about forty-five minutes. Someone resigned at Northern and there's a full-time tenure track opening. I've applied."

It's hard to read faces over Zoom and this is no exception. Tim looks simultaneously ecstatic and terrified is the best way I can describe it.

"Sooo you'd be moving back?" he chooses his words cautiously and takes a long time to say them. I think for a minute that he is in a relationship or that I just imagined his attraction to me. Maybe it was a phone in his pocket and not an erection. My mind is not my friend, pulling me into dark places where I'm suddenly feeling who the hell am I to go back? None of us can ever go back. We move ahead not backward. It's unnatural to want to relive the past.

"I'm almost scared to hope for this, Tess," he says and I realize that words are how we fuck things up. We attach meaning to them but it's inferior. "What does Luke think?"

"I haven't told him. Don't have the job yet, Tim. Just an interview."

"You'll get it. It's yours to turn down."

He's right. No way Dr. Dillman would have called me if he didn't want me back. There are other adjuncts out there salivating at the thought of a tenure track position in an English Department. Most of them don't have newborns. Dr. Dillman knows my research and he wants me, not some anonymous post doc who needs to kiss up to everyone to advance her career. I feel my shoulders relax. Nanny Anne is out with Natalie taking in the fresh air all babies need and I'm talking to a man who believes in me. That's pretty good for a Wednesday, the middle of a week in a country where gray is the national color.

"Can you text me after the interview and let me know how it goes?" he says.

"Sure."

He tells me about his daughter moving to California and how he's taking a break from the book group and joined a gym. He's planning to go to California for Thanksgiving. All I can think of is *it's yours to turn down* and how Luke used to be interested in my academic career and then he wasn't. Maybe he assumes I've found fulfillment in Natalie. Throw myself into mommyhood and it will replace my need for books and accolades. After all, if I'd done it right the first time, Serena might still be alive. Old stereotypes persist. Can a woman have a full career and also be a good mother? I'm in the yes column on this one. Maybe Natalie frees me up by flooding me with love — love for her toes, smile, and joy of life. I'd gone back to my research two days ago and found it lacking but with potential. Maybe Anne can take Natalie in the afternoons so I can finally finish the book.

"I started writing again."

Tim smiles, his face crinkling at the corner of his eyes though Zoom softens it and makes him look sickly.

"Good for you. That's exciting."

I promise to call back at night when Natalie is asleep but I will text him about the interview for the job he's sure I'll get. Serena once asked me what I did for work. I told her I teach students how to read between the lines, and find the hidden meanings in stories or poems.

"Like a secret code?"

"Sort of. It is a kind of private language. For example, what does damp make you think of?"

"I don't know, rain or the basement."

"Is there a way you feel when you hear it?"

"Sad because I can't play outside without getting all muddy. Or I want to hold my nose because it's stinky."

"A writer can make you feel sad or happy through words. Sometimes they can even make you think about the world differently."

"Like being a spy?"

Someday I might have conversations like that with Natalie. Maybe she'll be more interested in how engines work or numbers. It doesn't really matter. What matters is my life. I need to have one.

## Chapter 24

Heathrow is closed because of a terrorist threat so Luke is stuck in Dublin for a few more days.

"Security is crazy. I thought it was bad in the States."

"It is bad in the States. At least there aren't millions of guns here," I say.

He goes on about his research, peppering his conversation with excitement about Bronwyn's discovery of a manuscript in the Trinity Library. Not once does he ask about what I'm doing except to inquire about Natalie.

"She's fine. I found a nanny that Lucy recommended and she's coming in the afternoons."

"Can't you take Natalie with you when you go out? The fresh air is good for her."

What is this, a British dictum? One must take the baby out in the fucking pram with its grocery cart wheels. Wear your wellies because it's sure to drizzle. Who said the air is fresh? It smells like a basement, stinky, as Serena once so eloquently put it.

"I'm working on the book." I hesitate to tell him this. Not good to anger the muse. I thought of the days when I turned my computer on and just stared at the screen. Who would care about the bawdy writing of an ancient writer when a child had been run over like a squirrel? It seemed disrespectful to even try. Now I understand that I have a legacy to protect. I'm alive and this is what I can do. It is possible to love Natalie and also write.

"I thought you decided it wasn't a viable manuscript."

"Finding new angles," I say.

I want him to ask me what they are, and share the excitement I felt when I went to the library and looked at the material with different eyes. It was as if a stranger had shown me the research, a witty, well-read stranger. Luke and I used to share work, have late night conversations about literature. Now he works and assumes I'm nursing and wheeling a pram around in the relentless drizzle.

"Great. Just remember we need to be careful with money. Things are more expensive here."

Fuck you, I think. I've been in a stupor for ten years, making $5,000 a semester to teach one class and barely going out of the house. Now I'm back to writing, have a strong possibility of a tenure track job, and you're quibbling about a nanny. Fuck you, Luke. Stay in Dublin as long as you want.

The rage starts in my chest, a rush that moves to my face. The heat spreads across my cheeks and my hands ball up into fists. Maybe my depression is convenient for him because it keeps me passive and quiet. He throws himself into his research to further his career, even moving us across the Atlantic Ocean. Don't I deserve the same opportunity?

Little Natalie fits snugly in the front carrier. I head out for the requisite fresh air but really so I can go to the one place where it is possible to get decent espresso, The Missing Bean. They have a roasted aubergine and tomato on ciabatta that offers a possibility of lifting my dark mood. In front of the Bean, I spot Lucy staring at the tiny screen of her phone.

"Feeling a little peckish." she says. "How's Luke doing?"

"Stuck in Dublin because of the terrorist threat at Heathrow."

Lucy's face registers something like surprise but she's a hard read.

"Nigel came back two days ago on SailRail — the ferry from Dublin to Holyhead. He caught the train from there. He sleeps best in his own bed. Maybe Luke had more research to complete. I know Nige said there was an important manuscript they were poring over. He uses SailRail a bit because airports are dodgy these days, aren't they?"

It is a British habit to end sentences with questions that are not meant to be answered. It is a fact that airports are dodgy or at least a fact according to Lucy. I'd never heard of SailRail but I am fairly certain that Luke's extended Ireland visit has little to do with a manuscript.

Lucy peeks at Natalie, asleep in the carrier.

"Easier than a pram, I'd say. Leaves the hands free. Look at all that hair. Luke must dote on her."

I'm not sure it's possible to dote on a child you rarely see. He looks in on her during his short time at home. Mostly she is asleep. Infants do that a lot. To be fair, there isn't much to do with her yet except make faces or talk, and keep her comfortable. That is rewarding a lot of the time since she is a happy baby. Still, I look forward to my weekly phone calls with Bess, Tim and even Wyatt, though he rarely talks more than five minutes, mostly telling me that everything is fine. He's still with Belle.

I grab my espresso and ciabatta and tell Lucy I need to get back for a phone call. The first bite of the eggplant reminds me of home.

Suddenly I get a craving for Antonio's eggplant parmesan over angel hair pasta. I went there with Tim once and I was afraid I'd wreck my ugly maternity shirt because pregnancy made me the opposite of graceful. The thought of little speckles of marinara on my white blouse forced me to take tiny bites and pack up most of it to take home.

I can't stop thinking about SailRail and Nigel's return without Luke. Do they cover for each other? Lucy looks matronly. Did Nigel have a graduate assistant who held his papers and maybe something else? This line of thinking is doing me no good. I lift Natalie out of the carrier still asleep, her fingers curled like shells. How do babies do that? She's still light though the doctor said she's in the fiftieth percentile for height and weight, right on schedule. She doesn't flinch when I lay her down in the crib and turn on my computer.

The committee is impressed with my credentials. They want a second interview, preferably in person. Can I get there next week? They would pay for the flight, hotel, and rental car. There is a link to the travel department, a department I know well from all the invoices I completed back when I went to conferences and spoke on panels. I wonder if Gatwick is also closed. How the hell will I get out of there? A quick search tells me that Gatwick is open and flights to Boston are running about £500. I can rent a car and drive from there. What about Natalie? I wouldn't be comfortable leaving her, even for a short time. I text Tim.

*Second interview! In person. Thinking of flying in next week. Any ideas about Nat care?*

*Great! Could take a vacation day and watch her.*

*Too much to ask. Do you know a sitter?*

*I want to do it. Been a long time since I hung out with a little one.*

*Interview is next Thursday, assuming flight will work out. I get in on Wednesday night. Will rent a car.*

# The Shape of What Remains

*Excited!*, Tim texts.

I book everything and send the receipts to the travel department then I pull out my luggage, save my manuscript on a flash drive, and start a wash. When Natalie wakes up, I have sorted everything and I'm beginning edits on Chapter 19.

I text Bess but caution her that Luke doesn't know yet. I want her to be able to see her granddaughter.

*I'll be there. Dinner on Friday?*

I book my return flight on Sunday so that gives me Saturday with Tim. At least that's where my mind is going.

When Luke calls, I don't mention Lucy or SailRail. Instead, I feign concern over his dilemma, telling him I'd be going to Connecticut next week.

"What the hell for?"

"I have an interview at the university. Tenure track opening."

"C'mon Tess. We've been through this. You couldn't handle it before and barely got through last semester."

"I was pregnant and sick a lot of the time last semester. I'm neither of those things now."

"What about Natalie? You need to be there for her."

"I don't want to talk about this now. Just finish your research and come home. I'm leaving on Wednesday. The university is paying for the travel so it won't impact our budget."

Luke apologizes for the inconvenience of the problem at Heathrow.

"How did you get a flight?" he asks.

"I'm flying out of Gatwick. It never closed."

I tell him Natalie is fussing which isn't true. I just want to put him on notice about lying. He isn't stuck anywhere except in his own lies. I don't want him to think any of this is negotiable---my job, the care of Natalie, my book.

## Chapter 25

Kandi once said that we're all characters in a book. I wonder how my story will end and which characters will fade and which ones will become more vivid. It's easy to grow philosophical when I'm on a plane, Natalie sleeping against my breast, cloud swirls that look close enough to touch outside my window. I'm glad she's little and doesn't require a seat so I can hold her, feel her tiny heartbeat against me.

Luke finally said goodbye in a phone call this morning. He overestimated his ability to convince me that this is a foolish idea. Now the ocean is thirty-five thousand feet below and soon there will be a barista around every corner. I didn't want Tim to drive to Logan so I rented a car. He'll meet me in Northbrook after I've showered and changed. Long flights are exhausting and this trip is brief enough that I'll have no chance to get adjusted to the time. I've booked a hotel since the house is rented until spring though we still reserve the right to move back with a month's notice.

"How old is she?" The woman on the aisle leans over to look at Natalie's sleeping face.

"Three months."

"First time flying?"

"No. We flew to London with her when she was just a few weeks old. She doesn't seem to mind it."

"She'll be a good traveler."

I don't know what she'll be. Maybe she'll hate flying. It's not something I can even imagine.

I try to nap so I'll be at least a little less exhausted when we land. The woman is polite enough not to bother me again.

After a meal they call breakfast, a muffin snack, and beverages, we finally start our descent. Natalie is nursing but quiet. I know to keep her on my breast as the plane loses altitude so it won't hurt her tiny eardrums. I have a cotton blanket over my chest, as discreet as I'm willing to be.

I hadn't realized just how hard it would be to gather luggage, baby accessories, and my carry-on bag. Fortunately, the woman seatmate becomes a savior, helping me juggle everything until I get to the rental car kiosk. I tell her about the interview.

"Why would you want to go back to work? What will you do with the little one?"

I make up a story about a grandmother who is eager to watch her because I hate giving true details of my life to strangers. This fairy grandmother raised six children and two grandchildren. It's her calling.

"Oh, that's different. I used to watch my grandson a couple of days a week. As long as it's family."

I think of Bridget and how I wouldn't let her watch my dog if I had one, never mind a child. I'd trust Bess but I'd never ask that of her. She's earned her freedom and aside from the occasional weekend, she shouldn't be raising our child.

# The Shape of What Remains

I rented a car seat for Natalie and now I have to figure it out. You'd think they'd have a standard infant seat but there are literally hundreds of styles and they all seem to buckle in differently. Finally, a nice man who works at the rental agency helps me.

"I have a six-month-old," he says. "This snaps in and then you have to run the seatbelt over there." Glad I asked. I have no idea how he's doing it but in minutes the car seat is securely attached and a wide-eyed Natalie is buckled in, ready for our road trip. I've changed her and fed her so I'm hoping she'll go another hour and a half without needing anything. I can't wait for a shower and some American television.

After one drive-through coffee stop and another change for Natalie, I finally pull up to the Hampton Inn and ask for help. Who doesn't want a tip? I just had a baby three and a half months ago and though I'm recovered, I'm grateful for someone else to do the lifting. I had asked for a first-floor room with a crib and they delivered. King-sized bed. I check out the tiny shampoos and conditioners and hair dryer. God, I love American hotels. This one even offers breakfast, a boon for me since I'll be on the run. Going out to eat with an infant has its challenges.

After I shower, I text Tim.

*The bird has landed and is sleeping in the nest.*

He wants to come over right away but I'm not sure that's a good idea. Even though I can feel a distinct tremor in the lower region, I still have some command over those feelings. I tell him I'll call back after a nap.

Natalie wakes me after forty-five minutes. I've always been told it's better to get used to the time change though I can't see how five days will make much difference. I feed her, wishing my dinner could be that easy — ready-made and perfect temperature. No harm in having dinner with Tim.

When I call him, he answers immediately.

"What do you feel like? Thai, Mexican?"

I've been salivating throughout the flight thinking of Mexican food. It's hard to find in Oxford and what I've found is almost a fusion of Indian and Mexican with chutneys and tacos. No, I want real Mexican food.

"Is a half hour too soon? Is Natalie awake?"

She's awake all right, kicking her little legs and flailing her arms in the carrier.

"She's fine. I'm starved."

I am not sure what meal this is supposed to be for me but it doesn't matter. I just want to sink my teeth into some food that isn't a scone or a hardboiled egg in a cup.

Out comes the eyeliner, the nursing bra without stains, hipster underwear in orange and teal. I brush my hair until it is shiny, clip part of it back then step back from the giant mirror to survey the results. I still have a small roll of baby weight but it continues to shrink and most of my old clothes fit me. I decide the fitted jeans and a bright blue sweater with boots will make me look thinner. When was the last time I obsessed about the act of dressing? I put Natalie in a bright blue onesie, long-sleeved. Some of the clothes from *Jennifer* still fit her. A flowered sweater goes over the onesie because it is cool outside. Fortunately, she has blankets and a cute fleece hat.

When he knocks, I can feel my chest thumping and I wonder if it will make my milk let down. The tingly feeling comes when I see a baby or watch something emotional, sometimes finding the front of my shirt soaked with breast milk. Super inconvenient.

This really happens. I fall into Tim's arms and before I know it, he is kissing me, the real kind of kissing not the kind we'd done at the end of our lunches. I mean his tongue is in my mouth and his arms are around me so tightly, I think my swollen breasts will pop like balloons. Natalie is asleep again so there are no witnesses to what I'm about to do. I shut the door and pull him down on that king-sized bed and he unbuttons the sweater, unzips the jeans, unhooks the industrial strength nursing bra, releasing my milk engorged breasts.

"You have to use protection," I whisper because let's face it, one pregnancy in one's forties is more than enough in a lifetime.

Tim pulls out a condom. Later I thought, sneaky bastard. He *knew* he was going to get laid because we had about a year of foreplay. At my age, that's way too much waiting around. It is the first time since the baby so I feel a bit like a virgin. The episiotomy made me tight. Maybe doctors do this as a kind of present since a vagina stretching enough to allow a baby's head through definitely changes the anatomy.

"Am I hurting you?" I guess he could feel me wincing. Yes, but keep right on doing it. Pain is pleasure. Finally, I relax into it and remember the steps to this particular dance, the one you can do without music. He is softer than Luke, less muscular and definitely taller. His mustache tickles me when we kiss.

"I've been thinking about this for months."

"I've been thinking about this for years," he says.

I guess we both agree that this was bound to happen. The erection I felt poking me after book group most definitely was not a phone.

"Not kidding about the Mexican food." I sit up and try to stuff my breasts back in the silly bra with its Velcro flaps.

"The lady has many demands," Tim pulls on his boxers and jeans.

As if on cue, Natalie wakes up and lets out her *feed me* whimper.

"I might as well just walk around with my breasts out."

"Fine with me," Tim says, stroking Natalie's head as I settle in the chair to nurse her.

"Adorable. Great head of hair," he finds a diaper and wipes so we can be ready to leave after I'm done. This man knows the routine.

I expect to have a twinge of guilt but there is nothing except that sense of well-being that comes after a good orgasm. I can't remember the last time I had sex. I didn't have enough experience to rank lovers but Tim is better than expected, attentive and he definitely knows his way around a woman's body. Luke used to be like that but most of the lovemaking we've done in the last year was distracted and quick.

I pass Natalie to Tim so I can clean myself up and he puts her on his shoulder and burps her, causing a little rivulet of baby spit to go down the back of his shirt.

You've been christened," I say dabbing at it with a wet towel.

By the time I get out of the bathroom, he has changed Natalie and packed the diaper bag.

"Fiesta time," he says.

## Chapter 26

As soon as I walk into the conference room, I am brought back to the time I tried to return to work after the accident. Everything felt dangerous; students crossing the street without looking, the delivery trucks pulled up by the dining halls. On my third day, I froze up, completely forgetting what I was talking about. A fluke, I thought until it happened again the next day. I'd go into the bathroom and splash cold water on my face and the tears would flow. Once I left campus without notifying the administrative assistant so she could put a sign on the door. Students complained that I never showed up to teach. After that the English chair gently suggested I try just one class a semester.

Sitting across from two people who know that particular history is unnerving. I clench a fist under the table and my underarms grow clammy. The interrogation goes on for two hours. Any time it is about my subject, I am on solid ground. I can talk about English Literature without missing a beat. What trips me up are the questions about my teaching philosophy and my technology expertise. Fortunately, they aren't allowed to ask about my mental health or if I have children.

A man with a unibrow and waxed mustache seems to specialize in intimidation. He asks me what I have to offer that is better than anyone else with similar credentials. I cry a lot, I think. No one else watched their child bleed to death in the road. I survived a midlife pregnancy because I was stupid enough to open my heart and my legs again.

"I have experience and empathy. I taught a range of literature and writing classes and I enjoy developing new courses," I say.

He keeps grilling me and I bite my inner lip to keep from saying something I'll regret.

"What kind of new courses can you teach that would be relevant to students today?" Unibrow asks. "How do you keep up with current teaching philosophy, the latest pedagogy?"

I hate these kind of questions and I dislike this man. He doesn't let up.

"What technology platforms do you use? Are you aware that Northern is transitioning to a new platform?"

Of course I know this. I get the emails, asshole. I'm not crazy about learning a new platform but I'm not a complete Luddite. Dr. Dillman shoots me a sympathetic look. He knows my past and invited me to interview anyway. I remind myself that this is a second interview, which means I'm competing against a select few — maybe two others. They paid my travel expenses. Doesn't that indicate that I am a serious contender? By the time they let me go, my legs are weak and my milk is dangerously close to soaking the front of my professional blouse. When I finally stand up, I feel wobbly.

"We'll be making a decision by next week. You'll be hearing from us. Thank you."

I can tell that Dr. Dillman wants to ask about Luke. If I am offered the job, would it be a package deal that includes his definite return? That would sweeten it for them since Luke brings in funds. He is officially on sabbatical and I honestly don't know if he's even told them about the job offer.

Bess is walking around the lobby with Natalie when I get back.

"Here's Mommy. This little girl is ready to eat."

We move to my hotel room and I nurse while Bess fills me on the news since my departure. They have gone on a few trips, Ira's arthritis is acting up, and Wyatt spent a weekend with them.

"You know Belle broke up with him last week, right?"

"Oh my God, no! He didn't tell me. He must be heartbroken." I say. Why didn't he call or text? Does Luke know about this?

"Yeah, he wasn't expecting it. Everything seemed to be going fine but they're both young. She wanted to date others," says Bess.

"How is he taking it?" I feel ridiculous having to get information about my own son from my mother-in-law.

"Not well. You should reach out. Seems depressed."

"I'll call tonight. Maybe I can drive out there tomorrow." I am calculating how much time I have left and when I can see Tim again.

"Aren't you happy in Oxford?"

"Not particularly. I can't sit around nursing and washing clothes or having tea. I'm ready to finish the book and get back to teaching," I say.

"Does Luke know?" Bess furrows her brow.

"I told him about the interview. He's been in Ireland doing research. We don't see each other much."

I am careful with my words. This is her son and I know better than to reveal too much. Dr. B-S would have said it is circumstantial anyway and that I should confront him about Bronwyn and the SailRail option. It took no effort for me to book a flight out of Gatwick instead of Heathrow.

"Well, I'll let you rest, sweetheart. We can talk tomorrow. I know traveling with an infant is difficult though she is a peach. She just cooed and napped." Bess hugs me and I almost don't want to let go. I want to tell her about the shitty interview and the unibrow professor. I knew she'd tell me to pick myself up and show my worth. *No one is going to give you an opportunity if you don't let them know what you can do.* I just couldn't tell her any of it any more than I could tell her that my first postpartum shag was with Tim. I love this woman but I am not sure how I feel about her son. These are choices I'm not ready to make.

Tim texts me to find out how it went.

*Couldn't get a read.*

I tell him I'm too tired for him to come over and I know he's thinking that I regret our lovemaking. I don't. What I regret is attaching it to any decisions whatsoever. As a pure act, it was the exact right thing at the right time. Emotionally, I'm not so sure. I will see him tomorrow. I pull off the interview outfit and cuddle with Natalie on the giant bed. When I wake up, my phone is pinging and the sun is streaming through the edges of the blackout curtain. I'm still in my underwear and Natalie is fast asleep.

## Chapter 27

It takes me a few seconds to orient myself to the fact that I'm in Northbrook, not Oxford and there will be breakfast choices waiting for me downstairs. I'm happy for the respite. Luke is finally home, tells me how empty the place seems without us there. I imagine him walking from room to room, leather loafers clicking on the polished wood floors. Even in a vulnerable moment where I think I blew the interview; I don't care if Luke is lonely. It's been a way of life for me since I arrived in Oxford. Sometimes I'd bundle Natalie up in the pram just to walk around and see people. Almost no one talked to me except to say something about Natalie. Like dogs, babies are a conversation starter. The problem is, it doesn't go anywhere. *Lovely little pet* is not an intro to *tell me about your book on Chaucer*. I would have been happy to talk about climate change or politics. I'd even offer unsolicited commentary on American gun violence, immigration, or racism.

Tim is taking a half-day and wants to hang out. It's chilly and I don't relish the idea of going to his house. Too many ghosts. I'm also trying to fit Wyatt into my schedule. He didn't respond to my text even though I avoided mentioning Belle. It's still early. I don't know his class schedule but without an early class, he'd probably still be asleep. Friday, and I leave on Sunday morning to go back to that place of ancient architecture, tea, and mediocre coffee.

When I finally reach Wyatt, he sounds half-asleep and gives me minimal answers. I arrange to take him out to dinner. He doesn't have a car but can get a bus to a town twenty minutes away. Even as we talk, I'm mentally calculating the time to see if Tim will come back later tonight. Yes, dear. Mother has a lover. Not only did she get pregnant at forty-two, she's taken on another man. Gives you something to look forward to, doesn't it?

Natalie is uncharacteristically fussy when Tim arrives. He bounces her, makes faces and even lifts her up and down enough times to build some serious biceps but nothing seems to be working. Her whimper gives way to a full-throated shriek. I try the shoulder position, which sometimes eases her stomach if she has indigestion but she's inconsolable.

"Maybe she's teething," I say, thinking that I wish I had an excuse like that. Babies have it easy. They can spend an entire day grumpy and no one decides they should get over it, cheer up, and give everyone a fake smile. After Serena died, I spent a lot of time wallowing, even to the point of ignoring my personal hygiene. Sometimes I didn't get out of bed or eat. Depression, Luke proclaimed, offering a diagnosis because it came with solutions in the form of drugs. When I refused, he felt as if I was sabotaging my own recovery. Grieving isn't alcoholism or clinical depression though I'm sure I teetered on the edge of the latter for some years. It was the most and the least I could do to deal with the incomprehensible loss. Even all these years later, Serena feels like a phantom limb. Every day I am aware of her, even though I've adapted to functioning without her.

Finally, Natalie exhausts herself and I lay her down in the crib.

"Maybe we should stay here for a while. I hate to move her and risk another meltdown," I say.

Tim nods and I know he's thinking what I'm thinking. Let's make love while she's sleeping. Who knows if we'll get the chance again and my body is already preparing for a possible intruder. I drape her blanket over the side of the crib in a sudden wave of prudishness. Natalie can't differentiate Tim from any stranger and I'm not even convinced she has attachment to the elusive Luke. Still, I don't want her twenty years from now describing to her therapist a scene she swears she witnessed from her crib.

Tim kisses me tentatively at first and then builds to a soft open mouth encounter. He's not one of those lovers who thrusts his tongue in and out at the back of your throat, which always reminds me a bit of the gills on a fish. He takes his time and I like that. By the time we kick off the duvet and roll around on the clean sheets, he's ready with a condom. I'm not sure where he pulled it out of but I pause a second to appreciate the seamless move. He's pacing himself to my rhythm, a quality I notice briefly and then ignore. Thankfully, Natalie is still out, making little breathing noises behind the blanket. We curl up together and nap, awakened an hour later by Natalie's whimper.

I'm tired of living for the future. For most of our married life, I followed expectations, suffering through pretentious dinner parties, and publishing papers so I could move up the academic ladder. This has been a nice interlude though I have no idea where it's headed or even what I want other than the affirmation that I'm still desirable, and the release of a good orgasm. What does Tim want? As a widower, he has nothing to lose. His grown children would be delighted to know he's taken care of, though a married girlfriend with an infant would certainly test their unconditional love. I have a son with a broken heart and a husband who likes other women. If I get the job, would I live with Natalie in Northbrook? I don't see myself as a single mom but I don't see myself as married either. I pull Natalie to my breast and she takes a long draw, chubby hand on my upper arm.

When Tim gets out of the bathroom, he kisses me on the forehead.

"Tomorrow?" We both know it's the last possible day we could see each other and I've arranged brunch with Bess. Bridget hasn't even met Natalie but she's on St. John doing whatever rich women do on St. John. She expressed her regrets that she couldn't see us on our brief American tour.

I'm already feeling guilty about what I'll tell Bess so I can get out of spending the entire day and evening with her. I don't think it would be possible to love her any more than I do and I know she's aware of at least some of Luke's shortcomings as a husband. She was solidly in my corner during my decade long paralysis, never forgetting an anniversary of that terrible day, always available to listen to me rant and wail.

"Not until 6 or so. I want a day with my mother-in-law," I say. I can sleep on the plane or when I get home and the days stretch in front of me like cars on a train.

"Your call. How about you text me when you're on your way back and I'll meet you here?"

I think we've both decided that discretion is advisable. I don't know what this thing is, a fling, revenge, mid-life crisis, or maybe even love. I'm not willing to give it up but I don't want it to knock me around or jeopardize my family. Tim knows about Luke's affairs, probably the only reason a moral guy like him would even think of shagging another man's wife. He also understands that grieving is a lifelong pursuit, not an infection treated with medication and cured.

After he leaves and I'm changing Natalie, she gives me a look that makes me freeze. It's kind of a mischievous smile with eyes twinkling that looks exactly like Serena. When the tears start, I can't stop them and pretty soon I'm sitting cross-legged on the bed sobbing and holding the pillow as if it were the limp body of my daughter.

"It was bound to happen," Bess tells me, holding Natalie on her lap. "Even though Natalie doesn't look like Serena, she has the same genes. There are similar traits. Sweetheart, you've got to be ready for her to give you homemade Mother's Day cards, make you burnt toast, pick dandelions and put them in a juice glass with water."

I tear up again, remembering the buttercups in a peanut butter jar that Serena brought me on my birthday. Luke told her that dandelions and buttercups were weeds but she thought that meant a type of flower. *I want to pick some weed flowers for Mommy.* Memory is a cruel master, storing smells, sounds, and texture for a lifetime. The smell of banana muffins is a trigger. *Who let the Dogs Out* by the Baha Men is a trigger. Vanilla scented candles, corduroy, and the sound of a squeaky voice saying *Mommy*.

I know she doesn't tell me any of this to be cruel. She believes that recovery is the realistic coping of a person who lived every parent's nightmare. Bess is grieving too, even if it may not be as all-encompassing as my grief was and is. Besides Dr. B-S, Dr. Scribner, and Rachel on rare occasions, there aren't many people with whom I can talk about Serena. Not everything can be fixed. On National Public Radio I heard a horrible story about a child refugee. He had nearly every bone in his body broken by mortar. There would be no recovery and the doctor described holding the child's hand as he died. Comfort is what Bess offers, and most of the time, it's enough.

## Chapter 28

I am the exemplification of a bad mother, the apotheosis, embodiment, quintessence of a maternal influence that is literally and emotionally out to lunch. Wyatt looks despondent, his hair unwashed and his body thinner than it ought to be. The bags under his eyes make him look older than his nineteen years. I pull him close and he doesn't protest even though he's old for this kind of hugging. He pretends to be interested in Natalie, complacent in her infant carrier. I don't want to pressure him to talk nor do I want to imply that there was anything he could have done to keep Belle, gorgeous young women not being exactly my area of expertise. I know my role is to be present, a witness to a grief I fully understand.

"I thought we'd go to The Fried Pickle," I tell him, knowing it's probably a place he hasn't been since it's in another town and he doesn't have a car. He nods though I don't think he'd care if I brought sandwiches or decided that we didn't need to eat after all. He helps me buckle Natalie in her car seat, hands her the tiny stuffed doll I brought along. She gurgles and smiles at him, kicking her pudgy legs.

"How come you applied for a job here? Don't you like it in England?"

"There isn't a lot for me to do. I'm not the type to walk the baby and drink tea all day," I say.

He knows this. My domesticity is limited to cooking, choosing wine, and setting a nice-looking table.

"Do you feel well enough to work full-time?"

It's an honest question and deserves an honest answer. A few hours ago, I would have said *no* because of a tiny expression Natalie made. On the drive to the bus station, I started thinking about a class I wanted to teach on Women in Victorian Literature and I had to pull over to jot down titles of books that would be applicable. I've been toying with a modern rewrite of one of the Canterbury Tales, and even thought of writing a children's book that incorporates mythology.

"I think so. Most of the time. There will always be setbacks, you know. I have days when I can't get past them but it's not often and I'm more in control."

"Did Grandma tell you that Belle broke up with me?"

I don't want to lie to him. "Yes. I'm so sorry."

Wyatt is trying not to cry, maybe because of some code of manliness or maybe because he knows, like I know, that emotion, once unleashed, is unpredictable.

"She said we were too young to be that serious. She wanted to date other people."

I want to say *good idea* but I remind myself that I would have hated to hear that at his age. He was convinced she was *the one* and he needs to grieve that she saw something he didn't see — maybe cultural differences or his inexperience or just that he wasn't what she wanted for the long term.

"That must have been hard to hear."

"Yeah. It blows. She is the hottest girl on campus so lots of dudes want to hook up with her."

I stop myself from chiding him for the blatant objectification of Belle. Let him rant. She *was* gorgeous and brilliant. Both Luke and I were stunned when he brought her home, not because he's unattractive but more that he was completely unversed in the cryptic ways people communicate attraction. The fact that it clicked at all was a minor miracle to both of us. We later talked about his complete disinterest in women in high school. We had pegged him as a loner, questioning, or just scared of girls. Not only did he bring home a woman that no one could take their eyes off of, he brought home a woman with intelligence and social skills — in short, the whole package. Huge loss. We expected a breakup because nineteen-year-olds go through lots of blunders in the pursuit of sex and love. The fact that Belle initiated it wasn't surprising.

"She texted me. That was low. She said I was nice which means boring." he says.

"I don't think nice is the same as boring but I agree that she should have told you face-to-face. It's not respectful to break up in a text," I say.

"Nice means boring. What else could it mean?"

"It means she liked you. She just wasn't ready for it to be more than that."

I want to tell him that nice can mean agreeable, courteous, pleasant. Nice isn't exciting but it isn't boring either. Wyatt might be clueless about women but he's a quick learner. I think of telling him to get back on the horse even though that's a disgusting metaphor.

"Do you want to come to England? You could transfer, you know."

As soon as I say this, I regret it. Translation: you lost Belle and there will never be another woman for you at a university with 20,000 students. What would he do? Drink tea and meet Abby's friends? Go to pubs. What if I leave? He'd be alone with absentee father Luke. Luke could give him tips on how to get women.

For a minute I think Wyatt is going to go for it, the perfect out. It's a face-saving measure to leave the country after being rejected. Then he does something that I'll always remember, something that makes me unspeakably proud.

"No. If I went to England, I'd be running away. There's this girl that I help in my programming class. Thinking of asking her to the *Misplaced Dragon* concert on campus tomorrow night. You said you're ready to go back to work and that's great. I'll be okay."

He leans over and tickles Natalie and she makes her almost giggle noise.

"She's cute. Kind of looks like me as a baby."

Yes, Wyatt. She does look like you. May she be lucky enough to get to college and weather a heartbreak with poise and courage. God, I love this unkempt boy-man. He leapt into adulthood when I wasn't looking and I wanted to kiss his scruffy face. Instead, I drape an arm around him. He unbuckles Natalie from her car seat and holds her in his boy-man hands.

"She hardly weighs anything," he says.

## Chapter 29

I didn't expect to run into anyone ten miles from his school but one of the servers has an unmistakable dimpled chin and high forehead, fishtail braid of auburn hair. When she passes by, I stiffen. "Maisie" on her nametag and I know immediately that this is Serena's friend from gymnastics years ago. She recognizes Wyatt because she is a year older than Serena and a year younger than Wyatt. I remember Maisie's mother said she kept her back from kindergarten so she is actually closer to Wyatt in age. Even though we moved away, Wyatt continued with a local youth group and Maisie was in it with him. Luke would drop him off on Saturday afternoons so I wouldn't have to see any parents of Serena's friends.

"Wyatt! What are you doing here?" her eyebrows go up and she grins, showing perfectly even white teeth.

"I go to UConn. What about you?"

"Same. Freshman. What dorm?"

"Buckley."

"I'm in Shippee, right next door," she says.

"How come we never ran into each other? I mean, you're practically my neighbor," he says.

She hands us laminated menus.

"Hi, Mrs. Calvano. Good to see you. Who's this?" She turns to Natalie, settled in a high chair Wyatt pulled over to the table.

"My little sister, Natalie," Wyatt says.

"Nice to see you, Maisie," I say but it isn't nice at all. In fact, it's terrible. Can't my past behave and stay in a drawer or in the house we sold eight years ago? Why do young people move around and pop up when I am trying to have lunch with my heartbroken son? Wyatt doesn't seem interested in the menu.

"What's your major?" she asks.

"Not sure. Maybe computers but my gender studies class is fire."

"Yeah, Dr. Balinski is the best."

I want Maisie to move off and wait on other customers but the place isn't crowded and no manager seems ready to swoop down to challenge her priorities.

"What about you? You have a major yet?" Wyatt asks.

"Musical theater. Hey, you should totally come see *Pippin*. I'm a player but I get to dance. Opens Friday."

It's coming back to me, Maisie and her tap lessons. Serena wanted to take tap but we limited lessons to two a week. We weren't going to be the kind of parents who shuttled their children from activity to activity. Maisie took ballet and gymnastics and we carpooled with her for gymnastics because that was one of Serena's choices. I remember a sulking Serena when she saw the recital costumes Maisie got to wear — a black flouncy skirt and top hat for her tap class and a yellow tutu with a glittery bodice for ballet.

## The Shape of What Remains

We order sandwiches and Maisie finally moves off after Wyatt agrees to get a ticket to Pippin and meet her after the show. His eyes track Maisie whose fitted black skirt and white blouse reveal grown-up curves. She might not be the goddess Belle but she's a female and he's nineteen.

"Can't believe she's living next door to me. We were kind of friends at camp." I didn't know Maisie went to camp with Wyatt but then I don't remember much about those years except I was grateful to Luke for handling all the transportation so I wouldn't have to face parents who looked at me with a combination of horror and sympathy.

Wyatt is animated now, maybe because of the prospect of a date with a pretty young woman. I don't want to talk about Maisie's gift for singing and dancing because it makes me think of Serena and her love of art and science. The interests of children may develop into a career or at least a lifelong passion. I'll never know and that makes me unspeakably sad.

"Cool, huh? I mean Serena was friendly with her. Weren't they in some dance thing together?" Wyatt doesn't mean to unhinge me. He thinks I'm together enough to talk about this.

"Gymnastics. Serena was going to take hip hop in the spring."

"Yeah. I remember a show we went to where they were tumbling and doing somersaults and cartwheels."

I'm hoping this is the end of it. Please don't marry Maisie. I don't want to face a parade of old neighbors at the wedding, the ones who brought casseroles and cookies and then faded out of my life one-by-one. Only Rachel stuck by me though she annoyed Luke with her bluntness and swearing. If I listen closely, I can hear a virtual Greek chorus of criticism of what I did wrong. I failed the test of stoicism. Dr. B-S said it's because my former friends felt awkward. They didn't know the proper response to my unrelenting grief. I'd never been given instructions on grieving but I still needed friends. It was lonely in those early years.

Maybe that's why Oxford doesn't work for me now. I don't want to be isolated. I need some semblance of a social life. Wyatt exchanges contact information with Maisie before we leave. She helps me clean off the crumbs from the bread Natalie sucked on during our meal.

"She looks like you, Wyatt," she says.

Thank you. If she said Natalie looks like Serena, I would have to excuse myself and cry in the stall of the women's bathroom.

"How old is she?"

"Three months," I say. Maybe she's thinking that I'm too old to have a baby. The mothers and fathers in my age group are raising teenagers or packing firstborns off to college. I was a young mother though. Maisie's mother is easily ten years older and she has a younger brother.

"I bet you're a great brother," Maisie says to Wyatt and I can see that she regrets it as soon as it comes out of her mouth. He had practice and she knows it. She was there when they made snow forts and came in the house for hot chocolate. Her mother was one of the parents who disappeared out of my life after six months.

It's obvious to me that Wyatt will be fine. He's got more dating prospects in the near future than most.

He buckles Natalie in her car seat like an expert.

"Are you really interested in gender studies?"

"Kind of. I mean Belle got me into it but I like it. We talk about how gender roles are just socially constructed bullshit," he says.

I don't know much about this but I agree that sexuality and gender traits are more fluid than I originally thought. I know he has to declare a major by next fall and I don't want to influence this. Luke thinks he should go for computer engineering because it would guarantee a lucrative career and he has aptitude in this area. My own passion for ancient text clearly didn't come with a financial payoff. In my ideal world, talent and passion would matter. No one should starve or have to compromise a career. My students tell me they feel pressured to choose a career that offers the maximum payout.

"I'm glad you're exploring. College is a good time to try things out, see what you like," I say.

I pull up to the bus station.

"It would be cool to have you back. Hope you get the job. I could see Natalie more," he says.

Maybe he saw Maisie's reaction to his sister. Best way to practice for parenthood. So considerate of me to provide him with an opportunity to change diapers, spoon cereal, and calm a squirming baby. Belle had been excited about it. He's suddenly cool for having parents young enough to produce a baby sibling. But Maisie knows what happened to the last one. Would that be a topic on their dates?

I hug Wyatt, taller than I remember.

"I'll let you know what happens. Best of luck with all the women," I say.

He smiles.

I'm mentally calculating whether or not I have time for Tim if I also will see Bess again. The hours are running out though I managed to cram a lot into these few days.

Will it ever be okay to face the people in my past? My old neighborhood is like a ghost town. I go out of my way to avoid it. A few old friends attempted to contact me through Facebook but I didn't accept them. I couldn't bear to see postings of their children growing up, going to proms and college, and later getting married and producing grandchildren. I deleted my Facebook account after a couple of years. Luke still has one because he uses it for his contacts from college and research. He keeps in touch with his brother and cousins. Once in a while he'd tell me about a mutual friend who had moved or had another child. Social media has made us all privy to the intricacies of each other's lives. If Serena had been old enough to have a Facebook account, perhaps there would have been a memorial page. When a high school acquaintance of Wyatt's died in a car accident, his family kept the Facebook account so people could post memories. A cyber existence after the corporeal one has ended. Six years isn't enough life to chronicle. She hadn't gone out into the world. Her short life was lived in one house with a close circle of friends and family.

Tim texts me and I parse out my remaining time. Natalie fusses while I primp. A pang of something like guilt washes over me but I dismiss it. After Maisie and the flood of memories, I need something to pin me to the present and its promise of a career and a life. Then Bess calls and I tell her about Maisie.

"I remember that gymnastics show. Is she the one with the dimples?"

I'm visualizing them in their zigzag patterned tights and green shirts tumbling on the mats while parents took photos or videos. We have those photos along with kindergarten graduation, first day of first grade when she was mere months from her last day. The photographs are important, Dr. B-S told me. We chronicle the moments. Moving on is not forgetting.

Natalie gurgles and smiles. I make a decision to keep my visit to Tim public and short, saving the rest of the time for Bess.

## Chapter 30

"I don't know why you applied, Tess. What the hell will you do if you get it? I mean, you're not going to live in Northbrook with Natalie while I'm here, are you?"

Luke sips from his mug of tea, his latest concession to British sensibility. I steadfastly stick by my coffee addiction, hand-grinding the beans for my French press cup each day.

"I'm ready. I put my career on hold in the beginning and after Serena died, everything seemed pointless. Now the work excites me again. That's what you wanted, wasn't it? You kept telling me I needed to get back to life and now that's suddenly a bad thing?"

"You're twisting my words. It's not a bad thing to get back to life, it's the manner in which you're approaching this. Why didn't you apply for something here? This is where we live. You have a nanny you like. There's no reason why you can't teach a few classes."

"I don't want to teach a *few* classes, Luke. I want to be paid for travel and research like you are. It's a life, not a dip in the ocean."

"We have a baby. She needs a mother. I can't see how full-time work would be best for Natalie, can you?"

"I don't think having her mother unhappy is a good thing either."

"Why don't you finish the book? That university press was interested in it years ago. I'll bet you could rewrite the proposal," he says.

I rinse the breakfast dishes in the sink and put away the cream. Talking to Luke is like talking to Bridget. There are certain people in the world who have formed an opinion before a person starts to say anything. I thought of Tim and how he cocked his head when I spoke as if there was no one else he'd rather hear. I know I'm romanticizing everything he does but I wish it was his warm bulk next to me in bed instead of Luke's occasional visits to my bedroom. We still haven't made love and his late hours aren't helping any possibility of intimacy. I am glad in a way. I can hold the memory of lovemaking with Tim for a while longer. Sometimes I think about it when I'm nursing Natalie in the morning. I linger in bed remembering the heft and thrust of him.

"How is Wyatt doing?"

I tell him about Wyatt's maturity, his tentative step toward dating again. I don't tell him about Maisie since my memory is still fresh and I don't need to give him evidence that I'm not ready for full-time work.

"Smart man. Girls like Belle never stick around."

"What's that supposed to mean?"

"She's stunning. I'd imagine it's hard for her to sort out who really cares about her as a person," he says.

"Wyatt cared about her. He seemed oblivious to her beauty." As soon as I say this, I realize it is completely untrue. Our son isn't blind. I still find it offensive to objectify her.

"C'mon, Tess. He had a good time and it wasn't likely to last."

## The Shape of What Remains

Natalie needs a change and so do I. I scoop her up and pick out another tiny outfit, fuming all the way to the bedroom. Is he trying to be an asshole or have I just been blind to it for years? I think of how supportive Bess is, even as she gently expressed her concerns about leaving Luke in England. She is his damn mother and she gets it. Why is it so hard for him to remember that the intellectual connection we once had is related to my continued growth?

Tim texts:

*How was reentry?*

*Rough.*

*Sorry to hear that. Wish you were back here.*

*Me too.*

I don't know what I wish. I want Luke to morph into a combination of Tim and Bess but it isn't going to happen. He is grateful that I can take care of myself and Natalie now, giving him the freedom to pursue whatever it is he pursues.

Lucy invites me to lunch and I think about the lunches I used to have with Bridget back when she thought that lunching was what mothers and daughters did. We'd sit at a table with linen tablecloths and pick at salads and drink iced tea. I never could come up with much to talk about since I didn't care about shopping or her travel. Sometimes she'd tell me about a trip they took to St. Kitts or Cozumel. Palm trees, turquoise water, waiters tripping over each other to offer drinks. Since Lena was inaccessible, I was the token lunch daughter.

"Do you want to pick out a new outfit?" she'd offer.

"All set. Thanks," I'd say.

Bridget would flatten her lips into a line like I'd said the absolutely wrong thing. What woman doesn't want a new outfit? I admit I went out of my way to dress down when I saw her. It never bothered me that

Bess paid attention to her appearance because she didn't laud it over me. It was more like something she chose, like a model of car or musicals over dramas.

I agree to go to lunch with Lucy only because I have no other plans today. If I stay home, I'll obsess about when I'll hear about the job and what kind of upheaval might be around the corner. Fortunately, Natalie doesn't care what I do. As long as my breasts travel with me, she's all set. She doesn't mind gender neutral clothing or being wheeled around in a pram. I decide I'll bring Natalie instead of wasting nanny hours on an unnecessary outing like lunch. If Lucy is impatient with it, so be it. I know enough about this culture to know she'll pretend to be thrilled.

We arrange to meet at Banana Tree on George Street. Because Oxford University is not campus based, there are academic buildings scattered throughout the city. I don't even know where Luke works since he's never invited me to visit him. We have long established boundaries dating back to an impromptu visit to his campus at Northern Connecticut when I interrupted him giving a neck message to Tyra.

Lucy is folding her umbrella when I get there. No one travels without a "brolly" and macs are raincoats, not computers. I don't have any wellies but I've acquired a serviceable mac. She stands up but doesn't move to hug me so I'm not sure what I'm supposed to do.

"Isn't Natalie getting big?" she says though I don't see it. She's still wearing six-month clothes. I expect it's just what people are supposed to say when they see babies. Our waiter serves our tea. Then Lucy tells me that Nigel is dying.

"Advanced pancreatic cancer. No cure, really, just that dreadful chemo. We're thinking of going to the States for a promising new treatment. Nigel is mixed, but I'm all for it. I thought you should know though Nigel has kept it quiet from most people. Luke has been indispensable in helping the department run without a snag."

"Oh, Lucy. I don't know what to say. If there is anything I can do, please let me know. I'll help in any way I can," I say.

"It's the devil you know versus the devil you don't know. He could stay and slowly lose his strength or he could try the treatment, which might offer more years if it doesn't kill him. Abby thinks he should go. The doctors at Yale have had some successes. One patient has been in remission for five years," she says.

"What a difficult choice to make. We have a house in Connecticut. It's rented now but you could certainly use it if you were to spend an extended time in the States. It's about an hour and a half from Yale New Haven Hospital."

"How kind. I don't know what he'll choose and it's his choice to make now, isn't it?"

I didn't know what else to say even though I have more questions. Would Luke be replacing him as chair of the department? Was that why they recruited him for the job? Coming from a state school to a place like Oxford was surely not a common occurrence. We eat silently for a moment or two until Natalie awakens and needs to be fed. I pumped so I could offer her a bottle, knowing that in many places it is considered rude to breastfeed, even discreetly, in public.

"She's taken to the bottle quite handily," Lucy said. "Abby is adopted so I never had a chance to breastfeed."

Lesson: Don't assume anything about other people. I'd pegged Lucy as the dull wife of an academic with little life of her own other than philanthropy. I also thought Abby resembled them. Now, I suspect there are volumes about her and the family that I'll never know. Was she infertile? Was it a late marriage? How long has Nigel known he had cancer? What is it like to plan for the death of a loved one? We walk a little after lunch in the windy rain. I'd grown somewhat used to the dampness and Natalie is well-insulated in her pram.

"It's most enjoyable to see a little one. How is her brother taking to her?"

"Adores her. I was hoping he'd join us in England but he seems to have made friends at the university and prefers to stay."

"That's one thing that's different about Americans. We make those decisions for our children until they're out of school. Abby will stay nearby though we both think a semester abroad would mature her."

I don't tell her that I'd already lost one child and it is hard to let go of another one, especially since we are getting along right now I'm not certain of my marriage, my career or whether I want to stay in England much longer but I share none of this. These are decisions that I will need to make over the coming months.

When I return to our flat, Luke is there.

"Why didn't you tell me about Nigel?" I ask.

"Would it have made a difference?"

We sit in the living room and he cradles Natalie. She reaches her little fingers up and touches his chin.

"I'm sorry about Dublin, Tess. It was thoughtless of me to stay away that long. I don't blame you for wanting your career back, in fact I'm thrilled about it, really, I am."

He puts out his finger and Natalie grabs it.

"Another strong woman, huh?"

## Chapter 31

*Dear Dr. Calvano:*

*Thank you for applying for the position of Assistant Professor in the English Department at Northern Connecticut State University. After a long and difficult process, we have chosen another candidate. Because of your credentials and relationship with Northern, we would like to offer you an alternative. There will be a half-time teaching position in the fall that can be expanded to include ten hours a week directing the writing center. As a three-quarter position, you would be eligible for health and retirement benefits. We will need a decision by December 1. The position would be for the calendar year beginning in August.*

*It was a pleasure to see you again.*

*Sincerely,*

*Gerald M. Dillman, Ph.D.*

When I walked out of that conference room, I knew I hadn't prepared correctly for that kind of grilling. Like Tim, I assumed the job was mine to refuse. Now I had been offered a consolation prize, teaching and directing a writing center I helped to champion. I also had the possibility of delaying full-time work until Natalie is over a year old. I didn't know whether to cry or open a bottle of champagne. Of course, I'd take the job. Every academic knows that any position with benefits is a good offer. It might even be a better offer than the Assistant Professor opening because the union rules might force them to hire me at my former Associate Professor rate. Champagne seems suitable although it's ten in the morning.

I pick Natalie up and dance around the empty flat.

"Mommy's got a job!"

Natalie giggles, something she's just learned at around the same time she outgrew all those overpriced onesies. I had to make a trip to Sainsbury's for clothes and the next size of nappies, as they call them.

I text Tim first.

*Didn't get job. Offered another one. Starts in August!*

*What kind of job?*

I tell him and he reacts with suitable enthusiasm.

*Moving back? I hope so!*

What a mess of complications. My lover cheers me on but my husband is sure to be incredulous that I'd even consider the job, especially in light of poor Nigel's health. It isn't a good time for Luke to leave but that can't be a consideration in this decision. I've already made too many concessions.

When I tell Wyatt, he congratulates me.

*They have a writing center at UConn. You'd be good at that.*

I don't know what classes I'd teach but it hardly matters. Having my own income and decision-making ability is foremost. I can't exactly tell Bess until I tell Luke. Sometimes I wish they weren't related so I could have a clean relationship with her.

# The Shape of What Remains

I text Luke but he doesn't respond. Probably in class or at some important meeting. Dr. Dillman follows up with a phone call.

"Sorry for the form letter, I fought hard for you but the committee chose a candidate with more of a technology background."

He tells me how much the department values my expertise, so much so that they came up with the position for me.

"Please consider it carefully, Tess. I don't want to pressure you but a lot of us would be delighted if you return."

I want the job, an office and interesting colleagues. Natalie is a calming force in my life but at forty-three, I need research and new learning. It's her time to begin and my time to continue. In spite of what Luke thinks, I believe that a mother with a fulfilling career is the best gift I can give her. I don't want her to settle for less.

Lucy calls to thank me for listening. Nigel has decided to go for the clinical trial at Yale. He will fly in next week to undergo tests. She plans to go with him and stay in North Haven.

"We'll have to be at the hospital every day so we need to be nearby. If he is accepted in the program, treatment will start immediately."

At least you have a choice, I think. A child hit by a truck is a moment that changes lives forever. A disease you get at sixty-four is devastating but gives a person time to prepare. He may go into remission and continue his prestigious career. If he's forced into retirement or dies, he'll have left volumes of work and a legacy of academic achievement. I know it sounds as if I'm trivializing his life but it devastates me that I will never know what Serena might have accomplished. Her story is like those of the first graders at Sandy Hook Elementary School or in Uvalde, killed by a mentally ill shooter, their potential erased in an instant. I had to turn off the television coverage of those horrible days because I was crumpled up on the floor sobbing.

The small biography of the child who loved music or dancing or a particular color just made it worse. What is the point of listing what might have been when it is ripped away? What we love at six isn't what we will love at ten or fifteen so desperate attempts to immortalize children is just that. There is no good reason for children to die — sometimes they just do. I've never had the courage to visit a children's cancer ward but a girlfriend in our old neighborhood worked as a pediatric oncology nurse. I used to think she was a hero until she avoided me after Serena's death. I guess her noble work was limited to life-threatening disease, not sudden death. I understand now. How can we face each day if we think about the danger that lurks everywhere? When I fly, I rationalize how many planes take off every day and how few accidents there are. Small consolation to the loved ones of plane crash victims.

I tell Lucy I'm glad Nigel will try the treatment. Yale is an excellent place and the Smilow Cancer Center is known for innovation. I tell her everything she wants to hear, that I'm sure he'll be accepted into the program, that they can visit New York City and go to shows on Broadway when he's up to it. I promise to give her links to train schedules, Long Wharf Theater, and museum exhibits, as if this were a pleasure trip instead of a last attempt to save her husband's life. I do this because I would want someone to offer that if I am someday in a similar situation. I'd be happy for friends to pray for me even though I'm an atheist. I don't think prayer would have saved Serena but who knows? Maybe the collective unconscious unleashes an energy I don't understand.

When Luke finally answers my text, I'm pulling up old curriculum on my laptop, sorting through what might be usable.

*What's up?*

*Got a job offer. Different job but still with benefits. Starts in August.*

He calls immediately.

"What's the job?"

When I tell him, the phone goes quiet for a few minutes. Luke does this to indicate he's thinking, trying to formulate a response when he isn't immediately sure of what to say.

"I guess congratulations are in order," he says slowly.

"Thanks."

"You're not taking it, are you?"

Ah, here it comes. The assumption that I applied to test the waters, see if I am still viable in an academic world.

"I'm seriously considering it. Natalie will be over a year old by then. It's three-quarter time and quite manageable. Gerry Dillman called me and mentioned that there would be an opportunity for full-time down the road. The timing is good."

"But you know the situation with Nigel. They're leaving for Connecticut. I have my hands full here for the foreseeable future. This is a once-in-a-lifetime for me."

"Yes, I know. So you do what you have to do and I'll do the same. We have nearly ten months to prepare."

He tells me he'll be late again tonight and I think he's testing me to see if I bite.

"Fine." I say. "I'm having dinner with Lucy."

When I call Bess, she answers on the first ring.

"Is everything okay? How's Natalie?"

"Fine. Growing like crazy. I had to go on a shopping trip because she outgrew everything."

"Is she eating solid food?"

"Yes. Rice cereal and mashed fruits and vegetables. I've become a bit of a neurotic about it, pureeing the stuff myself. She loves avocados and bananas, hates peas even though we used to call her peapod. She's not living up to her name."

I tell her about the job.

"What does Luke think?"

Of course, she would ask this but I'm disappointed. Who cares what Luke thinks? He didn't ask me what I thought about the position at Oxford. The fellowship was a sabbatical appointment, not supposed to be a permanent move. I figured we'd get a semester and then go back to New England. Maybe not Northbrook but somewhere near Wyatt, and Bess and Ira.

"He's mixed about it. Did he tell you that the department chair has cancer?"

"How terrible. We haven't talked in a while," she says.

Yeah. He could call his own damn mother. If I had a mother like Bess, I'd talk to her at least once a week. I do that now and she's my mother-in-law. She tells me they're going to visit Ben and Cal in California. Raoul is graduating this year, thinking of graduate school. Ben and Cal got married quietly last year, just a civil ceremony without any reception. They had been together twenty-five years. They are planning a bigger celebration in July. She hopes we can attend.

Then she says what I most want to hear.

"I'm proud of you. This is a good thing for your career and Natalie will be fine. You need to get back to doing what you love and though it's great you're making your own baby food, if you start telling me you're embroidering cloth diapers or sewing her clothes, I'm going to get worried."

"Since I can barely sew on a button, not much of a chance. Thank you. It means a lot to me. I'm excited and I want to be near Wyatt and you and Ira again. Hanumas and Sunday brunch."

I didn't know that Cal and Ben got married. I wonder if Luke knew and didn't share it with me. I would have sent a card, maybe a present though after twenty-five years, what does one need? I want to go to the celebration. It is amazing to stay together twenty-five years in a country that didn't even allow same-sex couples to marry until 2015. They raised a child together and that alone is an accomplishment. We'll be married twenty years in August, for better or for worse. Neither of us is the same but I'm beginning to see that change is inevitable.

Natalie squeals and I think, *that's a new noise*, kind of like a sound Wyatt used to make. I silently offer a word of thanks that it isn't a Serena-like shriek. Her dark hair is growing and now she has a soft fringe of it over those blue eyes. I pick her up and she smiles at me and grabs my nose.

## Chapter 32

Luke's phone rings on a Tuesday, just after I'd made a pot of coffee, finished dressing Natalie and started the scrambled eggs. Pouring rain outside so it never grew lighter out though it was after nine. He rushes in with his shirt still unbuttoned. I thought Nigel had died or something happened to Bess.

"What happened?"

"The funding. I've lost the funding," he says, his face registering disbelief.

I'm not sure what that means. He'd been offered a full-time position beginning in the fall.

"I don't understand," I say.

"The fellowship. The one that brought me here. That ends in January. The position isn't going to be re-funded," he says.

"But you've been hired full-time, haven't you?"

"That position wasn't supposed to officially start until late summer and now it's uncertain. There is no money to hire someone who isn't a British citizen. It has to do with international funds or something."

193

"What about Nigel? He's off in Connecticut. You're already doing a lot of his job," I ask.

"Not really. I'm helping, sure. But there are others who can cover just as well."

I don't understand any of this. A month ago, he was indispensable, flying off to conferences, staying late. Now he's expendable.

"Did you give your notice at Northern?"

"Well, I did tell them there was a chance I wouldn't be back. I'm not sure that's the same as officially giving my notice," he says.

Natalie whimpers, probably smelling the eggs. I stick a plate of eggs in the freezer to cool them for her.

"I can't believe it. I thought funding was a sure thing," he says.

"What are your options?" I remember Dr. B-S breaking down steps for me. When I realized that it didn't matter what Serena saw that made her run out in traffic that day, it changed my perspective. I'd been obsessing about what it was that could cause a perfectly reasonable six-year-old to do that when it was the result, not the cause, that changed my life.

"I guess I'll have to leave at the winter break. We can't afford to stay here without my salary and I don't know how much longer I'll be on the payroll," he says, balling his hands into fists as if he wants to punch something.

I didn't know what Luke made, though he was still paid by Northern during his sabbatical so money hasn't been much of an issue.

"Northern won't pay after January unless I go back and teach in the spring."

"Have you called them?"

"I just found this out minutes ago. It's really early there," says Luke.

I forgot about the time difference.

"Well, I have a job beginning in August," I say.

"Did you accept it already?"

I guess we don't talk as much as we should. That was weeks ago and I not only talked to Gerry Dillman, I wrote a letter of thanks to the committee. It wouldn't hurt to let them know how much I appreciated the opportunity to return, I reasoned.

"Yes. Talked to Gerry a couple of weeks ago. I let the renters know that we'd be back in the summer but you can give them a month's notice if you want them out," I say.

I pull the cooled eggs out of the freezer. Natalie kicks her legs in anticipation of her favorite breakfast. I spoon mashed egg into her open mouth.

"Hungry girl." I give her a little more.

I mentally do the math. If we leave here in time for Hanumas, we'd have no place to stay. Winter break is only two weeks away and that's not enough notice for our renters. Although most of our stuff is in storage in Northbrook, we've acquired enough to make this challenging. Wyatt will be on break soon but he's already arranged to stay with Bess and Ira. Their two-bedroom condo can't accommodate all of us. I'll have to see if the renters can be out earlier. I think of offering them the two weeks for free since I know they bought a house and might be able to get in earlier.

"I can't reach Nigel. He's at the hospital and I certainly won't bother Lucy. Everyone else in the department seems stunned by the pull back of funding. It's impacting equipment orders and repairs — and of course travel," Luke says.

"I'm sorry." I feel for him. His identity has always been wrapped up in his work. It is one of the things that initially attracted me to him although his dedication adversely impacted our family life at times.

"Well, I'm going in. Maybe there will be more information I can find out when I get there. Will you be around today?" he asks.

"Sure. It looks miserable out there. I'm thinking of working on the book and starting on my curriculum plans."

"Call you later."

When he walks out of the room, I sit still for a minute watching drizzle pock the windows.

## Chapter 33

We land on a gray December day, claw branches and light sleet. Wyatt arranged to get our car to the airport but he's not here to meet us so we navigate the turnstile, Natalie, and our many bags alone. Bess will be back in two days. Since the news, Luke's mouth seems pulled downward by gravity or emotion. He's taken to wearing plaid shirts and a wool sports blazer every day. Northern had filled his position with a visiting professor for the spring semester. Because of his seniority, they'll fit him in somewhere but there is a good chance he won't get choices. I'm excited to see my office and thank Gerry Dillman and Brett for speaking on my behalf. Brett has already invited me to an English Department lunch the week before classes begin even though I'm not teaching until fall.

I'm carrying Natalie so Luke is left handling the bags, and he swears softly when he wheels my large luggage over his foot.

"Shit. We need one of those cart things. Tess, get one of the carts. I can't do this alone."

# The Shape of What Remains

I slip the money in and bring him a cart, Natalie kicking her legs in the carrier.

"I'm going to need to feed her soon. Maybe we can sit in the car for a little bit so she can nurse."

"It's freezing out there," Luke says and I think *turn on the heater then*. Finally, we pile all the bags in the trunk and I cradle Natalie who has gone from a whimper to a full-blown scream in the last five minutes.

"This is a parking lot," Luke says, like I hadn't noticed the yellow lines and the signs directing people to the terminal.

"I'll be done in about fifteen minutes. It will be a lot more unpleasant if we try to drive when she's hungry. It's not her fault that her schedule is all mixed up. In England, she'd be sleeping by now."

Luke sighs and flips on the radio. I'd forgotten how long it had been since I heard National Public Radio. There's a show about drones so he flips to another station where a pop singer is talking about her process. I pull the blanket up because even with the heat on high, it's damn cold.

When we pull out of the lot, I think of Tim and the Hampton Inn, how he barely got in the door before we were kissing and moving toward that king-sized bed. I switch my phone over to the local network and find a text from Wyatt. *Welcome to the land of fast food. Oh, and the rest of your family.* It's hard to pull intent from a text, which I suppose is a problem for everyone in his generation. I'm not sure if he's being sarcastic.

*On our way back to the ghost house.* A name I'd taken to calling our shell of a house in Northbrook. None of us were fond of it but I wondered if I'll feel differently with little Natalie eventually running up and down the halls. Luke doesn't talk at all, just looks straight ahead as if he's in a Driver's Education vehicle and I'm observing to make sure his hands are at 10 and 2.

It's dusk when we pull into the driveway. Luckily the renters were delighted with a rebate of two week's rent and vacated in time. I hope the cleaning service sufficiently sanitized the place. The furniture and boxes were pulled out of storage and delivered yesterday. Did our neighbors notice?

There's a light on in the foyer, perhaps on a timer. When we unlock the door, the pungent odor of Pine Sol and bleach hits us. Boxes line the hallway, piled up on the kitchen counters. Thanks, Wyatt. He moved them into the correct rooms, it seems. I scout around for a box of Natalie things since she's soaked through her fleecy pajamas. He's put her boxes in his room. Thankfully, there was never a Serena room in this house. Maybe he thought that was up to us to decide.

I find toys and blankets but very little in the way of clothes that will fit. Luke is wheezing as he hauls in the last of our bags. Somewhere in one of those bags are Natalie's clothes but I'm too exhausted to sort through them tonight. I pull out the last outfit I packed in the diaper bag and change her on the floor.

"Do we even have a wastebasket or trash removal set up?"

I'm holding the soiled diaper, unsure where to put it since the only flat surfaces seem to be the floor or the kitchen table. Luke locates a plastic wastebasket in the garage. I want a hot shower and a long sleep. There is only one bed set up, the queen-sized one we used to share. While it isn't the option I'd prefer, I'm tired enough to sleep on the floor if need be.

"Can you take her so I can shower?"

"Do we have any towels?"

I look for a box with bathroom stuff and find it in the garage. The towels smell musty but no time for a wash. At least I labeled the boxes. The hot water loosens the knots in my shoulders. I had missed my pulsating showerhead and the heat lamp. The plumbing in our flat was basic.

"Going to bed." I say.

Luke holds a sleeping Natalie, her hands curled into fists and her face angelic.

"You can put her in the portable crib in Wyatt's room."

Luke doesn't answer, just touches Natalie's fist and her head.

"Okay. Well, good night."

I make up the bed with floral sheets from a box in the hall. They are threadbare and I wonder why I never noticed that before. I don't know where the duvet is but there are fleece blankets. I crank up the heat. As raw as it could be in Oxford, it was not as cold as this. I have no idea what time it is when I awaken, only that a hand is on my stomach. For a minute, I think it's Tim and roll closer until I see that Luke is asleep. It's 9:00 and I slip out of bed and dash across the hall to check on Natalie.

She's in her portable crib, awake and looking around. No cry.

"Hey there Nat. Want to get out?" I lift her, marveling at her small scowl, tiny fingernails and thick hair. She warms to my voice and gives me a huge toothless grin.

"I think you're going to be a morning person. Either that or you're ready for teatime."

We didn't shop for food and there's nothing in the house. Easy for Natalie who can last for a while on breast milk. I'm starving and the last thing I feel like doing is bundling both of us up to go to the local grocery store where I'll be sure to run into a former neighbor or student. *Ghost house. Ghost family.*

I hear the shower running. When Luke emerges, he seems surprised that there isn't coffee made.

"Isn't it in the kitchen box?" He points to a box on the counter.

"We wouldn't have stored food, Luke. Those are just dishes and silverware."

I want to go into a lecture on mice or grain moths just for emphasis but I stop myself, that pregnant pause that was supposed to be his cue to offer to shop and pick up breakfast.

"Why don't we go out for breakfast?" he says.

Given that we're both unemployed right now, we should do the American thing and spend money we don't have. Since the alternative is breast milk, I nod and grab Natalie's jacket.

"We do have to shop, you know."

"I can do that later. You stay home with Nat."

"Thank you."

Luke is way better at dodging nosy neighbors. He's got this method he tried to teach me one night when I'd had a little too much Cabernet and was sitting on his lap.

"You pretend to be examining the fruit. If it's a melon, even better. You can pick it up, sniff it, press it. If that doesn't work and Mrs. Zinler is waiting for you to look up, fake a messy sneeze and then rummage through your pockets (or in your case, a purse) for a Kleenex. Blow your nose noisily and cough as if you have the flu. Definitely contagious. If the germs don't deter her and she keeps on advancing, pretend you just got a call on your phone. *Oh my God, not Mother. Let me check out and I'll be right there.* By then I was laughing so hard I almost had an accident. We did have a Mrs. Zinler down the road and whenever I ran into her, she gave me running commentary. *Do you know a red car stopped in front of your house last week? Did you get a new washer? I saw the Sears truck in your driveway. There are weeds by your mailbox choking out the tulips you planted.* Luke used to say that she kept a little notebook of our infractions — waited an extra day to bring in the recycling bin, played music on a

*Saturday with the windows open, left the newspaper in the tube for the whole weekend*. A widow, she probably didn't have much on her mind but that didn't stop my annoyance. Would I be the kind of mother who harped about things that didn't matter — bare feet, music, friends with bad haircuts or tattoos? I hoped not. Wyatt hadn't been social in high school so our house was never the site of teenage parties or sleepovers.

I feel almost human after eggs and good old American home fries, plus a strong cup of coffee. Luke still looks haggard and he needs a shave.

"It's depressing to be back," he says.

"Oxford wasn't exactly a laugh fest for me."

Luke opens his eyes wide so he looks kind of drugged in the fluorescent light of Morning Sun restaurant.

"I thought you liked it. You seemed to get on well with Lucy and you even mastered prams and tea."

"Conforming to the mores of a culture is part of travel. Short dips into the customs are fine. I'm still a fan of a foldable lightweight stroller and a mug of Americano."

"Drink all the coffee you like. I'm already missing a good pot of English tea."

"What was it about the scones? I never did understand it. They're hard, dry, and make more crumbs than is proper," I say.

"Done right, a scone is a work of art. Hard exterior, soft interior, slightly tangy. Kind of like you, my pet," he says.

He's laughing and it's a whole lot better than the silent plane ride and the grim moment when we opened the door. I don't feel defeated. I am at peace. This is the country that held Serena and now it feels like home.

## Chapter 34

Tim bounces Natalie up and down and she's making the same shrieking noise Wyatt used to make when Luke did this.

"You look great, Tess. I like your hair."

I'd cut my hair to shoulder length, my attempt at losing the middle-aged mother look. I'd also lost most of the baby weight though the last five pounds were doggedly hanging on. I decided not to worry about it. Natalie is worth carrying a little extra weight. In preparation for our lunch, I'd gone shopping and was wearing one of my leggings and skirt combinations with a new fuchsia sweater. Tim raises a glass of water.

"To you and your career as an academic."

We clink glasses.

"I have a present for you, actually it's three presents," he hands me a large wrapped box.

Inside the big box were three small boxes. I opened the smallest to find a name plate for my desk, *Teresa P. Calvano, Ph.D., English Department.*

"I was going to put Assistant Professor or something but I know you're really an Associate Professor and will someday be a full professor so I didn't want you to outgrow it. It's also portable, for when Yale or Harvard come calling."

Once again, Tim causes me to choke up. He thinks of things no man in my life ever thought of before. Luke was too caught up in his own fall to even acknowledge my ascent.

"How did you know my middle initial?"

Tim squirms a little.

"The Internet. It isn't hard to find out nearly everything about a person. Your middle name is Penelope, the one who keeps the home fires burning in The Odyssey. I love that name. I hope you don't think I'm stalking you."

"No, I'm impressed with your Internet snooping. I wouldn't even know how to do that," I say.

I open one of the larger boxes and find a figurine of *Doctor of Physic* from Canterbury Tales. The next box has a figurine of the *Wife of Bath*.

"I know you'll have two offices — the writing center and your academic office. This is so you can be close to your research in both places. I hope you will finish the book."

God, I want to run away with this man. His thoughtfulness is like discovering a new cuisine where my tongue tingles to welcome the spices, *where have you been all my life, cardamom and turmeric?* In his slightly rumpled way, Tim did exactly the right thing.

I squeeze his hand though I'd rather be squeezing something else. This is Northbrook, home to Mrs. Zinler and a hundred others like her. Although Serena isn't a part of my narrative here, our failed escape to the U.K. and the abrupt return are common knowledge. Small towns have big ears.

I give him a look that I hope says I would jump you in a minute if I could. He meets my eyes without flinching and winks.

"I know. No pressure. Confusing time. I'm doing a lot better. Started playing racquetball and joined a climbing gym. Grandchild on the way."

"That's great. Congratulations." I'd almost forgotten he had grown children. I think of the daughter at the funeral. I thought she might be pregnant but when she stood up, it looked like she was just big.

"You helped me to move to a different place. I felt guilty for Chantal's death but I understand it better now. I think I might have felt the same if I were in her situation. I'm not a man who wants to be dependent."

"You helped me as well. I was feeling....well, undesirable and lonely. I'm not sure my marriage will make it. Luke has to redefine himself outside of academia. I think he got lost and his busyness helped him through the grief. Now he doesn't have that luxury."

"Is it really a luxury?

"I guess not. Loss has a way of redefining us. I feel as if I'm back to being productive but Serena is still here. She's as much a part of who I am today as she was before but I'm not paralyzed by it. I look at it from the outside instead of carrying it like a tumor inside of me," I say.

"I know what you mean. We are changed by our relationships, brief or long. You've changed me, Tess," he says.

A warmth washes over me and I want to lean across the table and kiss him but I can't. I'm Dr. Teresa P. Calvano, part-time professor and I have a reputation just beginning. I will not be defined by my dalliances and Tim deserves a woman who can commit, not an affair. I know if my marriage doesn't work out, he will be at the top of my list for an alternative but I can't tell him that.

"We've changed each other and I'm grateful. I'm confused, Tim. I need to do what our son had to do when his first love broke up with him over text. I have to get back to life."

Tim smiles but it's a sad smile. I know he's thinking that our lunches will be infrequent or maybe stop altogether.

"Thank you seems inadequate." I put my hand over his hand. Natalie is still on his knee and she grins at me. Easy to be a baby and absorb love without interpreting it. We make no plans. I promise myself that I will check in with him regularly. He deserves that and so much more. I know he'll be an involved grandfather and maybe that will prove a welcome distraction. It takes all my willpower not to suggest a motel and an afternoon in bed. He buckles Natalie in her car seat and she grabs his hand.

"She knows a good man when she sees one," I say.

"She probably understands how much I like her mother."

I give him an enigmatic smile and wave as I drive away. I can see him in my rearview mirror growing smaller in the parking lot.

## Chapter 35

It happens when we're driving to pick up Wyatt for Hanumas at Bess and Ira's house. He'd been staying with a friend, spending as little time as possible with us. Luke insists he doesn't need Google Maps because he knows the area. He turns right, then left. There is a road closure due to construction and then a detour that takes us behind a shopping center. It directs us down a side street that looks familiar.

"Wait, that's North Street," he says.

Oh, shit. I know exactly where we are. How could this happen when we've carefully avoided it for close to a decade? We've crossed into Kendall, that pastoral suburb where children ride bicycles and they still have block parties on summer nights. Kendall, home of the Memorial Day Parade where bigger children pull smaller children in decorated wagons and parents carry toddlers on their shoulders and put red, white, and blue bandanas on their dogs. Kendall, where Duane Anderson III killed a blonde-haired child who ran into the road, carrying her *Dora the Explorer* lunchbox.

"Fuck fuck fuck." Luke pulls over, puts his head in his hands. "God, I'm sorry. I didn't know we were that close. I was just following the detour signs."

Once we moved, we would go out of our way to go around the town, even if it was inconvenient. Marigold Court. The pretty tree-lined street with colonials and capes and even one restored Victorian. The backyard with its swing set and climber. The sandbox we later filled in with mulch to plant flowers. A climbing tree that Wyatt had loved and Serena was just beginning to use. We had talked about building her a tree house where she could bring her stuffed animals and her little Lego houses. We are exactly a block away from where it happened. It is more than eleven years later. Serena would be seventeen, probably complaining about Hanumas, how her friends had more defined holidays like Kwanza or Christmas or Hanukkah. Why did we always have to be weirder than other families? Maybe she'd revel in it, bragging to her friends about our embrace of two traditions, bringing along a friend or a date. Would she have clear skin or pimples, be tall or petite? Luke's brother is over six feet tall but he's five foot eleven. Wyatt is just edging into six feet. I'm average at five foot five. It's hard to even imagine a seventeen-year-old Serena. What kind of music would she listen to? Would she be passionate about social issues, spend her free time reading about physics or climate change or would she be a social media addict?

Luke slumps over the steering wheel and Natalie starts to cry. It's cold in the car.

"Let me drive," I say.

He doesn't say anything, just opens his door and gets out.

I go around to the driver's side and plug in my phone. We are about fifteen minutes away from where Wyatt is staying and forty-five minutes away from Bess and Ira's but I can't do it. I have to go there. We haven't been this close in years and it's Hanumas. I can feel Serena directing me to go back and at least acknowledge what happened in Kendall all those years ago.

When I drive by our old house, it's lit up with Christmas lights. They are the kind projected by a laser so it looks like there are literally thousands of red and green lights but it's actually just dots of color. A trick of light like the shadow of a child I think I see in the road. I slow down and park across the street from the house.

There was yellow police tape after the accident. Scene of a crime or a fatal mistake. Neighbors huddled. Diane was inconsolable because she knew it just as easily could have been her daughter. We hold onto our children with invisible thread. It's an illusion that we can keep them safe. Natalie in her red velvet overpriced Christmas dress is protected. She stays with us all the time. We've only left her with Anne, the veteran nanny, Wyatt, or Bess and Ira. When I go back to work, we'll have to trust a stranger. I was right there when Serena died. I had made her a breakfast of cinnamon toast and yogurt, her favorite. She was happy to have cookies in her lunch box. We had been talking about Thanksgiving and how she would help with the pies again. She had asked me why the President pardons a turkey every year.

My hands are numb even though I'm wearing driving gloves. Warm tears pool in my eyes. Luke lets out a garbled noise that sounds like a cross between a scream and a sob. Then he's wracked with sobs, hunched over so that his face is almost hitting the console.

"Jesus. Oh, God. I miss her so much. Oh God, oh God."

I've never seen him like this. Natalie starts to whimper and then it gives way to a full-blown cry. I take her out of her car seat, push back my seat and nurse.

## The Shape of What Remains

"Shhh. It's okay, little one."

Luke's shoulders continue to quake as he sobs, more quietly now. I hand him a clean cloth diaper and he dabs at his eyes, blows his nose.

The Christmas tree is visible from the picture window in the living room, exactly where we used to put our Christmas tree. Serena would jump on Wyatt's bed to wake him up though all those years ago, he was an early riser too. They'd knock on our door because we had trained them never to barge in.

"Wake up, wake up. Santy Claus came, Santy Claus came," Serena said. "Mommy, Daddy, wake up."

Luke would pretend he was fast asleep and they'd tickle him. Finally, we'd allow ourselves to be dragged out of bed and Luke would start the coffee and heat up the almond torte I made every Christmas. We'd eat later. First, fat stockings would be passed around. Little gifts like vouchers for a forgiven chore or breakfast out and small toys like Silly Putty or matchbox cars were dumped out. We filled each other's stockings and Luke would often give me a gift certificate for a massage or a pair of earrings. It was never anything fancy, just fun. The house smelled like cinnamon and pine. I thought I couldn't bear it when I realized we would never again have a Christmas like that but somehow, we went on. Luke stayed away and I removed myself from the world, first symbolically, then literally.

I see now that Marigold Court belongs to another family. They are rewriting the story with their own traditions and I hope they will have happy endings. Luke doesn't say a word when I change Natalie, buckle her back in the car seat and pull away from the white house speckled with festive lights, peace wreath on the door.

# Chapter 36

Luke has taken over Natalie care in the morning, which allows me to go to the gym or to campus. He's only teaching a night class and supervising a male graduate student. After the Hanumas breakdown, he's been spending inordinate amounts of time at home, more than I can ever remember him doing in the past. Sometimes I'll come home and he'll be on the floor with Natalie trying to interest her in the plastic stacker or a creepy jack-in-the-box toy Bridget gave her. She is usually more interested in his face though sometimes she'll stack the colored rings in the wrong order and giggle. Wyatt was all too happy to go back to UConn, staying with us just a week and spending the rest of the time with friends. The new woman from his class didn't work out but he's mentioned Bree a few times. I invite him to bring her home anytime but so far, he's not interested. In March, Lucy calls to tell us that Nigel died. It seemed like he was responding well to treatment before she left that day but the hospital called to tell her he went into cardiac arrest in the early morning. Attempts to resuscitate him were unsuccessful. I'd forgotten how stoic Lucy could be, especially since I've come home to find Luke crying over the misshapen star that Serena had made us that we had laminated or her baby cup on the mantle. We had turned it around so no one would ask about the initials SJC as if anyone examines baby cups on mantles. Having three isn't unusual. I still have mine from childhood.

"Oh, Lucy, I'm so sorry. We're coming up on spring break for Luke. When is the memorial?"

Although our budget is tight these days without either of us bringing in much income, the university was kind enough to continue our health insurance since we'll both be working more in the fall. It's the right thing for us to go. Nigel and Lucy extended themselves to help us in that country and it's the least we can do. She tells me about a memorial fellowship they've set up in his name, how the department misses Luke.

"You know Bronwyn Cooley dropped out. She did your husband a grave disservice."

I have no idea what she is talking about. Did Bronwyn accuse Luke of some impropriety? Our exit was stressful enough, caught up in the sorting out of monies that came from sources outside Britain. No way to tell and I wasn't going to press for more information.

"Please let us know if there is anything we can do. Our thoughts are with you and Abby, you know."

When I hang up, I remember Luke took Natalie out for a walk. It's one of those thaw days, not bitter cold. Ever since England, he has a thing about fresh air for children. I call Dr. B-S. Although I haven't seen her since I returned, we've had a few phone calls. She recommended a therapist for Luke but so far, he hasn't been willing to go.

When I tell her about Lucy's phone call, she asks me how I feel, reminds me that I might be jumping to conclusions. Bronwyn's "grave disservice" could have been academic in nature. Perhaps he called her on her research or she complained because he demanded too much of her. I shouldn't assume he slept with her though I want to describe Bronwyn's long red curls, tiny waist, and her habit of wearing tight skirts and boots. I saw the way she looked at Luke. Older man, distinguished scholar. Hard to resist if you're a graduate student looking to advance. My younger self had once been infatuated with Dr. Carlton Freeling, a well-published medievalist who specialized in Chaucer and Gower.

He was a fellow at the Medieval Academy of America and urged me to become involved in the New Chaucer Society at St. Louis University. Already married, I suppressed my urge to visit him in what he called his "rooms," a converted duplex in his turn-of-the-century house. His ex-wife lived on the other side since they had forged what he called a "civilized" arrangement. In my twenties, nothing seemed civilized. I was trying to balance family with a demanding Ph.D. program. I'm still not sure how I finished the coursework but Dr. Carlton Freeling had a lot to do with it. He acted as my cheerleader, giving me clear deadlines and copious revision suggestions. If I hadn't gotten pregnant, I would have sailed through. There were days when I would go without sleep, often working into the morning hours. But I never slept with Dr. Freeling though we shared bottles of wine, a few joints, and one neck massage that might have gone further but didn't. I want to believe Dr. B-S and her theory but I also know Luke's weaknesses.

Luke walks in, Natalie's cheeks flushed with the chill.

"She's hungry. I brought along some Cheerios but it wasn't enough. We had a nice walk though, went all the way to the park."

I tell him about Nigel, and I think he's going to cry.

# The Shape of What Remains

"How terrible for Lucy. And he had so much work to finish. God, I wish I could be there continuing his research." He looks lost for a minute, as if he's mentally in an office with carved oak doors. "I loved that place. Miss it every day." This isn't the time to mention Bronwyn so I ask if he wants to go to the memorial service next week.

"I can't do that, Tess. Going back would be too hard. I put so much of my life and energy into that place. I don't think I could bear it."

"I think we should support Lucy. They did a lot for us when we first moved — finding the flat, hosting us for dinners, helping me find a nanny. Lucy is a strong woman but she'll need support during this time."

"We don't belong there anymore. I have no place in Oxford. We can send a nice note, make a donation in his name," he says.

I decided to drop it for now but plan to check airfares online. I don't make friends easily and I feel as if Lucy really took me into her confidence at the end. I came to regret my early judgment of her as a middle-aged woman who spent all of her time on philanthropy. It wasn't her style to talk about herself and her needs. I only found out about her scholarly work later. I'll consider going alone if Luke won't travel. I pull out Tupperware containers of mashed carrot and applesauce, take Natalie from him and put her in the high chair.

"I'm going to shower and then run some errands," Luke says.

More time to think about England and what Lucy meant by *a grave disservice*.

## Chapter 37

"Even though he didn't do anything wrong and was a victim of funding decisions, Luke feels as if he failed. One minute he's at the top and then next he's on a plane returning to a lesser assignment," Bess says.

She doesn't diminish her personal hero title and encourages me to go alone.

"If Lucy supported you, it's right for you to support her, woman-to-woman. She'll appreciate your presence and Luke can handle Natalie for five days. I'll drop by to help out."

I'd already told her that Luke had lost it when we mistakenly ended up in Kendall.

"I still do that when I see a toy that Serena would have loved or a man who looks like Dom. I don't think I'll ever be able to eat another cannoli," she says.

Dr. B-S wrote a book for clinicians about grief and loss. On page 143, there's a section about what she calls extended denial and it could be dedicated to Luke. *A client in extended denial might throw him or herself*

215

*into work, make radical health decisions like gaining or losing weight, accept a position that forces a move far away, divorce or end a long-term relationship. Displaced grief can negatively impact the family structure and have long-term consequences. Meanwhile, the client hasn't done the necessary work of grieving.*

I book my ticket and email Lucy. I've arranged to stay at the Travelodge Oxford Peartree Hotel, described as reasonably priced and well-located. I hate driving in England so I need to be able to use public transportation. Natalie is mostly weaned, only nursing at night. I have pumped enough milk for a week. It's spring break and Wyatt is going to Florida with his new love interest, Maisie, to meet her grandparents. I was hoping he'd stay with Bree or another anonymous woman but it didn't work out.

When Tim calls, I'm organizing my luggage, trying to figure out the best thing to wear for a funeral. I can still fit into the black sheath dress and gray and black striped blazer I wore all those years ago for Dom's funeral. I splurge on a pair of black pumps even though it will probably be raining and I'd be better served by wellies.

"Leaving tomorrow. I'll be back on Sunday. I'm a little nervous about leaving Natalie for the first time but bringing her would be hard."

Tim tells me he misses me. He's been seeing a woman named Laura. She's an eighth-grade teacher. I think of my own eighth-grade year and I shudder.

"Tough age to teach," I say.

"Yeah. She teaches art though. For lots of kids, it's one place without judgment. She's a good artist, and has a little studio off her garage. She gave me a painting of trees in autumn and I know that doesn't sound like much but the way she captured it, you can almost smell the dry leaves and feel the air turning cool."

I feel a tug as his voice becomes animated. I can practically imagine Laura with her painting smock and curly hair. I don't want to imagine Laura. While I wish him happiness, I miss his warm bulk and the way he cared so much about pleasing me — even when I didn't know how to please myself. He kept me from falling over though I'm not sure he knows it. In a different life or perhaps without Natalie, we might have ended up together in his colonial house with its row of hemlocks and Andromeda and slate pathway lined by emerald and gold euonymus. My own yard is ragged, given my tendency to kill plants. I have the name of a reasonably priced landscaper and plan to add that to the list of things I'll spend money on once I'm gainfully employed. Grown-up clothes, a new computer, furniture for Natalie's room, a garage light, and maybe a screened-in porch to keep out the mosquitos. He wishes me safe travels and tells me we should have lunch or take a walk together when I return.

I hoist the luggage in back of the Subaru. Luke doesn't want to drive me to the airport. His refusal to do things he doesn't agree with is damn inconvenient. I wish I had a contact list filled with people I could ask but I do not. It isn't fair to ask Tim to do things when my husband is unwilling to help out. I finally decided to go for long-term parking because Luke has his own car. I'd rather not ask anyone for anything.

Dr. B-S says I actually do have friends but I don't want to trouble them to ask for anything. She's both right and wrong. I have three sets of people in my life — before Serena died, after Serena died, Rachel, Bess, and professional contacts. Rachel is *before* and Tim is *after* since he *knew* and was kind enough not to tell anyone. I don't live in Kendall and even though it's only thirty minutes away, except for that one wrong turn, I will never go there. When there is a sale at Green Lily, my favorite women's clothing store, I recycle the flyer or buy it online. Eleven plus years is a long time. The *after* group is small, consisting of my book group, yoga class, and people I see at the university, gym, or grocery store. Because of Natalie, women with babies come up to me though I wonder if they think I'm the grandmother, not the mother.

I'm leaving early tomorrow morning and Luke has promised to make dinner tonight. He's become a better cook, settling into his temporary role as stay-at-home dad. If he'd rise from the funk, I'd be all for it. I don't give a shit about money as long as we have enough to pay our bills. The problem is, he looks awful. He's dropped about ten pounds and dresses in all the ratty clothes I thought we'd given to Goodwill. Unless it's his teaching day, he sometimes doesn't bother to change from sweatpants when he comes back from the gym.

When I go downstairs, he opens a bottle of Chianti and pours me a glass.

"I know I owe you an explanation," he says.

The bottle is half empty.

I'm wondering what explanation — the wine, the dinner, my solo England trip, Bronwyn. There are many things I'd like him to explain.

"I wasn't exactly truthful with you," he says.

About what exactly? Which lie is he referring to?

"I mean the funding *was* cut suddenly. It's possible they might have found the money elsewhere but then there was another issue."

"Huh?" I down the wine faster than usual.

"Remember Bronwyn?"

Yeah, perfect body, gleaming red curls that reached down to her tiny waist. That Bronwyn?

"I guess so. Red hair?" I sip more wine, more of a gulp than a sip.

"Well, she complained to Nigel and the committee that I was sexually harassing her. We had kind of a fling in Dublin, only one night,

I swear. We'd both had too much to drink and it just happened. You and I weren't getting along and you were wrapped up in Natalie. I told her after that I wouldn't do that again. When she got back, she went to the Dean of Humanities and told her that I'd deliberately gotten her drunk to get her into bed."

"Bit of a conflict of interest to bed your own graduate student," I couldn't resist.

"I know," Luke's voice is barely above a whisper.

*He's ashamed of himself*, I think.

"It was a big fucking mistake," he says. "I tried to make it right, apologized to Bronwyn, the dean, Nigel, everyone. Nigel said he'd had a few indiscretions in his time and it was nothing to worry about. He'd make it right but this dean is newer and an ardent feminist. She hates what she calls the "old boy network" where academic men protect other academic men who take advantage of women. It didn't cost me the position but when the funding dried up, it gave them more of a reason not to look for alternative sources."

This must be what Lucy meant by "a grave disservice". Perhaps she knew about Nigel's indiscretions, thought it came with the territory. Maybe she'd had a few of her own. I spent valuable time being jealous of Bronwyn's beauty. My breasts were sagging with milk, my belly had a postpartum roll, and she sailed in on those stylish heels with cascades of copper curls trailing down her back. Now I wanted to hug her. No, Luke. It is not okay to have sex with your own graduate student even if you both had wine and she went along with it. Bronwyn dropped out of a prestigious program, and I can only think it was because of this. She probably figured if this is the bullshit a smart and gorgeous woman has to put up with to get a Ph.D., maybe another profession would be safer.

I gulp more wine and Luke refills my glass. Lust makes even the smartest of us into fools.

"I wanted you to know because people talk. I can't go back there, Tess."

"Fine. This is me making a decision on my own. This is about Lucy and I'll do my best to pay our respects."

He hasn't really made dinner so we throw together some leftovers that he barely touches.

"I'm a mess," he says.

"See someone, Luke. Do I need to make the appointment for you like you did for me? Get some help."

He nods and picks at his plate.

"I'll miss you," he says.

Morning can't come fast enough.

## Chapter 38

An impressionist painting. That's what I thought of the rain-soaked days. Oxford was lush at this time of year, violet-blue Pulmonaria, Pink Lady, and Magnolia Fairy Blush with its pale rose blossoms. Gardeners (people not like me) had done the spring clearing and mulched and eagerly anticipated the variegation in what is otherwise a drab landscape. It was almost a sport, the juxtaposition of hue and shape in gardens. One more way for me to feel inadequate in England.

All of that is a blur now that I'm back at Heathrow, ready to board my flight home. Bronwyn had nodded her head at me but we never conversed. It wasn't the time to ask Lucy anything. Flanked by Nigel's brother, Abby, and a disheveled young man who might have been Abby's boyfriend, I barely had time to give Lucy a perfunctory hug. She whispered her thanks to me, invited me back to the house. Hundreds of academics showed up at Christ Church Cathedral, St. Aldate's. I saw a few familiar faces but couldn't remember names though one gentleman came up to me and asked about Luke.

"You must be Teresa Calvano. Where's Luke?"

"Unfortunately, his schedule is less forgiving than mine."

Where did I learn to lie so effortlessly?

"I enjoyed working with him. Peter Jones," he offered his hand. "We collaborated on Shakespearean research. So unfortunate he couldn't complete the academic year."

"Yes, it was," I said, before I was saved by Abby inquiring about Wyatt. There are occasions that one should attend because protocol asks that of us. I didn't regret the trip though it drained nearly $1,000 out of our strained budget. Bronwyn didn't drop off the face of the earth after all so perhaps she'd return to school and choose a female advisor. I felt a kinship with her even though we never had a conversation. I'm listening to Vivaldi with my ear buds, grateful for nine or so hours of quiet though the pain of being separated from Natalie has taken over my body. It's as if I just gave birth and she was ripped away. Even two Facetime calls did nothing since Natalie is really too young to make the association. She turned to my voice but seemed distraught so we ended both calls quickly and agreed not to try again. Luke is managing, bringing her to the park and spending time with Bess. I'm sure he'll be glad for my return but I also think it's useful for him to be the responsible parent for a while.

About three hours into the flight, the plane begins to sway and jerk. Air pockets. The seatbelt sign comes on and flight attendants sweep through the narrow aisle to collect anything that might spill. I remind myself that plane crashes rarely happen when a plane reaches altitude though that's a small comfort during these times. I'm ashamed to say I scanned the other passengers when I boarded, looking for anyone that looked suspicious. I don't trust airport security. More than once I've forgotten to remove a pocket knife or scissors from my carryon bag and it passed through the x-ray without a hitch. The child in back of me is crying and though Natalie is mostly weaned, I feel my breasts begin to tingle. My milk is sparse now but there is definitely some moisture.

After bobbing up and down for about ten minutes, everything calms and they're serving a meal. Not my time to die I think, though I don't even know what that means except it would be awful to check out when my career was finally back on track and I had a little girl to raise. When Serena died, I thought a lot about the afterlife and wanted some sort of proof that I could see her again. I would have killed myself in an instant if I thought that was a possibility. I talked to a priest but his confidence in heaven did nothing except reinforce my skepticism. His unfaltering belief in both a higher power and an afterlife was enviable. *As long as she's been christened, she'll go directly to heaven.* We'd had a naming ceremony for Serena but given our mutual dislike of dogma, never affiliated with any religious community. Serena wasn't old enough to make those choices for herself. We had both agreed that our children could choose any religious path they liked once they had enough experience in the world. Wyatt shows little interest in any of it.

I suppose it's possible that Serena will be waiting in some plane of consciousness when I die. My pragmatic self wants proof. I hate studies that make sweeping conclusions without empirical data. Even then I'm sometimes suspicious of the results. Will I overprotect Natalie? Can safety ever be guaranteed? Although she's only been in the world for a short time, I know her smell, her sounds, her love of eggs and avocado, her dislike of tomatoes and broccoli. She smiles at classical music but reggae often makes her cry. This will change, I know.

When we land, it's one of those teaser days, sunny and dry. I didn't sleep during that bumpy plane ride and now I have to drive the ninety minutes to Northbrook. I text Luke to tell him I've landed but he doesn't respond. Luke has a habit of leaving his phone in strange places.

# The Shape of What Remains

I stop at Starbucks for a large latte because the long ride and a couple of sleepless nights is making me feel like taking a nap in the front seat of the Subaru. Hopefully the caffeine will kick in. The interstate is a mess of traffic and my phone keeps making the noise that directs me to alternative routes that may save me ten minutes. Travel throws a twenty-four-hour day up in the air and the hours land randomly. Like airplane meals, breakfast may be dinner depending upon the time zone. Our rituals are dependent on a clock. Why the hell wouldn't Luke pick me up? It's a bad idea to drive oneself after an international flight. The latte doesn't seem to be doing enough.

By the time I get on the Mass Pike, the traffic has slowed somewhat. My phone tells me there is an accident ahead. Shit. I don't know why it feels as if the cars are going too fast, blurs of red or black passing me. I'm in the right lane when an SUV merges but doesn't seem to slow or yield. I pull the steering wheel hard to the left trying to avoid a collision without going into the next lane. There's a dull clunk as the SUV bounces off the passenger side of my car and I hit my head on the steering wheel before I make my way to the breakdown lane up ahead. The SUV slows but keeps going. Black Ford Explorer. I try to make out the license plate number. Massachusetts plates L-41 something. My head is throbbing.

By the time the police get there, the Black Explorer is long gone. The passenger side of my Subaru is heavily damaged. I can't open the door.

"Are you okay, Miss?" the officer asks. "I'll call an ambulance."

"It's not necessary," I say, though I'm unsteady on my feet and nauseous.

"You've got a gash on your head. I'm calling for help."

He's a young man and I wonder if he has children.

"Is there someone you can call?"

Luke still hasn't responded to my text so I try Tim. He answers on the first ring.

"Teresa. Are you back?"

"Yes. I was driving home from Boston when an SUV sideswiped me. My car is a mess but I'm mostly okay, just a gash on my head. Can't reach Luke."

"Did you call the police?"

"They're here. Trying to find the SUV and my car needs to be towed. I can't think straight."

"Where are you exactly?"

"Exit 10 on the Mass Pike. Auburn."

The officer says something about Harrington Hospital in Worcester.

"I think they're taking me to Harrington Hospital."

"I'll leave now. Can be there in an hour."

I think of Bess after I hang up, wonder if I should call her or if she knows how to reach Luke. Maybe they're together. Officer Tom Marks lets me sit in the cruiser, and passes all my information over to the tow truck driver. How much will this cost? I have AAA but just the budget plan. Towing this far will be expensive.

Officer Marks opens the door.

"We found the SUV. Good you had part of the license number. Too many people don't yield on that entrance ramp. I'm writing in the accident report that the other driver was at fault."

Small victory. I tell him I'm lightheaded and he tells me to put my head down between my knees. He's given me paper towels for the gash. By the time the ambulance arrives, I can't stand and they lift me onto a stretcher. I don't think I've ever ridden in an ambulance before except the one they put Serena in even though there was nothing that could be done. Two paramedics flank me in the back. BP 90/60. They start an IV and I barely feel anything. I see Serena wrapped up in a blanket. She's floating. *It's okay Mommy. It doesn't hurt.* I try to reach out a hand to touch her but one of the paramedics tells me it's better not to move. Pretty soon I'm drifting, looking at the white around me and the blurry faces of the woman and man attending me.

When I arrive, there is a flurry of activity as they move me from one stretcher to another. Then I'm in a cubicle under bright lights. A man in green scrubs shines a light in my eyes, asks me my name and birthday.

"What day is it?"

"Sunday," I say, though I'm not sure. Did the day change when I arrived here?

"You're going to need some sutures. How many fingers am I holding up?"

I tell him three and he seems satisfied with that answer.

"Does it hurt anywhere else?"

I shake my head. I feel stiff but seem to be able to move everything.

Luke. Did anyone reach Luke?

Where is my phone?

I didn't see Tim right away because I was in x-ray when he arrived. They decided to keep me overnight for observation since it's possible I have a concussion.

"Tess," he kisses the good side of my forehead. "Thank God you're okay. I've been trying Luke but no luck. I left a message. I can call anyone else if you give me the numbers."

That would involve locating my pocketbook and cell phone.

The green scrubs doctor asks Tim to wait outside.

"Nothing broken. We need a CT scan to make sure there is no internal bleeding but I think you just got a good conk on the head. You'll be good as new in no time."

Tim has the plastic bag with my purse and phone.

"I told them I was a family friend and we haven't been able to reach your husband. Do you want me to call Bess?" Tim asks.

How many times will Tim be a stand-in for my husband?

I nod. My eyelids are heavy and my body feels like Jell-o.

When I awaken, Bess is by the bed holding Natalie and Tim is gone.

"Where's Luke?" I can't quite focus.

Bess doesn't answer my question. "The doctor says you'll be fine. You can go home tomorrow."

How long have I been here? What happened to Tim?

"Your friend Tim called me. I've had Natalie since Friday night which is why I couldn't get here immediately," Bess says.

Natalie starts to cry.

"Here's Mommy," Bess passes her over. "You're probably bruised up so be careful because she kicks a bit. We've been playing peek-a-boo."

"Hey little Nat." Natalie starts to wail. Where the hell is Luke? Bess pulls a bottle out of her bag and passes it to me.

"I guess you're weaned now. I think my milk is all dried up." Natalie latches onto the bottle and sucks hungrily.

"Where's Luke?" I try again.

"I drove him to the hospital late on Friday and they recommended inpatient at Rose Hill. He's been crying, not eating or taking care of himself. I think having Natalie to himself pushed some buttons. He called me on Friday afternoon and he wasn't making sense so I drove over. When I got there, he was sitting cross-legged on the floor just sobbing, Natalie screaming in her crib."

"Oh, God. I'm sorry. I had no idea it would go this far."

"Don't worry about Natalie. We can keep her until you feel strong enough. She's a sweetheart though she gets mad when she's hungry." Bess stands up.

"I'll pick you up tomorrow. Your car has been towed to Mack's in Worcester and it will be in the shop for a week or more. Luke's car is at the house though," she says.

She kisses me on the cheek and I kiss Natalie. As soon as they leave, I call Tim. It goes to voicemail. *Thank you for rescuing me. Luke is in the hospital but I'll be home tomorrow afternoon.*

He calls me back just as my square of overcooked lasagna and iceberg lettuce with a plastic cup of Italian dressing on a tray is delivered by a woman in a bright blue uniform.

"My gourmet dinner of lasagna and iceberg lettuce just arrived. No wine."

"Maybe you didn't sign up for the deluxe plan," he says. "I guess not. I think they get mixed greens instead of iceberg."

"Probably, with candied walnuts and chevre. Bess is picking me up tomorrow. Luke had a breakdown of some sort. He's at Rose Hill," I say.

"Shit, Tess. I spent so much time feeling sorry for myself but you're the hero. I can help out when you need it."

"How's Laura?"

"She's okay. Busy working and dealing with her teenage daughter. We're taking it slow."

"You're a good friend," I say and it's true.

"How about I stop by after you finish your lasagna al dente? I'll bring ice cream. Give me an hour or so," he says.

"You don't have to. It's a long drive and I'll be back in Northbrook tomorrow."

"I hate eating ice cream alone," he says.

## Chapter 39

I had no idea the amount of red tape one had to go through to handle an accident claim. My insurance company is fighting it out and there is a good chance I'll get a settlement for medical bills and my stress. I have that kind officer to thank for the detailed accident report, which formed the basis of the case.

Bess helped me find a sitter for Natalie. Although Wyatt has taken to coming home some weekends to help, he's nearing the end of the semester and needs to study. I have a part-time graduate student, Gina to help on Wednesdays and Fridays. Luke is back home but his ability to handle responsibility is minimal. He spends a lot of time in his office on his computer.

"You're stuffing your feelings again," he says when I dump the burnt toast in the compost.

It's fucking toast. Would it be better if I said I burned the fucking toast? Maybe I should scream *fuck the fucking toast!* I can't decide if I liked him better when he was sleeping with graduate students and not showing emotion. When he's not in his office with the door closed, he's compiling a digital archive of Serena photos. He's been writing her brief history, punctuated by all the photos he's scanned and arranged artfully. I get it. My letters helped me to say the things I needed to say and I know this is his process. I just don't see him moving through it. Who am I to judge how long it will take for him to accept a death he denied for nearly eleven and a half years? The problem is: we have a living daughter. Luke shows no interest in Natalie whatsoever and he's missing all the milestones. Yesterday she pulled herself up and moved from the couch to the coffee table standing up. She'll be an early walker. Even her crawling is all about getting to a place so she can stand. Her hair is straight and thick. I cut the ends so it would lose the ragged look. She still looks a lot like Wyatt as a baby. She sits in my lap for stories, particularly if there are animal noises involved. She also loves ice cream and cubes of cheese. I wonder if she'll love pesto like Serena.

I have a department meeting this afternoon. They've taken to inviting me to the meetings and I'm even getting reimbursed for about ten hours a month of my time. Gerry Dillman is trying to get me on the payroll by June so I'll have time to do some writing center planning. I have to hire a few tutors and interviews will need to happen over the summer. Regular paychecks can't come soon enough. We've been blowing through our savings at a distressing rate.

"Gina will be here to watch Natalie at 1:00. I have a meeting at the university," I say.

Luke looks up uncomprehending. I repeat myself.

"I could watch her," he says.

No way, buddy, I think. You just started regular personal grooming a few weeks ago. I don't think you change the sheets on your bed more than once a month and I know for a fact that you don't eat unless I put food in front of you.

"Thanks, but I'm all set."

"It's a beautiful day. I could take her to the park," he says.

It is one of those late April days when the sun feels warm, not hot. Crocuses and tulips are up and my lilacs and rhododendron are budding. The air smells like flowers and sun. In a different reality, we'd bring a picnic to the park, spread a blanket and eat sandwiches, giving Natalie chunks of fruit, avocado, and cheese. Maybe we'd go for soft-serve ice cream from the vendor at the corner of Main and Prospect. The food and ice cream trucks returned last week, in preparation for the students who will be flocking to open spaces just before finals. The farmer's market opens in two weeks.

"Thanks. I'm glad you're feeling up to it but I hired Gina so Nat could get used to her before the semester starts. Gina has to work two days a week. You're welcome to tag along if she takes Nat to the park," I say, choosing my words carefully. I will text Gina and let her know what's happening. She's a psychology graduate student and Bess already filled her in on the sorry synopsis of our current life. In August it will be Gina three days a week, and Bess one day a week. I'll be off on Fridays. I'm not counting on Luke for anything.

"You're treating me like a child. Natalie is my daughter too. You can't keep me from spending time with her."

The irony. Fatherhood isn't something you take on when it's convenient, like volunteering at an animal shelter or helping at the church bazaar. I slept on the floor of her room when she had a fever last month. She still wakes up in the night when she has a stomachache or is teething. She looks adorable in her yellow cardigan and green and yellow pants, holding a stuffed frog and alternately eating Cheerios. My need to keep her safe, fed, and happy takes up all the space in my chest. I've got no room for anything else. It's all I can do to keep from snatching her out of the highchair. Luke has cut up a banana and is watching her gum and chew the slippery bits, smearing her hands on the hapless frog.

"Good, huh, little Nat," he says.

He dabs at the frog with a wet towel and Natalie bats at it as if they are playing a game so he drags the towel across the tray of her high chair and she grabs it, wrestling him for it with her fingers.

"Quite a grip you've got there," he says, laughing. His face is pulled tight like it isn't used to smiling.

I can't take a chance that he'll fall apart when he's out in the park and sees a six-year-old who looks like Serena. It used to happen to me all the time. Blonde-haired six-year-olds with squeaky voices are everywhere. He'll see her on the swings or by the flower garden, asking her mother and father what that pink blossom is called or why bees like flowers. He won't know what to do because Natalie will be heavy in his arms or in her stroller and she'll suddenly become an afterthought. There was no Natalie when I was wiping off my smudged mascara, blowing my nose with a Kleenex on the park bench. I wanted to scream to every parent texting, *Pay attention*. I don't know how the Uvalde or Sandy Hook parents go anywhere when there are so many living six-year-olds in parks and playgrounds with missing front teeth, pigtails, little sneakers and favorite hats.

"How about we go to the park together this morning?" I say.

It's a concession, I know, but also a way to see how he handles public places. Luke is home pretty much all the time except when he's teaching his class. I don't know how he'll handle full-time work plus all the committee and advisory responsibilities in the fall. He looks at me as if he doesn't know either.

"It's a beautiful morning and I could use the exercise."

I try to make it about me, not him. Do this for me, Luke. Just a mother and father out with their daughter on a spring morning.

"Okay. I'll clean her up," he says, unbuckling her and lifting her out of the high chair, the grungy frog still in her right fist.

He hasn't changed her in a month or more but I let it go, text Gina to tell her that Luke may ask to take Natalie out alone and under no circumstances should she allow this to happen. *Call me if you have any questions.*

When we get to the park, it's crowded with strollers and mothers flanked by toddlers. Fortunately, it's a weekday so six-year-olds would be in school. I had forgotten about that. Never go to the park on a weekend when families gather with their school-aged children. Natalie is shrieking and kicking her legs, pointing her finger at a golden retriever puppy.

*Ba-bow*, she says.

"That's right. It's a bow-wow," Luke says though I'm not convinced that Natalie has any idea what he's talking about.

We head over to the garden.

"Look at the irises and lilies, Nat," he says. A hummingbird is hovering and I'm transported to the moment Serena first spotted a "bee-bird."

"Are you sure it's a bird? It looks like a big bee," she had said.

"Look at the body. Doesn't that look like a bird body? And it's green."

She looked again. Hummingbirds don't stay in one place for long so it's a lucky thing to see one.

"Wow. It's a bee-bird. A green bee-bird," she was jumping up and down with excitement.

I put up a hummingbird feeder for Serena so she could watch them from the breakfast nook at our house in Kendall. We had a large window by the table and I hung the feeder off a post that Luke adjusted so it would be at a good height for Serena. Sometimes I'd find her there in the early morning singing a little song she made up about the bee-birds.

*Teeny bird, not a bee, drinking nectar from the trees.*

Luke sees the hummingbird too and his eyes fill up. His lips are a flat line when he takes Natalie out of the stroller to show her. Natalie shrieks and waves her hands and the bird flies off.

"Remember that Serena used to love hummingbirds. She called them bee-birds," he says.

"Yes," I say in almost a whisper. "Hey, look at the squirrel, Nat. He's got an acorn in his mouth." Natalie turns to where I'm pointing and watches the squirrel scamper across the mowed grass.

"Why don't we take her to the swings? They have a baby swing," I say, not sure what he remembers since he's been such an infrequent visitor to this park.

We strap her in the swing and Luke pushes her lightly. She's laughing and kicking her tiny legs, her messy hair blowing in the spring wind.

Finally, we walk around the perimeter of the park, Natalie mostly on Luke's shoulders. We could be any family. A few people stop to say how cute Natalie is, ask her age.

"Thanks for suggesting the park, Tess. I know this has been hard. Can I tell you something?"

I look at him. His hair is thinning but he's looking better, wearing jeans and a denim jacket. At least he's shaving and showering again.

"I didn't understand why you took so long to deal with Serena's death. I thought you'd never function again and that was terrifying. I've always been able to compartmentalize, you know what I do with work — Iago, Shylock, my spreadsheet of graduate students and their dissertation proposals. I had our life set up that way too, date night, vacations with my parents and later Mom and Ira, weekends in Boston or New York. I even had a budget sheet so we could save for vacations. It kept things predictable. When Serena was no longer a part of it, I was devastated but I coped by adding to my work responsibilities, taking on more graduate students, and sending out proposals for my sabbatical year. It took six months to write the justification and then another six months of emails and phone calls with Nigel to finalize the semester in England. There wasn't a lot of time for anything else."

I don't mention Tyra or his consuming interest in Amanda's life. Forget about Bronwyn and the fling that cost him a job and may have cost her a graduate degree.

"My career was at a high point until it wasn't. Failure never seemed like something that would happen to me but when it did, everything else fell apart. That's what my doctor at the hospital, Dr. Thistlewaite said. Like fucking dominos."

I put my finger on my lips, a signal that we both need to watch the swearing. Natalie is beginning to talk and I'd hate for her first words to include *fuck*.

"You know what I mean. House of cards. Catastrophic fall, Thistlewaite said. Says I'm a control freak. Everything was copacetic as long as I had my little boxes and spreadsheets. Even in your depression, you were predictable. When you came out of it, you did it in a big way — going to England without me, making plans with friends I don't even know, like Tim. You applied for a damn job and didn't tell me about it until you flew in for an interview. None of this was supposed to happen. You don't really need me and Wyatt is out of the house. My academic career was in freefall. It hit me that I should be teaching Serena to drive, meeting her prospective dates and finding all of them lacking, giving her an idea of what to look for in a relationship. Except she is gone. I don't know. It was as if I'd convinced myself she was just out of the country or at a fancy boarding school or something — not permanently erased from my life."

I choke up at the word erased. It isn't possible to erase Serena. I see her in the hummingbirds, my own similarly shaped fingernails and blonde hair, the laminated star we keep on the mantle.

"So I fell apart. Men aren't supposed to fall apart but I did anyway. You were in England paying our respects. The house was empty and Natalie was bereft without you. I called my mother and told her I couldn't handle it anymore. I think I scared her because she dropped everything and came right over."

"What does Dr. Thistlewaite think about your progress?"

"I was well enough to be discharged. I know I haven't helped much with Natalie but I don't know who she is yet. I want her to be Serena and she's not."

*Thank God.*

"Remember when I wanted to have another baby right away and you kept telling me that Serena couldn't be replaced, that you needed to feel the pain. I thought you were being selfish, denying me that opportunity. Now I understand the purpose of that pain. It's the other side of love. Grieving is a tribute to love. It honors every moment we had even though we can't relive any of them. As long as we remember, we keep a part of Serena with us. It makes her life matter," he says.

I'm losing it. I start to cry and put my hand on his hand. All of this makes sense though it still doesn't engender any confidence in Luke's ability to care for Natalie.

"What about Natalie?" I say.

"I have to let her in and I'm afraid. You must have been terrified when you were pregnant. When you leave her with Gina, don't you worry about something happening?"

"Of course, I do. I use the same rationalizations when I fly or drive. Millions of people fly and drive every day and the overwhelming majority will be fine. Most children grow up and become independent adults, like Wyatt. I resort to clichés like lightning won't strike the same place twice. There is no reason for tragedy. We can fight for better gun control, enact stricter traffic laws, and make planes safer. Children still die at the hands of an abusive parent, war, guns, or disease. It's part of the human condition. My challenge has been to live in smaller increments of time. This morning, Natalie pointed to tell me to change her diaper. She laughed when she saw the hummingbird."

"Doesn't the noise of the world overwhelm you? There is so much crap going on and I have a hard time shutting it out," Luke says.

"I know. I have days when I think we were irresponsible to have children at all. Who knows what the world will be like when Natalie is an adult. Dom once said to me that every generation has challenges that seem insurmountable and I think it's true. Think of Hiroshima, the Cold War, 9/11," I say.

Luke takes Natalie down from his shoulders.

"What do you think, Natalie?"

She grabs his nose and screams, little waves of laughter shaking her small body.

# Lisa C. Taylor

"What a happy baby," a woman pushing a stroller says. "I wish my son was that cheerful."

## Chapter 40

Brett MacDonald lobbied for me to get a private office. Although it's currently being used by an adjunct filling in for a professor on sabbatical, it will be mine shortly. I can pick up the key after grades are in next week. They've even put a printer in the room, and it's one of the coveted offices with a window. I think I'll go to Ikea for a small cabinet to put next to the bookcase. I can finally move the boxes of books I never unpacked in Northbrook.

Wyatt will be coming home on Sunday, working in town for the summer and saving to buy a car. Maisie is "just a friend" he tells us but he needs to drive to Kendall to visit her when he's not working and he met her grandparents in Florida. Natalie gets animated when she sees him and he's good with her, stopping short of changing diapers. He's agreed to watch her for a half day a week so I can organize my lessons. Is it terrible to think that I trust him more than Luke?

I feel like I understand a little what it must have been like for Tim. Chantal's disability made many activities impossible — long walks, kayaking and even some performances. Everywhere they went had to be handicap accessible. I think of all the places we've gone where I took for granted that I could climb stairs, walk on a beach or row a boat. Luke isn't physically limited but his moods are unpredictable enough that I hesitate to go anywhere that may trigger memories. No more park visits in the summer until he can cope without falling apart. I have basil in the garden but I won't make pesto. I try to remember all the things that were difficult for me in those years; holidays, her birthday, bleeding heart flowers, honey and cinnamon toast. I stopped making almond tortes years ago. I couldn't wear blue or yellow and I'll never buy Natalie a stuffed monkey.

Luke's office will also be available over the summer and I'm hoping he'll spend time there organizing or compartmentalizing as he calls it. He'll only have one graduate student to supervise in the fall and three classes. It's not a heavy load and I wonder if they did it on purpose.

We don't sleep together but we're congenial roommates. He might have said that about me years ago though I don't have a penchant to bed graduate students. Although I'm lonely, I'm trying to keep my mind on my return to work.

"How did you get past the depression?" Luke asked me last night. I stopped myself from mentioning his insistence that I try a cocktail of drugs, all of which made me feel like a zombie. They may have deadened some of the feelings but they did nothing to further my healing. Grief is a process. Each stage can last hours or years. I was stuck in anger for a good five years — anger at Duane Anderson III, Luke, Serena for running into the road, Diane for distracting me, and most of all myself. Denial only lasted a day or so for me though Luke was stuck in it for years. Even with all the therapy and the books I've read, losing a child was a bit like swimming with sharks. You know you're going to be hurt, the only questions are how much and will you survive?

Acceptance isn't what it sounds like. I don't accept the loss though I understand its permanence. She isn't coming back and no amount of belief in an afterlife or magical thinking can change that. Acceptance means having a life. Natalie and Wyatt need me and I have the possibility of continuing my research. It's a world of pale blues and dusty rose instead of indigo and magenta but I can live with that. Maybe the colors will become vivid again someday.

I tell Luke about my shark metaphor and he nods.

"Yeah. I feel like I have newborn skin. The sun, hot water, and shaving hurts."

Maybe that was why he didn't shave regularly for months after we got back.

"I got used to it. But I'm no model. Took me almost eleven years," I say.

"It feels unfair to enjoy anything when Serena won't have that opportunity," he says.

"She can't miss what she never had," I say, knowing that sounds harsh.

The dead don't feel, I've told myself over and over. If they exist in another plane, it's not of our making. We can't control it.

"It's just that we'll never know what she would have become."

How many times have I cycled all the possibilities through my brain? Because of the bird project, I was sure she was destined to be an ornithologist. What about her love of gardening? Maybe she would have been a botanist. The passions we have as children may remain in some form in our adult self but there are so many things she never experienced. I wanted to be a doctor when I was her age — mostly because I had received a doctor's kit as a present. Once I found out they had to do autopsies, I lost interest. I also loved dressing up and fancied

I'd be a model because they wore cute outfits and could change clothes several times a day. It's hard to think of a profession I would be less suited to than modeling.

"That's true. We might have been thrilled with her choices or had to face disappointment that she didn't live up to our expectations. Bridget is disappointed in me and I am a professor," I say.

"Your mother is crazy. She doesn't understand what you went through to get that level of education. Most parents would be proud of you. My mother certainly is. She brags to all her friends about her professor daughter-in-law," he says.

"And son," I add.

"We aren't like that. We would have been Serena's champions even if she chose a different path," he says.

"How do you know? What if she wanted to drop out of high school?"

"She loved learning."

"Six is easy, Luke. Fifteen is harder. Some kids get caught up in peer expectations. Sometimes smart girls fake ignorance," I say.

"It doesn't matter. What matters is she never had a chance to fail or succeed and that just sucks," he says.

"Yup. It does. We will get to see Natalie grow up though. She may be a motorcycle racer or astronaut," I say.

"Chocolatier or Senator," he says.

"Stuntwoman or Supreme Court Justice."

He's smiling.

"She has good hair. That matters," I say.

"More than you know," he says, running his hands through his thinning hair.

## The Shape of What Remains

"Getting back to your original question, I stopped fighting depression. I let myself wallow in the feelings even when they paralyzed me. I reminded myself that my love for her was tangled up in the grief. Parents in the Compassionate Friends group described that feeling, the idea that everything seems pointless. I watched people going about their day and thought it was absurd when someone used a directional signal or took too long to respond to a green light. A child died. What could be more important than that? Eventually I began to see that minutia is a good distraction. I like shucking corn because it's mindless. When I paint a room or roast a chicken, I'm working toward a reachable goal. It's that balance of finding out what you can control and adding more of those things to your day. You did that with work but you did it to avoid what you couldn't face. Now that you've faced it, start adding back in doable tasks. Celebrate something you finish — grades, a chapter in a book, changing Natalie."

I add in the last one because Luke seems oblivious to Natalie's discomfort. He lets her sit in soaked diapers until I come in and notice.

"I've gotten nothing done over the last six weeks," he says.

"I don't agree. You've done more emotional work than you had done over the past eleven years — maybe longer. You're different because of it. It will either bring us closer or destroy us." I hadn't planned on saying that last part. It's a bad habit I have sometimes of saying what I'm thinking.

Luke's eyes open wide and he stares at me.

"Are you going to leave me? Is it Tim?"

"No. I didn't mean to say it that way. It's just that things have been challenging for a long time. First it was my depression, then your affair, then your work, and so on. I'm getting used to the idea of making decisions for myself. I don't know how our relationship will fare over the long haul. How could I? You stayed with me but only on paper. Your world was definitely outside the house for many years."

Luke nods. "I'm a fucking idiot."

"At least you're a fucking idiot who shaves every day."

Luke rubs his chin. "Remember when I used to shave twice a day so I wouldn't irritate your face when we kissed?"

"I do remember. It was sexy."

"Not good that you put that in the past tense." Luke moves closer, kisses me lightly on the lips. I'm not ready for a romp but I go along with it. He pulls away when he hears Natalie whimpering.

"I think our daughter is determined to ruin all our intimate moments for the foreseeable future," he says.

"It is her job. She's trying to prevent us from producing an unexpected sibling. We're too old, as Wyatt said."

"That boy knows nothing," Luke says.

He takes the steps two at a time and rescues Natalie from her crib. When he brings her downstairs, her hair is sticking up in all directions and she's rubbing her eyes with tiny fists. Sometimes she's so cute, it hurts to look at her.

"Here's mommy. She wants to change your wet diaper," he says, passing her to me. She's dry and I can see that he's even changed her outfit.

"No, I'm sure she said daddy. He's better at picking out the best outfits."

Natalie looks at me and starts laughing. Pretty soon we're all on the couch laughing. When Wyatt walks in, he takes a look at us and goes back outside before coming in again.

"I thought I walked into the wrong house," he says.

## Chapter 41

I used to love roller coasters. The dips and the sheer speed made my stomach flip around and goosebumps form on my arms. On a roller coaster, I was the kind of person who would get in a fast car with a stranger, travel alone to a foreign country, or go skydiving. Once the ride was over, the ground seemed to move under my feet as if I'd been forever transformed. I wondered if people who live through earthquakes expected the ground to be unsteady, ready to shake any moment. After I had Wyatt, we left him with a friend and went to an amusement park. I dragged Luke to the roller coaster, a new feature that promised to turn us upside down and take us through long minutes of hairpin turns and dips at a death-defying speed. I checked my harness more times than necessary and felt the panic rising with the speed and simulated disaster. Exhilaration was replaced by scenarios of what might go wrong, I clenched Luke's hand.

"I'm too old for this," I told him, even though I was young. He led me to the water park where we floated in the lazy river and dodged waves in the wave pool. After an hour or so, we left, earlier than planned. We had expected a return to an early time in our relationship but it wasn't possible to get it back. All we could think of was the baby at home and a quiet dinner.

We returned to roller coasters with Wyatt when he turned ten, a rare post-Serena outing. He screamed and begged for a second run. A tiny piece of who I once was made a cameo appearance and I waited in the long line with him six times.

"Your mother was crazy for roller coasters when I met her," Luke said.

"Yup. Every chance I got until you were born."

"Why'd you stop?" Wyatt's face was flushed with wind and excitement.

"It felt different. Too real."

"Just a ride, Mom."

I don't know if I'll ride the coasters with Natalie. Already I can see that wildness in her as she careens into corners, tries to climb on the coffee table or rickety chair. Yesterday she pulled a sugar bowl off the edge of the kitchen table and it smashed on the floor, little pottery shards and sugar everywhere.

"Uh oh," she said.

She likes uh oh and says it a lot. Luke says maybe she'll be a demolition specialist.

Serena was careful to the point of fastidiousness. She compartmentalized like Luke, her stuffed animals in plastic bins, stacks of books, and crayons returned to their tin. Once, she spilled hot chocolate on her favorite dress and she was inconsolable even when I reassured her that I could wash it out. I had to show her the stain remover, hold her up to watch it spinning. Natalie would happily smear mud all over herself. Last week she had chocolate pudding for the first time and quickly shunned the spoon. Pudding was in her hair and all over her face, on and under her king-sized bib.

"Archeologist," Luke said. "She'll be digging for artifacts."

"Mud wrestler," I said.

Serena's fondness for order might have been what killed her. She hated things out of place. What was in the road that day that didn't belong?

Natalie strings together sounds as if she knows that words have power.

"Me bop. Me bow."

When she gets what she asked for, she stretches her hands out and shrieks with joy. Once she's done with an item, she throws it on the floor.

"You have to stop picking it up," Luke says.

It's hard to know if she's throwing it for effect or if it's a careless move. Babies can only keep a short sequence of thoughts going. Once thirst is satiated, the cup has outgrown its usefulness.

We're back to work and by appearances all seems fine. I return to my research and teaching, drop the book group because I can't add anything else to my life. Wyatt returned to UConn and we're like any other middle class overscheduled couple except we spend little to no time together. Luke's therapy takes up free time so I use the gym at the university, have coffee with colleagues or occasionally meet up with Rachel. The silence feels like something I can't break, an impermeable skin over us. When Tim calls to invite me to lunch, I grab at the chance to change the narrative.

I meet him in the next town on his light day and my free afternoon. Natalie has taken well to her schedule, reaching her arms to Gina or Bess as I dash out the door.

"Been a while," Tim says, kissing me lightly on the cheek. "You look so professorial."

"Thanks. I never did properly thank you for the figurines and the nameplate. Wife of Bath lives on a shelf in the writing center. Doctor of Physic is in my office along with that classy nameplate."

"How is it going?"

"Good. A nice balance of teaching and administration. I hired tutors and they're getting the word out about the writing center. Next semester I can propose a class."

"Was it hard leaving Natalie?" Tim asks.

"Not as much as I expected. She's pretty adaptable. Loves Gina and Bess. She doesn't seem to have much separation anxiety. How are you doing? How's Laura?"

Tim looks at his iced tea.

"She wanted a commitment and I'm not ready. I almost talked myself into it because I'm sick of being alone but I thought it would be unfair to her. We're taking a break," he looks at me and I know what's coming before it's out of his mouth.

"I have to say this. I don't need you to respond or do anything. I'm in love with you. You probably guessed it a while ago. It started as an infatuation when we were in the book group but it's not that anymore. I respect your desire to keep your family together but I had to tell you."

I put my hand on his.

"It's okay. I have strong feelings for you, too," I say knowing that is not what he wants to hear. He wants me to say that I'll leave Luke, move into his house and have a life with him. A part of me relaxes into the warmth of this decent man. I wish I could continue the fling without hurting anyone, spend a night a week in bed with him, no demands.

"I've been trying to make it work with Luke," I say. It feels like betrayal to tell him that it's been a colossal failure, that the best part is Natalie. Luke is progressing but he's not the man I fell in love with and maybe he never will be again. I don't understand the elusive qualities of love. Was I drawn to his lack of emotion? Now he cries at shampoo commercials. When he talks about denial and acceptance as if they were taps to be turned on or off, I zone out. I'm sick of psycho-talk. Memory is a lock of hair, a photograph, but it isn't life. My living, breathing daughter needs me.

"Going well?" he says as if he doesn't believe it.

"No, it's hard. Most days it feels like I'm suffocating. God, I'm sorry for telling you this," I say.

"It's okay. I felt like that with Chantal. Everyone viewed me as a hero but I resented it a lot of the time. I didn't blame her but the woman I loved was hijacked by her limitations. You have a right to happiness, don't you think?"

"I don't know. I have a responsibility to raise Natalie in the best way I can. Luke has gotten better with her."

"No pressure, Tess," Tim looks at the menu.

I want to pull a screen over my mistakes, hit the back button to keep Serena out of the road. No. Then there would be no Natalie and there's something about Natalie. She's brash, funny, and messy. All things I want to be. This career is different but exciting. This child will bring new challenges. And Tim. Tim is my *not Luke*. When I think about it, I realize that Tim is the total opposite of Luke and that is what makes my relationship with him so compelling and hard to leave.

"You deserve someone unencumbered," I say.

"I hate that. I don't deserve anything. Feelings are unconditional. Perhaps there is someone else out there but there is also someone sitting right here. You're the one I want to be with and failing that, I'll cope. My grandson will be born next month. I'm going on a cruise to Alaska in the summer. I wish you could go with me, eat salmon, and see the glaciers before they disappear."

I think of Natalie staying with Luke while I go on a cruise, see Denali National Park and glaciers. I've never been to Alaska or on a cruise. Would we make love for hours in our cabin, have bottles of wine delivered? Will there be cheesy entertainment and hordes of people?

"I've never been to Alaska," I say.

"I have a cabin with a balcony reserved. Ten days. Side trip to Denali and the Yukon."

I think of Natalie with her wild hair and zest for everything. Will she grab at opportunity as if it were a streak of light across the sky that a cloud might render invisible? Serena would have considered pros and cons. She was a pleaser. Natalie is a doer. I remember one time in therapy when Dr. B-S asked me what I want.

"What do you want? What do *you* want? What do you *want*?" Inflection led to different answers. Serena back. A life. Peace.

"Thank you. I can't tell you today," I say.

"I know. It's part of what I love about you. You're thoughtful and discerning. Life is brief, Teresa. I don't have to tell you. No pressure. Even if everything stays the same, I'm glad I told you. I don't want to be in your book group or the person you call when you can't reach anyone else. I want to discuss books with you in bed and be the first person on your contact list," Tim says.

"You deserve that. I just don't know if I have it to give," I say.

I put a card on the check. "My treat."

## Chapter 42

There are times when quiet is exactly what I want, especially after a long day of students filing in and out of my office with issues that range from a course overload to a professor who graded unfairly. Unfortunately, it's hard to get a moment to myself with Hurricane Natalie. She chatters and destroys everything in her path. Childproofing is a misnomer. For Natalie, I had to look up and down and sideways. She's a climber so plugs in the middle of a wall are no deterrent if there is a chair nearby. I used to think toddlers on leashes were abusive. They looked like dogs. *I* would never do such a thing to my civilized child. Serena doggedly held onto my hand and sat for hours just looking around while we ate dinner. Natalie eats with two fists, refuses to be socialized and breaks free anyplace she isn't strapped in. Thank God for car seats. Luke likes her personality, says she's spirited. I wonder if I was like that. No way to know. Bridget considers it distasteful to reminisce about my childhood. The past is the past. Just today, Natalie learned two new words—bye and bot. She's in love with the letter B, which reminds me of Sesame Street. *Today's show is brought to you by the letter B.* Serena asked what that meant. I told her that the show focused on a different letter each day so she could learn her alphabet. *That's silly. I already know my alphabet.* For Natalie, it's the process of discovering how much of her world begins with B. Bottle, bed, bowl, banana, baby, bye bye. She rocks back and forth or bounces up and down, bending her chubby legs. If she tires of a toy or book, she throws it. We work on this a hundred times a day. I can't even imagine her at two. The other side of her temperament is demonstrative and loving. She kisses and hugs, snuggles against me, a warm ball of energy. She also goes from wakefulness to sleep in a minute and then back again in the morning. She's an anchor.

In less than a month the semester will be over. Wyatt will return and we'll celebrate Hanumas. I'll have a glorious month to think about Tim's offer, my next semester, and a future that is longer than next week. I've not made much headway but I wake up looking forward to Natalie's hugs and my teaching. Luke seems low energy, grabbing a coffee on the run, going to bed by 10:00. He rarely shares breakfast with us except on the day that Bess watches Natalie. He tries to be there for her, demonstrating that he's an involved father. It comes in waves. Some days he'll be on the floor doing a puzzle with Natalie and other days he's looking around for me to take over.

Last night a neighbor was crying in his truck.

"Must have had a fight with his wife," Luke said.

This neighbor, a fiftyish man, had his head bent, hands over his eyes. It's late November so it's not necessarily outside weather. I had an urge to tell him it would get better but I didn't know what made him cry. I didn't want to watch him but I did with the same curiosity that people have when they slow down to look at an accident. Thank God it wasn't me or someone I love, they think.

# The Shape of What Remains

Luke tells me his name is George and his wife Merle has been diagnosed with early onset Alzheimer's disease. Their only child lives in California and they are both only children. Another neighbor told him. There will be a fundraiser at the Methodist Church on Friday. The neighbors will be meeting next Wednesday night to discuss support. Can we attend a meeting at 7:00? We can bring Natalie. I nod but I don't want to go. Is it wrong to feel as if I've just emerged from a tunnel and can't bear someone else's darkness?

We're bad neighbors, don't socialize or even know the names of most of the people in the neighborhood. Ghost house. Although I'm glad to be back, I still have a nagging feeling that I don't belong here, my destiny sitting on a screened-in porch elsewhere while a gardener tends the flowers. Luke wants to go, says it's important to be a good neighbor. This may be a side effect of his therapy, awareness that there is a world out there filled with needy people. One of them lives in his own house and tugs on his pant leg. Goodness is defined as something that happens outside the home so others can see. *He's a busy man but he took the time to attend and even volunteered to drive her to appointments.* I'm waiting to see what Luke takes on and how he fits it into his *to do* list.

"They're having a potluck at Meg and Brian's before. Do you want to go?"

I have neighbors named Meg and Brian? I vaguely remember a thirty-something woman with her hair clipped back wheeling the recycling bin into a garage. This is not a multiple-choice exam. I fail if I don't show up. Serena once got a certificate for good attendance, which I thought was absurd. I have students who show up but don't do the readings or hand in any papers. The brain needs to be engaged at some point. In spite of my best efforts, not everyone belongs in college. Students are the embodiment of their parent's desire to educate them but some never buy in. Given the price of tuition, it's a colossal waste of money. If I show up, I will volunteer because I know the drill. I went to fucking graduate school.

I make vegetarian stuffed cabbage hoping no one is gluten-free, dairy free, vegan, or has subscribed to a diet like intermittent fasting or keto. It's hard to keep straight all the diets out there today. American cuisine fuels the diet industry.

"I'm glad you're going with me. It will be good to get to know our neighbors."

This doesn't feel like a date. A date involves wine, a babysitter, and wearing something that isn't a blazer or jeans. It's more like a reality television show: *Total Marriage Makeover: Meeting the Neighbors*. We're sure to become besties with Meg and Brian. Do they have children? I'm out of the school-age loop with a nearly twenty-year span between children. I've seen a bushy-haired pre-teen waiting for the bus but he could belong to anyone on the street. There are dogs, picnic tables, lawnmowers, and grills here. It's an American neighborhood.

When I bring my Pyrex casserole dish of stuffed cabbage, Meg (the woman with the recycling bin) tells me how much she loves stuffed cabbage.

"Does it have hamburger and rice in it?"

"No, it's vegetarian."

She manages to mask her disappointment with a stretched smile.

"Sounds delicious."

I wanted to tell her that it really is good with onions, peppers, and tomatoes mixed in with brown rice but she's moved on to greet a large woman carrying what looks like a tub of mac and cheese. Luke is already moving toward the bathroom and I drop my casserole dish on the kitchen counter and follow him.

"Shit. Mac and cheese."

Will we ever be able to look at mac and cheese as just high fat, high carb instead of Serena's most requested dinner?

I put a hand on his shoulder.

"At least no one brought pesto," I say.

Mac and cheese is every child's comfort food. Pesto speaks to a more sophisticated palette. I don't tell him that I now order it in restaurants, sometimes with Tim. I love pesto and I've convinced myself that it's a way to honor Serena.

He ducks in the bathroom and I microwave my cabbage and place it on the dining room table. A potluck is a chance to see how the neighborhood eats. There are dishes I'd never touch like some kind of Shepherd's Pie and a ham salad. Ham was never meant to be in a salad. There is even that horror of a dish, Jell-o mold. I thought those went out of fashion with slow cookers and Panini makers. It's red with cut up bananas and other unidentifiable fruit in it. I would rather lick the tires on my car.

"Teresa, right?" Meg has perfect teeth though a little big for her mouth. "Strange we haven't really met. I guess everyone in the neighborhood is busy. Takes a crisis to bring us together."

You know nothing about crisis, I think.

"You work at Northern, right?"

I nod.

"My brother is in facilities there. Greg Marquette. Do you know him?"

This is a game people play. There are nine thousand students at Northern. I don't know how many employees there are besides faculty. We have forty-six in our department.

Facilities isn't anywhere near the English Department. I went there once to get a key but I don't remember who issued it.

"I don't think so. Big place."

"Do you teach?"

I nod. "English Department."

"Oh. That's great. I teach social studies at Northside Middle. Our son Keith goes there which is a little awkward. He's at that age where you don't necessarily want your parents around while you're at school."

"I can imagine. We have a son at UConn."

Meg looks confused. "Who is the baby?"

"Our daughter, Natalie." I watch her face. She's thinking second marriage but it doesn't fit. I don't look like he traded me in for a younger model. Maybe she's adopted or one of us had a relative who left us the child. I remember Wyatt's confusion when we told him. *You're too old*, he said.

"How does your son get along with her?"

"After his initial shock, he's fine. Not around too much but she adores him."

Meg needs to move on to find someone who isn't reminding her that she might have a birth control accident and end up stretching those toned abs again. I take the plastic wrap off the cabbage and stick a serving spoon in it.

After Serena died, neighbors brought desserts and casseroles for weeks. I finally donated them to the soup kitchen. We couldn't eat them all and to me, the message was clear. If we do this, the Gods will reward us and keep our loved ones safe. Like an amulet, kindness should protect you but it fucking doesn't. I'm here to say that George's previous life is over. I don't know him but I know he'll contemplate suicide unless his religion prohibits it. Even then, he may lose the religion. Their kid will visit briefly before flying back to California. This will be all on George and it stinks. Don't tell me about a greater plan. What kind of a God runs over children and robs minds?

Luke kisses me when we get home and he wants to sleep with me. I lay Natalie down in her crib. She was surprisingly mellow all night as if she knew that these strange people were gathered to remember that this was happening to someone else and for the moment their family was doing okay.

"Pretty depressing, huh?" I say.

"I thought the turnout was amazing. See what happens when neighbors pull together?"

"Merle has Alzheimer's. She isn't going to get better. You think a casserole or a ride is going to help anything?" I feel like shit saying this but it's true.

"The important thing is that George doesn't feel alone. What a great neighborhood," he says, pouring both of us glasses of Pinot Noir.

"What if she lives ten years? Are you going to offer rides until you're 56?"

"She probably won't last that long. Why are you being like this?" he sips his wine.

"There are problems that can't be solved with casseroles. If we had a better healthcare system, George would be able to get the support without losing his house. It's a drop of rain in a damn drought," I say.

"You're cynical," he looks at me as if I've committed a crime. The misdemeanor of telling it like it is.

"I'm tired, Luke, and I have a final to give tomorrow." I finish the wine and put the glass in the sink.

When I go upstairs, I hear the television on in Luke's room.

I call Tim's number.

"Tell me about the Alaska itinerary."

## Chapter 43

Sometimes it helps to think of floating on a cold sea, seals popping out at random intervals in the white crest of a wave. Serena loved the beach, her experiences limited to summer visits where we'd find beach glass and shells or crabs washed up at low tide. She always wanted to throw them back even if it was clear they were dead. Maybe dead things can be resurrected with a little hope and a good arm. Natalie is likely to eat the sand or run into the water. I won't look away.

It's still five months away from summer. A new semester recently started with cold settling over campus. We've had three cancellations, snow so deep even my Subaru waits in the driveway. Natalie wants to play in the snow so I bundle her in a puffy snowsuit and mittens. She brings her mittened hand to her mouth and licks.

"Um."

I remember snow cones we made with maple syrup though I'm sure there are all sorts of pollutants in snow. The greatest hazards are invisible and arrive unbidden. She falls over but the snow is fluffy so she tries it again, her cheeks rosy with the cold. I'm too old for this, would like a warm cup of cocoa and a movie but I show her how to lie on her back and make a snow angel. Hers looks more like a bloated moth. When I finally bring her in, she's crying.

"Mo, mo."

Nothing is ever over for Natalie. If she likes an activity, she won't tire of it for hours. I rarely have that kind of patience or cold tolerance.

I make her hot cocoa mostly to distract her from the snow still blanketing the roads. When I let her out of her high chair, she remembers, goes to the picture window and points, a plaintive cry rising until it hits a crescendo.

"Mo' snow."

It's the first time she's said snow so clearly but it's almost drowned by her distress that she's not old enough to put on her own jacket and go outside. Her mother lacks an adventurous spirit though I'd love to be boarding a ship bound for Alaska, come June. Luke won't be home tonight because he's paired with Meg to take dinner to George and help him navigate Netflix to watch a movie. He's been out a couple of nights a week. Luke put the finishing touches on his split pea soup last night. I asked to taste it but he told me it was for George and Merle.

"I want them to have leftovers. I can make it again."

But he won't. Luke cooks about once a month and that is usually a Sunday breakfast. Suddenly he's perusing Epicurious online to find recipes. I eat a lot of sandwiches for dinner, usually at my computer. The Calvano family life. Tim tells me to bring Natalie over and he'll make us dinner but I've never done that and it's snowing hard. She has a memory and her vocabulary, though limited, is growing every day. Until I sort out Tim's role in my life, I don't want Natalie to develop a relationship with him. I don't have any coverage at night other than Luke and he either assumes I'm handling it or he's off being a good neighbor. His brief interlude of involved fatherhood appears to be over. I don't even know if he still goes to therapy. That topic is in the category of *Things We Can't Talk About* like Serena, Dom, England, any of his former lovers, and his breakdown. He's gone back to being the Luke I know, efficient and emotionally unavailable.

I started back with Dr. B-S, every other week. She tells me I'm avoiding the real issue but won't name it. *That's what I pay you for*, I think, but I know it's more than a trick. It's an exercise to get me to reflect. What do I want? What do *I* want? Natalie wants to play in the snow until her hands are frostbitten. She can't know the consequence of too much cold. What do I *want*? I want a partner who is present. I want recreation and a meal I don't have to make myself. Surprise. Love. I tell her that I want love and surprise.

"Have you discussed this with Luke?"

That is kind of like asking your chair if it minds if you sit on it. Luke doesn't listen. He's back to antiheroes and department meetings and volunteering to help George cope. I don't look needy enough.

"He doesn't listen."

"Why don't you make a date with him? He's good with scheduled appointments. Maybe you need to get on his calendar."

Sure. Maybe we can schedule sex except I don't want sex with Luke right now. I've told her about Tim and she didn't judge it.

"That's a tempting offer, especially since you and Luke have a lot of obstacles right now. What do you want long-term from your relationship with Tim?"

I don't fucking know, I want to say. Can't I be like Natalie and just get taken care of? I want a home-cooked meal and adult lovemaking. A vacation. Conversation. Maybe a movie on a winter night.

She thinks Tim is wounded; I know. A sad man obsessed with a married woman. I see him as more together than most anyone in my current sphere. He likes his work, has a decent relationship with his kids and dotes on his grandson. Plenty of women would be interested in a man like that. He chose me, I told myself and then I tell Dr. B-S.

"He was with this woman, Laura, but he is taking a break because he's in love with me. Didn't think it would be fair to her."

"Is it fair to you?"

I look at her in her smart wool suit with the brown leather boots. Is she married? I assume so because of the hyphenated name. Does she ever question the status quo?

"I think he's sincere. He's not trying to force me into anything. He backed off when I said I was trying to work on my family and wanted to support Luke."

"What changed?"

"Luke doesn't seem to put much into it. It's like trying to keep a seesaw level with only one person on it. I can't be a mother and father, professor and counselor. When he started volunteering to help the neighbor whose wife has Alzheimer's, I wanted to scream."

"What did you want to say to him?"

"I think I actually said some of it. I wanted to say are you fucking kidding me? You can't handle your own daughter and you're taking on outside responsibilities," I say.

"What was his response?"

"He gave me some psychobabble about it taking a village and getting out of your own way. He doesn't see that he's detached."

"What if he does see?"

# The Shape of What Remains

I think about this. Was Luke deliberately detaching? I know this pattern because I've seen it before only I'm not depressed now, I'm angry.

"Maybe he's having another affair," I say.

"Do you think he is?"

"I don't know what I think. Tim is thoughtful and makes me feel cared for. Luke is preoccupied."

She tells me to make a date with Luke and write down my questions ahead of time.

"It's okay to ask him directly what you want to know. Does he know about Tim?"

"He thinks Tim is just a friend from my book group. I didn't tell him we slept together twice because I didn't see the point. I told Tim I wouldn't sleep with him again unless I leave Luke."

"Fair enough. I don't see any point in giving him more information than you need to right now," she says.

I'm thinking about a cabin on a cruise ship with a balcony, champagne chilling in a little bucket, the sound the water makes against the hull. It's enough to hold onto, unrealistic as it may be. I'm the same woman who rode roller coasters and made love in front of an open window on the ground floor of an apartment. I miss the wildness even though I love my work and the spontaneity of Natalie. I don't want to hurt Luke. I told Tim I'd let him know before Valentine's Day. He said it isn't a problem because he's going regardless. June. Ten days.

## Chapter 44

"Your father is sick," my mother says in a rare phone call. Bridget isn't a fan of intros.

My father, Lewis Brennan? I assume she's talking about my biological father, the one I haven't seen since I was fourteen. At first, he sent a birthday card every year, usually with fifty dollars. After I went off to college, the cards stopped. Bridget told me he remarried a Canadian woman and moved to Vancouver, just north of Washington State.

"He has cancer. His wife called me because she didn't know how to get in touch with you. Your sister Lena is on her way."

"What kind of cancer?" I ask this not because I give a shit but because I know Bridget wants to tell me. It's her kind of game, spreading bad news about others that she doesn't have to feel, just disseminate.

"Prostate. I know that's common but his is the bad kind."

There's a good kind? *We're sorry to tell you it's cancer but don't worry. It's the good kind.*

"The kind that is fast-growing, inoperable," she says.

"Is he getting treatment?"

"I don't think so. Did you know he had another kid with Paula years ago?"

How would I know this? I have a half sibling in Canada?

"I haven't heard from him since I graduated high school."

"He's not good at keeping in touch."

Understatement of the month, kind of like saying that a mass murderer isn't good at anger management.

"The kid is twenty-five. Paul. Smart, Lew says. In grad school."

"Not sure I can get away. I never even heard from him when Serena died."

"He probably didn't know."

"You're in touch with him and you didn't tell him that his granddaughter died?"

"In touch is an exaggeration. He knows how to reach me because we bought the Vineyard house together."

Yeah, and you took it and everything else you could get your hands on in that years-long divorce. I remember.

"When was the last time you heard from him?"

There is a long pause at the other end of the line.

"I guess a week or so ago. We've been talking a little more regularly since we're getting older. Lena has been to visit him a couple of times and Emilie and Mariah have met him."

"So, when exactly were you going to tell me? Why didn't you just wait until he died?"

"I know how you are, Teresa. You would hold a grudge that I didn't tell him about Serena. There was nothing any of us could have done so why be the bearer of bad news?"

"Isn't that what you're doing now?"

"He isn't dead. I thought you might want to see him before he is," Bridget says.

"Oh, I see. She was dead so supporting me would have been useless. I'd be over it in a little while. It's taken me over eleven fucking years to get back to life, Mother."

"You know I hate it when you swear, Teresa."

"Sometimes there's no other way to get you to listen, Mother," I say, suddenly aware that I'm pacing at an aerobic speed and Natalie, still in her high chair eating egg and toast is staring at me and staying unusually quiet.

"I'm sorry I didn't tell him but you haven't exactly been in a good place. You have no interest in my life. I finally became a bridge life master last week but I didn't bother to call you because you wouldn't care," she says, her voice trailing off.

Got that right. I don't give a rat's ass about your tournaments or Dr. Arnie Grayson. I don't need any more postcards from countries you visit. You didn't even send a card when I finally finished my Ph.D. As Luke said, any mother would be proud to have me as a daughter. Any mother except Bridget Brennan. My child died. My other children are flourishing but you haven't even met Natalie. Wyatt made Dean's list. I'm in line for a full-time teaching position in the fall. Are any of these events slightly interesting to you?

"Congratulations, Mother," I say, before I can stop myself. Getting on Bridget's bad side has serious consequences like the time she stopped speaking to me for two weeks because I ruined her Manolo Blahnik shoes when I borrowed them for the eighth-grade dance and wore them in the rain. I had no idea they were anything special. I liked them because they were two-tone and went with my retro dress. I had yelled into the next room to ask if I could borrow shoes and she said, yes.

Something about brown ones. The shoes had brown in them. How was I to know that Bridget spent $900 on a pair of beige and brown shoes with a chunky tapered heel? The moratorium on speaking was only part of her revenge. She also bleached my favorite jeans, removed all the books from my room, and cut off my allowance for six months. I can only imagine the divorce proceedings. All I remember is that when it was over, my father disappeared and my mother sold everything he left behind — except of course, the Vineyard house, the Acura, and his extensive wine collection.

How the hell can I get away? I don't have a break until March and even though I have Fridays off, Vancouver is across the country. Not exactly a weekend trip.

"It's up to you, Teresa. I never could get you to do anything. I mean I offered to pay to have your hair styled properly for your wedding but you insisted on that ratty look. I even told you that I'd pay for a facelift when you had that change-of-life baby so you wouldn't look like a grandmother at all those school functions."

I pick up the pace so I'm almost jogging through the living room and the kitchen. Natalie stops eating.

"Okay. I get it. We're different. Thank you for reminding me. I have to get Natalie changed and get to work. Bye." I disconnect before she has a chance to respond. Overdose on Bridget is bad for my health. Already my heart is pounding and I need another application of antiperspirant.

"Mama," Natalie puts out her arms to signal she's done.

"I'm done too, Nat." I kiss her egg-stained cheek.

When I text Luke, he tells me he'll call back in fifteen minutes when I'm on my way to drop off Natalie.

Lewis Brennan. I remember his sandy hair and a belly that spilled over the top of his belt. He worked a lot, some kind of computer job that made a lot of money. He also invested well which Bridget gloated over when her attorney told her she'd be a rich woman. Bridget had proclaimed loudly to friends that he was sleeping around. She doesn't want me to say the word *fuck* because it's low class but I overheard her phone calls.

*That bastard is sleeping with that woman from Briggs and Waterton. Can you believe it? Not the first time. I'm getting the best damn lawyer in Massachusetts. He's going to pay for this humiliation.*

I wonder what made him choose her. Surely there were less self-centered, kinder choices out there for a wealthy, decent looking guy. My mother had a great figure and kept herself primped. Manicures, hairdresser. When she hit fifty, she had a facelift so her cheekbones rivaled Katherine Hepburn's. At sixty, she had porcelain veneers put over her teeth so she looked like a model in a toothpaste commercial. How do I know this? Periodically Bridget offers suggestions on how I can improve myself.

Why did she tell Lena before she told me? Lena lives farther away even though it's the same country. She's not near anything; about fourteen hours from us and far from Halifax where she could get a flight. The only advantage is airport security since she has a Canadian passport. Lena also lives on the edge of poverty, having shunned Bridget's materialism in a big way. Maybe Bridget bought her guilt tickets. I'm sure she'd offer to pay for mine since she views the life of an academic as forced poverty. I could try to get writing center coverage on a Monday. A dying father is a legitimate excuse. If I left Thursday after class, I'd have four days. I did this for Nigel, a man who didn't contribute any DNA. I'm curious. Will I recognize inflections, habits?

## The Shape of What Remains

What about my half-brother Paul? He's twenty years younger, the same age difference between Natalie and Wyatt. He might have been friends with his nephew, and gotten to know Serena. I'll have to bring Natalie and I want to show her off. She's striking with those blue eyes and dark hair. Maybe her wildness is a Brennan trait.

Luke calls me back and I fill him in.

"You have to go, Tess. I'll go with you."

He has Fridays off too. For him, a day off for a dying father-in-law, even one he's never met would be justifiable. He returned with tenure intact. I don't want to test the fragile thread of stability in my life.

I hadn't considered Luke going with me but the more I think about it, the better it seems. We can pretend to be a healthy couple, doting on our toddler.

"We should tell Wyatt and give him a chance to come as well."

I didn't think of that either. Of course.

He suggests we leave on Thursday, come back on Tuesday.

"What about my classes?"

"This is a family emergency. They will understand. Put your assignments online and the students can complete them while you're gone. Do you want me to look for flights? I have a break for the next hour."

I slip into the last parking space that isn't a long walk. It's freezing out. The department will understand. I'm just new at this and afraid to test the one certainty I have. At least it's my second semester back and I've received good feedback on my performance.

Luke is right. Gerry Dillman tells me to take as long as I need.

"When my mother had breast cancer, I had to work a modified schedule but it was so important for us to have the time together. You can't get that time back, Tess."

As soon as those words are out of his mouth, I can hear that he regrets them. He watched me go from a competent professor to a weeping mess who forgot class times and office hours.

"Do what you have to do. We'll cover it. Luke is going with you, right?" Gerry says.

"Yeah. Wyatt and Natalie too."

"You can ask the tutor to cover the writing center. Don't worry about the classes."

"Thank you," I say.

"You know we're here for you."

Lewis Brennan, absent father who flew away to rewrite his life story. Bridget got him financially but he might have been the winner in the long run by extricating himself. I don't know why he had to cut ties with his children and grandchildren but I do understand the concept of a fresh start. I've been looking for one around every corner — new town, new job, new man. Serena peeks out when I go to wake a sleeping Natalie. I expect a blonde head and find a dark one and then I circle back to the present, grateful for the way she is teaching me what is possible — fistfuls of snow, chaos, love.

# Chapter 45

There is no snow on the ground with the temperature comfortably in the forties. I could like this kind of winter. Wyatt is making faces at Natalie who is wide-awake in her rented car seat. She's chattering, pointing to a cityscape of buildings. *Bye bye, uptie* (her word for something tall), *geen* (for green). She calls Wyatt *Ayatt*. Luke is *Papi* and Bess is *Nomi*. I'm *Mama* and she says that clearly and regularly now. Every day she seems to learn a new skill or short phrase like *all gone* or *go bye bye*.

We pull down a street when the phone directs us. The street is filled with boxy houses, mostly ranches and bungalows. It's a gray house with an old Toyota pickup truck in the driveway. Though there's a definite city feel, we passed a turnoff for Crescent Beach. I'm hoping we'll have time to explore. We also saw mountains, which always make me feel small.

Wyatt takes Natalie out of her car seat and passes her to me.

"Bop," she says and I dig out her plastic cup and fill it with the milk I bought at the airport.

What's the protocol for a visit to a dying man? When Dom had his heart attack, no one had a chance to say goodbye. We had seen him the weekend before for brunch and then we got the phone call. Bess had discovered him in the garage where he'd gone to find some WD-40 to lubricate a squeaky door. By the time she called 911, they were unable to resuscitate him.

A young man in a Simon Fraser University sweatshirt answers the door.

"You must be Teresa. I'm Paul." My half-brother smiles at me and bends down to say hi to Natalie.

"Thank you for coming."

Luke and Wyatt introduce themselves and he leads us into a sunny kitchen where there are platters of salad and Indian food set out on the center island.

"People have been dropping off food. Why don't you eat something? Beverages are over there. I'll join you and we can catch up. Dad is sleeping and my mom is taking advantage of the time to go shopping. She'll be back shortly."

I give Natalie a piece of Naan. The aroma of Indian food has awakened my taste buds and I take a plate. Wyatt does the same.

"Why don't I feed Natalie while you eat?" Luke says. "I can wait a bit."

Paul brings us into the living room where they've set up tray tables. Cards line the mantle next to a silver baby cup and a photograph of a blonde-haired boy holding a fishing pole. It must have been Paul. My heart stops at the resemblance to Serena.

"Yeah. I was a blond. Grew darker. Looks like you didn't get that side," Paul nods to Wyatt and Natalie. Luke shoots me a look that feels like a hand on my shoulder. He's seeing it too.

# The Shape of What Remains

"I knew Dad was married before and had kids but he didn't talk about it much. About a year ago he started telling us stories — you and Lena at the beach, how good you were in school. You're a professor, right? That's what I want to do once I finish my Ph.D. Lena has come to visit a couple of times with her kids," Paul says.

"What are you studying?" I'm not that interested but I sense that making him comfortable will also get him to talk about my father.

"Biological Sciences. Dad used to take me out on fishing trips and that's probably how I got into marine life."

"Good place for it. Seems like a beautiful part of the world," I say.

"It is. They say you can ski and golf on the same day. Up in the mountains, there is always snow but it's temperate here. We have beautiful springs and summers. Even the winters aren't as harsh as where you live."

"Yeah. We get snow, especially this winter. My classes have already been canceled twice."

"Dad is pretty emotional right now. He knows he's going to die because he's choosing it. He went through some harsh treatments and he doesn't want to do that anymore. We want to honor his wishes but it's hard on everyone."

A thin man with thick glasses comes into the room and stands next to Paul.

"Jaxon, this is Teresa, Luke, and Wyatt. Oh, and that's little Natalie. Jaxon is my husband. We got married last week because we wanted Dad to be there."

I shake Jaxon's hand. "Are you a graduate student too?"

"Happy to say I'm done. I teach in the English Department. That way I don't have to muck around on boats and pick up slimy creatures."

"Teresa and Luke are English professors," Paul says.

"Really. What are the odds? As my father-in-law says, one English professor is one more than is needed. I teach graphic novels, digital media, and whatever else they throw at me."

We tell him briefly about our work while Paul checks on Lewis.

"Still asleep," he says when he returns. "We have dessert but you probably want to hear more about the family. Mom should be home soon. I see a resemblance — in the cheekbones. Your kids look more like Luke," he says.

Except for Serena, the invisible child standing next to us. I think of the chalk silhouette the police drew on the road. A paper doll, legs splayed, hair matted with blood. One dimensional.

"We lost a child, a blonde like you." I pull out the worn photo that lives in my purse.

"Wow. That could have been me as a kid," he brings it over to the mantel photo and sure enough, they definitely look like siblings.

"What happened?"

Luke shoots me a *why the hell did you have to bring this up* look but it's too late. Serena has been invited to this gathering whether he likes it or not. She's probably wishing they'd put out desserts or someone would show her the beach.

"Hit and run. Right in front of our house. Six years old."

"God, I'm sorry." Jaxon is standing next to Paul nodding. "That's awful. How long ago?"

"Over eleven years. That's why there's such a big age difference between Wyatt and Natalie. Anyway, I brought it up because you look so much like her in that photo."

"Does my father know? He never mentioned it."

"No. I didn't even know my mother was in touch with my father. We don't have much contact."

# The Shape of What Remains

"Dad said she was pretty controlling. I guess she stuck it to him in the divorce. He finally took her back to court ten years ago so he could stop paying alimony."

"That's good. She doesn't need the money. She has a rich boyfriend and the house your father bought on the Vineyard is worth millions now. Why didn't your father get in touch?"

"He told me he tried to reach you a bunch of times but the letters would come back stamped *wrong address*. Did you move?"

"We moved twice after Serena died but we've been in Northbrook for a while now. That's strange."

"He probably addressed it to Teresa Brennan. I don't think he knew your married name."

No one in Connecticut knows my maiden name. I left it behind along with lunches, manicures, and conversations about my shortcomings. Even if I divorce Luke, I'm Teresa Calvano forever. All my published work is under that name.

"Too bad we lost those years," I say, though with the Internet, it's hard to believe he couldn't have found me.

A heavyset sixtyish woman comes in with a bag in each hand.

"More bags in the car, Mom?"

"Yes. Thanks, dear. You must be Teresa. Paula," she sticks out her hand. Jaxon takes the bags from her. "I'll put these away. You sit and visit. Do you want some lunch?"

"In a few minutes. How is he?"

"Still sleeping. Morphine knocks him out," Paul says.

She turns to me. "The pain started up last week so they put him on some strong painkillers. Hospice is coming twice a week."

I introduce Luke and Wyatt, who is holding Natalie. She's been good, still chewing on a crust of bread and playing with the toys Wyatt has pulled out of our *Entertain Natalie* bag.

"You must be about the same age as Paul," she says.

"Almost twenty," Wyatt says.

"Paul just turned twenty-five. Did you meet Jaxon? We had a little ceremony last week. Lew was having a good day, even proposed a toast."

When Paula comes back, she sits next to me.

"I know you've probably heard all sorts of things. I'm not saying your father is a saint but he's been a good husband and father. What do you remember?"

I tell her about the Christmas stories he'd make up, starting with *The Night Before Christmas* and adding verses. I remember him yelling at me to turn my music down but he loved a good Rock 'n Roll song and he was my Led Zeppelin and Janis Joplin connection. *Don't ever get into drugs, Terri. Janis and Jimi did themselves in. Big loss.* I don't tell her how Janis still guides me though I recently made that connection to my father. He liked fishing and had a little boat on the Vineyard. Sometimes I went with him. Lena used to get seasick which is ironic since her husband is a fisherman. My mother wouldn't clean the fish or eat the stripers or blues we caught. She preferred fish in restaurants or in neat packages in the grocery store. If my mother was away, he'd clean the fish on the picnic table, brush them with butter and throw them on the grill. I can still taste the buttery salt of it. He'd take us to watch the sunset at Menemsha and then we'd stop for an ice cream cone. Once he woke me up and we went to the beach to watch the sunrise.

Once I start reminiscing, the memories flood back in. He smoked a pipe, had a slight belly, favored pastel polo shirts. No one except my mother and father has ever called me Terri. My mother said he wanted a boy and they were going to name him Terrence. I guess he finally got his boy. There was a woman he'd visit, Joyce something. Joyce lived in Edgartown during the summer and in Cambridge the rest of the year. My father's company did business in Boston and he was often traveling there.

"How did you meet?"

"Lew was working in Boston and I had a scholarship to Northeastern. I grew up in a rural town and thought it would be good to try a city. I'd only been to Seattle and New York. Once I finished, I went to grad school for art history and was able to extend my stay. Lew was there about three days a week." she says. "He wasn't divorced yet but they were separated. He told me he'd be poor when it was all over and he was right about that. I got the job in a museum in Vancouver and we moved here. We married as soon as his divorce was final. He loves it here. Used to take Paul fishing which probably sparked his interest in marine science."

"Seems like a beautiful place," I say.

I'm thinking about lost time, how Serena never met the grandparent who might have taken her fishing. Wyatt goes occasionally with Ira and Bess and I suppose Natalie will join them when she's old enough if Bess and Ira are still able.

"We can't complain," she gets up to bring her plate in the kitchen.

I can see her through the doorway, talking to Paul. When she comes back, she puts a hand on my arm.

"I'm sorry about your daughter. Can I see the photo?"

I pull out the photo and she puts a hand over her mouth.

"Uncanny how much she looks like Paul at that age. Must be the Brennan genes."

Natalie wanders over to Paula and she smiles.

"Hey. Want some ice cream?"

Natalie knows exactly what she's talking about and takes her hand. They return with a little bowl and Paula tucks a towel into the top of Natalie's shirt.

"If she's anything like Paul at that age, she'll be wearing as much as she's eating."

Jaxon comes over to tell us that Lewis is awake.

"It's better if you go in one or two at a time."

"Don't worry about the little one. I'll entertain her," Paula says.

I take Luke's hand and he nods. Jaxon leads us down the hallway to a large room that was probably a study. There is a hospital bed, a few tables, a flat screen television, and a bookcase. He's propped up with pillows. Jaxon has brought him a bowl of chocolate ice cream. The first thing that strikes me is how thin he is. I remember his round face and a belly that protruded under shirts. His face is almost gray but his hair is mostly sandy-colored with some white strands. He wears bifocals and has a paper and the book *On Being Mortal* by Atul Gwande on the night table. I read that book last year. Although I know he's not much older than Bridget, he looks about eighty.

"It's Terri. All grown up."

I walk toward the bed. There's a chair next to it so I sit, not knowing if he's hard of hearing and it would be good to be close. I don't know whether or not to kiss him but decide against it, and put a hand on his bony shoulder instead.

"Good to see you again. Been a long time."

"Yeah. Too long. I tried to stay in touch but your mother wasn't helpful. She considered you and Lena part of her divorce settlement."

That sounds about right, using us as leverage with the court, not because she had any reservations about his skills as a father but because it was a way to hurt him.

I tell him about what happened to Serena, and her resemblance to Paul. When I pull out the picture for the third time, he scrutinizes it.

"It's uncanny. I am so sorry you went through this and I wish I had gotten a chance to know her. I understand you have another daughter, a little one. And a grown son."

I introduce Luke and my father smiles.

"Good-looking guy, Terri. Looks Italian."

Luke squeezes his hand. "Half Italian, half Lithuanian," he says and my father laughs.

"Mixed up like the rest of us," he says. "Doc thinks I've got maybe one or two weeks, maybe three if I'm lucky."

I'd forgotten this about my father, no subterfuge, just facts. Bridget liked to muddy issues but I remember his directness and I have emulated it without ever attributing it to him.

"I'm not so lucky though. Well, maybe a little lucky. Good son, found my daughters, and I'm about to meet some new grandchildren. And Paula is a gem. I searched all over for a woman like that — at least all over Boston. Didn't plan to marry again but she made me an honest man. No regrets. Do you still like fishing?"

I tell him that we don't live near the coast but I've gone out with Bess and Ira. I explain briefly about my mother-in-law.

"Next best thing to a good mother is a good mother-in-law. God knows you got the short stick with your mother," he says.

He tires easily so Luke leaves and I bring in Natalie and Wyatt. Wyatt stands there awkwardly. He's never been at a deathbed and he doesn't know this man.

"You're a nice-looking guy, like your father. I'll bet you're a computer whiz or something." He knows this because we told him.

"I like computers," Wyatt says.

"I was a computer engineer. Did you know that? We could have built our own system together or designed programs. Of course, when I started, computers were the size of that bookcase. I was sad to retire though. Technology changes all the time and it's exciting."

"Yeah. I like programming and creating apps and stuff."

My father has an iPhone on the table next to him and a laptop on one of the other tables. He's obviously more computer savvy than Bridget or Bess. I wonder if he could have helped me with my computer woes.

"I hope you stay in school. Lots of good jobs out there in computers. Got a relationship?"

"Kind of."

My father doesn't press him.

"We're going to talk again. I get tired easily but I'm better in the morning. You come by tomorrow morning, young man and we'll do some playing around on the computer."

Natalie is beginning to whimper. She's been sitting too long and is ready to climb or run. She's socialized just enough to know not to do that when there's a houseful of people in her way. Ice cream is no replacement for a good run on the playground or *paygo*, her word for it.

I bring a flailing Natalie over to the bedside.

"What have we here? Restless one. Wild, like her mother." He winks at me. "You never could sit still, Terri, always fidgeting. Long car rides were the worst. Are we there yet? Can't we stop for a picnic? You loved the boat though, would dive off the edge and go swimming even when the water was freezing. You'll have to get her swimming. You started when you were about three."

I had thought of signing Natalie up for *Mommy and Me* swims at our community center.

I pass Natalie to Wyatt. "Yeah. I'm going to take her. She already likes water but she's a handful — no fear."

"Good to be fearless," he says. "I let fear control a lot of my life. Don't make that mistake. As far as we know, we only get one spin. Might as well have it full of adventure."

I don't mention Serena and how her death made me afraid of traffic. I began to see danger in everything. Natalie won't put up with it though. She's determined to move in the world at her own rhythm and although it's my job to keep her safe, I now recognize that it isn't my job to pass on unreasonable fear.

Lewis is getting tired. Paula comes in with water and his pills. We promise to return in the morning. Our hotel isn't far away and we have four more days to get to know this man, my father.

"He's different," Wyatt says. "I expected an old man and he is one but he's a lot cooler than Grandma Bridget. He knows about computers. How come we never met him before?"

I tell him about the divorce and my mother's attempt to keep him away from us.

"Adults are really fucked-up sometimes," he says. I put my finger on my lips to alert him that Natalie is listening.

"Yeah. Who knows her motivation? Sad, we lost those years," I say.

After Wyatt goes to his room, Luke turns to me as he wheels our luggage into our room.

"I see a lot of your father in you."

"I wonder what..."

He shushes me, pulls me over to the bed and puts his arms around me.

"This is the part where we make up a different ending," he says.

I'm not sure what he means. Everything I thought about my family of origin is now in question with the introduction of Paul and Jaxon, and the realization that my father isn't the callous man I made him out to be. So many lost years. I lean on Luke's shoulder and he kisses the top of my head.

"We can't waste any more time," he says.

I think he means that being in the presence of the dying makes it more urgent to live the way we want to live. Unlike Serena, Lewis is making a choice to forgo treatment and go on his own terms. What choices can we make about the way we live in the months to come?

We separate with the knock at the door.

## Chapter 46

Wyatt is standing there shaking and we pull him inside.

"Maisie is in the hospital. Car accident."

Neither of us knew he was still seeing her.

"She's at Hartford Hospital. Broken collarbone, maybe internal stuff. I have to get back," he says.

We pull him onto the edge of the bed and put our arms around him.

"She works the late shift at the All-Night Store. I told her that's when all the crazy people come in. Anyway, this guy was hanging around and waited for her after her shift. She got in her car and drove too fast so she lost control and hit a tree. Her sister called me."

Working a late shift at a convenience store isn't the safest job. There seem to be an inordinate number of robberies.

"She called the police before she left. They just didn't get there in time," he says.

Couldn't she have waited inside until the police arrived? I remember thinking that the end of a shift was literal. Once a man hung around at the restaurant I worked at on the Vineyard. I grew more

284

panicked as the end of my shift loomed. Finally, I told one of the older servers and she asked him to leave, walked me to my car.

"You gotta be direct with these assholes. You come to me, Teresa, I'll tell them to fuck off," she said, rolling up her pink apron and lighting a joint.

It's eleven o'clock here, which makes it two in the morning back home.

"We can't do anything tonight," I say. "Why don't you get some sleep and call early in the morning? If you get up at six, it will be nine there. You should have some answers by then." Wyatt heads back to his room.

"Sometimes I think it's amazing that any of us are still standing," Luke says. "So much damage."

I nod. "I don't want to leave. If Wyatt needs to go, we could put him on a plane and Bess can pick him up. I need to stay the whole time."

"Yeah. I'm staying too."

We fall asleep with our clothes on, waking up at four in the morning to Natalie, on Eastern Standard Time, ready to eat.

By the time we've fed Natalie, showered and dressed, Wyatt knocks on the door.

He looks like he stayed up all night.

"She's doing okay," he says. "They're discharging her today. She has to wear a sling for six weeks and can't work or drive for a while."

"What do you want to do?"

"I guess I'll stay. I talked to her this morning and she thinks I should. She'll be back at school next week."

I can't turn on the news without seeing bodies from some bombing or rampage. It is the role of parents to balance protection with a healthy dose of realism. Wyatt remembers the day Serena died though he wasn't home because the Oakhurst School was K-2. He was in third grade and going to Robert Monteith School where the bus picked him up twenty minutes earlier. I'm grateful for that district oddity because it saved him the permanent image of Serena's battered body lying in the road, the *Dora the Explorer* lunchbox strangely intact and upright. I didn't even think to call his school. Luke did it, sitting on the stool at our breakfast nook, calling Bess first, then Wyatt's school. After Bess got there, she took over with the calls, cradling both of us. She managed to put out food and make arrangements that neither of us could possibly consider. She even picked out Serena's favorite dress to bring to the funeral home before we decided she should be cremated. I couldn't bear the thought of her rotting in the damp ground. A broken collarbone is a minor injury. I know this because my high school boyfriend broke his playing soccer. Maisie will recover, graduate UConn, stay with Wyatt or break up with Wyatt. This particular crisis has no bad ending. The sequel may show the return of her stalker or more reckless driving. I don't know if she'll stick around long enough for us to have an awkward moment with her parents, part of that posse of neighbors who lost interest in my extended grieving process.

I call the house to make sure everyone is up and we won't be imposing if we arrive by nine.

"We've been up for hours," Paula says. "He sleeps in shifts so we take shifts staying up with him. Paul did the last one. He's gone back to his apartment to take a nap."

We have breakfast at the hotel and Natalie tries a waffle, stuffing a huge portion into her tiny mouth, syrup dripping onto her shirt. I cut up the rest of the waffle and dab at the sticky mess.

"You okay?"

Wyatt nods. "Didn't sleep much." He takes a swig of the coffee.

When we get there, there are cars parked outside. Paula lets us in.

"Pot of coffee and water for tea," she points to the kitchen.

A small crowd of people we don't know are gathered in the living room.

"Friends," she says, and introduces us. "He's awake, wants to see Wyatt to talk about computers."

While Wyatt heads in, everyone fusses over Natalie. She's just learned that she can get a reaction by smiling or pouting so she's playing to the audience. We've already decided to head to the natural hot springs in Harrison tomorrow. It's only a couple of hours away so we can leave after the morning visit. Paula prefers to keep the evenings for just the immediate family and I know we're not included in that group. My father can't handle too much company.

Would I opt to have painful treatments to prolong the time with loved ones? I know it's an act of courage to choose death. I've talked about this with Tim many times. After his initial shock and anger, he came to view Chantal's suicide as both courageous and loving. My father deserves to be the one to make the decision but I'm not sure I'd do it. Life is paper thin, easily burned or crumpled. There is a certain allotment of heartbeats, a finite number of times to make love.

When Wyatt comes out, he's animated.

"He knows about AI, hackers, the dark web, and other stuff. He used to find security loopholes."

Paula tells him that Paul and Jaxon will be over soon and they want to show him around town. Wyatt turns to us.

"Great," I say. "We'll probably be here until the afternoon and then we can all meet up."

I haven't told him about tomorrow yet. I get the text from Tim while I'm waiting for the visiting nurse to finish up with my father.

## The Shape of What Remains

*Thinking of you. Hope you find the missing pieces.* There is a photo of a mountain somewhere I don't recognize.

I hadn't thought of my life of missing pieces but now I can see it. Lewis will not live long enough to fill in all the gaps or answer the questions I want to know. Was he a serial philanderer like my mother said? Paula said he was no saint but a good husband and father nonetheless. What constitutes goodness? Does it work on a percentage basis like grades? I achieved about ninety percent of the time but there was always ten percent *I don't care* in the mix. Wyatt seems to be the same with this. He makes Dean's List but not with a 4.0. When I go in, my father is on the computer, which is on a little table that pivots so he can use it from the bed.

"Terri. Not sick of me yet?"

"No. Back for more," I say. Maybe the questions I want to ask aren't the ones I should ask. Maybe there are no answers for what I want to know — why didn't he try harder to find us? Why didn't he fight for custody?

"Wyatt is talented. He understood everything I showed him and even showed this old dude a few things. You must be proud."

"Yes," I say, wondering if Wyatt knows that.

"He said he was at school when his sister was killed."

"Yeah. He had an earlier bus. He's lucky not to carry that image," I say.

"I'd imagine. Poor Terri. My worst fear was always losing one of you but I did it anyway by leaving. I'm not a strong man. Bridget could run me over with that tongue of hers."

"Why didn't you fight her?"

"No one wins in a fight, Terri. The victor is the last one standing but that's not winning. It's a test of endurance and I wanted to live, not endure. I was wrong not to fight for you and Lena but I wasn't wrong to leave. I just didn't think I could have both freedom and my kids, and freedom won."

"Couldn't you have found us on the Internet? It isn't hard these days and you did this for work."

"I did find you eventually. Lena is another story. She has a wacky off-the-grid life and her husband is a conspiracy theorist. No Internet for them. You were easy to find; published papers, Ph.D., academic appointments," he says.

"So you knew where I was and didn't try to contact me?"

"I didn't say that. Took some sleuthing to figure out the Calvano part. I was sending letters to Teresa Brennan and they came back. Once I found your married name, I figured at first that you would be too mad to want to hear from me. I remembered your temper. The diagnosis gave me the push I needed. Paula doesn't know any of this. My online life is separate from our relationship."

I sat down hard on the office chair next to the bed.

"Isn't it better to deal with anger than to lose part of your family?"

"I hate conflict. Had fifteen years of it with your mother and that's enough for two lifetimes. When I have strong feelings, I shut down. It was hard to even work after I left. I spent years in a funk. Paula is the one who pulled me out of it, got me back to life. I used to cry when I saw a father with daughters on the T or riding on those stupid duck boats in Boston Harbor. I tried to reason with Bridget a few times but she had this high-priced lawyer who said I exposed my daughters to a lurid lifestyle by having affairs. Yeah, I had an affair. You probably remember Joyce. Not proud of it but there wasn't any love in the marriage."

"I don't remember much about Joyce except you met her a few times when I was with you. I thought she was a friend and I guess later I kind of got it," I say, remembering my father looking at Joyce and giving her a short kiss goodbye.

"It's easy to have regrets now that I'm a dying old guy. Messed up lots of things but I brought up a good son. Knew Paul was gay when he was about twelve and he came out to us at fourteen. Paula had a hard time with it because she's Catholic but she's come around. You know losing my daughters was the biggest tragedy of my life. There wasn't a day I didn't think about you and Lena. Not one day." He points to a box on top of the bookcase, tells me to bring it over.

A photo of the three of us on the boat, Lena in braids and my hair blowing wildly. Me holding a striper. A report card from second grade. *Excellent reader, too chatty in class.* A piece of fishing line, shells and beach glass and a silver ball with a chime in it that my father gave me when I was ten. I thought I'd lost it. Father's Day cards and letters. *Come downstairs at 9:00. We're making breakfast.* A certificate to wash his truck. We keep the lives we lost in artifacts. Luke donated Serena's clothes and toys but I secretly saved the stuffed monkey she loved, cards and notes, a purple dress, bracelets and collected rocks. There is a shoebox of these artifacts in the far reaches of every closet of every house.

"I want you to know I never forgot you," my father is crying. I lean over and give him a half hug. He's so bony I can feel his collarbone and I'm reminded of the parts of all of us that can easily break.

"There is a letter on my computer that I'll have Paula send you when I'm gone. It's long —added to it over the years. May fill in some of the gaps, answer questions this old man might not remember in the few days you're here."

We sit quietly and I think about the blue stone Serena gave me. I attached a kind of power to it because she touched it. Her DNA was on that rock and everything else she owned. I'm here and my father gets to close the circle.

"I'm dying. You get to live and raise Natalie. That's an incomparable gift. What a feisty little girl! Can't regret what I did wrong because it won't do any good. Just wanted to tell you that I never stopped loving you even though I did the wrong thing over and over. Who was it that said life would be simple if it weren't for people? We definitely complicate things. If I could go back, I'd stand up to that bitch, excuse my language."

"If I could go back, I wouldn't have said 'hello' to my neighbor or I would have driven Serena to school that day," I say in almost a whisper.

"Playing it over and over in your head doesn't change the outcome. Power of thinking only goes so far," he says. "Getting tired, Terri. Come back in the morning and bring the little one for a bit. Cheers me up to see that kind of energy."

I kiss my father then go back to Luke in the living room. He's brought in more Indian food.

"Paula has enough to worry about," he says.

When we pick Wyatt up, he's in a better mood.

"They have a great apartment, mountain view. Took me to the university. Paul showed me his lab but his experiments are off limits because they're in progress. You can't change any of the conditions or it skews the results."

He seems to have forgotten about Maisie.

I remember Tim's text and missing pieces. Maybe my father is right and we don't get to do over anything. Tim showed me what was missing with Luke but Luke carries Serena with him, the broken parts of our marriage. When my father opened his box, I remembered with him: *that was the day I caught my first striper*. Luckier than some, less lucky than others. He's dying. I want to bargain for more time, go out on a boat or have had him at my graduation and wedding.

I look at Tim's photo of the mountain. There is snow and a tiny someone at the summit, and I imagine myself there, standing in the thin air waiting for direction but no sherpa or guide in sight, just the wind cutting through my jacket, and ice that makes it hard to stand in one place without slipping.

# Chapter 47

My father doesn't die in a week. Paula says there is something pulling him. I'm not religious but I secretly pray for another Facetime call where he attempts to fill in thirty years for me. We play Scrabble online and I send him pictures — Serena digging in the sand, her first day of school (though I can't bring myself to send any where she's carrying that lunchbox), her last Christmas. He sends me photos from Paul and Jaxon's wedding, and even a few of the Vineyard and his old boat. I save them all in a file I call *Lewis Found*.

Valentine's Day. Luke takes me out to dinner, gives me a single red rose. We actually hire our first babysitter that others in the neighborhood recommend. I remembered Dr. B-S and her assignment to go on a date and write down questions ahead of time.

*Why should I stay with you?*

I have trouble coming up with anything else. Luke still volunteers with Meg though he's slightly more involved with Natalie. He's taking her on Saturday mornings so I can go to the gym and meet a friend for a walk or coffee. Having more female friends is something I neglected for over a decade. Now I treasure the opportunity. My new friend, Adrienne, has a two-year old.

Luke turns off his cell phone, orders champagne.

"To us."

*Why should I stay with you?*

"I've decided that Natalie is going to be a long-distance truck driver," he says.

She's taken to making *vroom vroom* noises to indicate she wants to go for a car ride. We bought her a variety of toddler cars and trucks and she uses them to run over other toys like stuffed animals and foam blocks.

"Scary thought. Diner food, hemorrhoids," I say.

"Rock music. And she'll see the country, develop biceps and triceps from unloading freight."

*Why should I stay with you?*

Luke takes a deep breath. "We need to talk, Tess."

He's going to leave me. I'm trying to decide about Tim and he's beat me to it. Is it Meg? Another graduate student? Is Bronwyn coming to the States? I sip the champagne for courage.

"I need to sleep with you again. The separate rooms aren't working for me," he says.

My bedroom has become my sanctuary. I can watch a movie, read, look at Serena memorabilia or photos on my iPad. Sometimes Natalie snuggles with me on weekend mornings or I talk to my father over Zoom or Facetime.

*Why should I sleep with you?*

"I want to make love again," he drops his voice since the restaurant is full.

"I don't trust you," I say, and it's true.

"I'm not fooling around, if that's what you're asking. Won't say I haven't thought of it and there's no shortage of willing women."

"Is that a threat?"

"I didn't mean it like that. I feel undesirable when you shut me out. In therapy I've come to realize that it's not that. You're shutting me out because you're still angry. It's counterproductive for both of us and I don't think it's good for Natalie either."

*How do you know what's good for Natalie?*, I think. He only takes her on Saturday mornings and it took months for me to trust him with that.

"I'm attracted to you, Tess. Even after all the crap. And we have kids, jobs."

"I know that."

I tell him I'll be right back and duck into the women's room. My phone is vibrating.

*Happy Valentine's Day, Teresa.*

Tim resends the same picture of a mountain with that tiny person who might be me or someone braver or more careless. I power down my phone. I can't go to fucking Alaska with a man I slept with when I was desperate for any human contact. He wasn't there when Serena slithered out of my body and whimpered. He didn't call people to tell them she was gone or scatter her ashes on the waves in Cape Cod. He doesn't come up with professions for the intrepid Natalie who just yesterday tasted cherry juice and smiled as if she'd won the lottery. I don't know who Luke is anymore and I'm not so sure about myself but I'm sure about Alaska.

I go back to the table where Luke has ordered us a house salad for two. He's refilled my champagne glass and there is a small wrapped box by my plate.

"I didn't get you anything," I say.

"Good. You'll owe me."

I open the box to find a gold bracelet.

"Read the inscription," he says.

*The course of true love never did run smooth.*

Midsummer Night's Dream. Lysander to Hermia before all the mischief and complications. A lover's conflict similar to the one in Chaucer's The Knight's Tale where Palamon and Arcite fight over Emily. Luke knows I'll make the connection.

He puts it on my right arm, and kisses my hand.

"But Lysander isn't an antihero."

"Neither am I, love. Just a flawed man trying to navigate the obstacles."

Dr. B-S assigned me to write a list of good moments in my week. This is definitely one of them along with the cherry juice-stained smile on Natalie, my father's surprise rally to live long enough to fill in the gaps and Paul, a half-brother who will visit us this summer with Jaxon.

"I don't know about the room thing. Can we go slowly? Maybe a few days a week?"

"I'll take what I can get but I'm not backing down. We need to connect."

Luke has a citrus spicy smell that used to distract me. When I was finishing my dissertation, he'd come up behind me, lift my hair and kiss the back of my neck. Pretty soon I'd lose my train of thought and the words would seem senseless, like random typing. I don't know how I finished, only that I used the all-night room at the university a lot. I'd come home bedraggled and flushed with accomplishment and he'd have espresso ready.

"She returns from the underworld," he'd say. That was his name for the room with its spartan study carrels and metal shelves of books.

Sometimes I'd put my feet up and he'd massage them, ask me how the paper was shaping up. He'd been through it all, knew about the many rewrites and my upcoming oral defense.

"You'll do fine," he'd say, though I still don't know how I did it when I had a baby and a teaching assistantship. We lived in a small apartment just off campus. Dinner out was a pizza or Thai food to go. We had loans and his Corolla was sputtering and leaking oil. My car needed new tires. When I walked up to receive my diploma, Luke was there with Wyatt and Bess. I was pregnant with Serena.

"Plenty of room in the gown," Luke had said. "Could have twins and it would still fit you."

Serena wasn't a twin; she was singular in her short stay.

My father said he's learned to live in moments; a bowl of chocolate ice cream, the sunset. Paul took him to the beach last week, against the advice of his doctor though hospice was all for it. *Screw that doc*, he told me over Zoom. They got a portable wheelchair and wheeled him to the edge of the parking lot, then Paul and Jaxon lifted him onto a blanket. *Damn cold, Terri, but not the kind of cold you have. My Paula brought so many blankets; they could have buried me in them. Paul brought me a Naughty Hildegarde, got to love a beer with naughty in its name. I had a few sips and they finished it off. That big boy of a sun looked like it would plop right into the water and I thought, that's a reason to be here, isn't it? You remember that, Terri. Don't piss off time.*

I'm not sure what would piss off time but I've come to expect that snow may turn to ice and Natalie will probably break something I care about, maybe tomorrow. Maybe what pisses off time is not using it, assuming that it will always stretch in front of me like the path to the beach on the Vineyard. Tim told me that he loved that my middle name is Penelope because she was the one who kept the home fires burning while Ulysses was out screwing around and wreaking havoc. He didn't say it like that but Ulysses was no saint---like Luke, like my father, like me. When Natalie put both fists in the bowl of chocolate pudding, I didn't rush to stop her, as Bridget would have. I just watched her eat it, paint with it, smell it. That's what I want from life — a do-over. A chance to sit in the muck and not be disgusted, to drink it in before it's gone.

When we leave, there's a scrim of ice on the windshield. We crank up the defroster and heater. It's damn cold, as my father said. Luke turns on the audio and there she is, belting out *Piece of My Heart*. What would Janis do?

"I hope Natalie went to sleep for the sitter," he says.

I visualize her curled up in the crib, stuffed puppy in her hand. I see us opening the door to Luke's bedroom, the one where we made Natalie. Tomorrow is Sunday and Bess offered to take her for a few hours. We had picked out his blue duvet at Ikea, joked that it wouldn't be long before we'd have matching shams and swags on the windows.

I had no way of knowing that my father had died in his bed two hours ago or that Natalie would be sitting up in her crib when we got home, smiling and wide awake. My phone was still turned off, and for twenty minutes we drove home slowly in the icy dark, blasting Janis Joplin and singing off-key.

## Acknowledgements

This book has been many years in process and revisions were impacted by events that happened after I began writing it, most importantly the untimely death of my friend and neighbor's beautiful young daughter, Demi Grace from neuroblastoma. The strength of her mother, Mia, motivated me to research and address the issue of long grief for this story. Compassionate Friends is an organization that offers support to bereaved parents. https://www.compassionatefriends.org

I am deeply grateful to the team at Between the Lines Publishing/Liminal Books—Abby Macenka, Morgan Bliadd, Penny Dowden, and Siân Hyleg. Your belief in my story and your energy in moving forward to publish it is much appreciated.

A heartfelt thanks to my early readers, Raymond Rose, Donna Chase, Christina Peterson, and Mark Stevens. Your observations made me rethink scenes and characters. Christina Peterson helped me to update my characters in terms of gender references and I am grateful for her expertise. I am appreciative of the many people who helped this story along.

My longtime critique groups, Still River Writers and East-West Writers continually challenge me to experiment and take leaps: Charlie Chase, David Morse, Garrett Phelan, Margaret Plaganis, John Suroweicki, Joan Sidney, Claudia McGhee, Gabrielle Zane, Jane Katch, Suzy Lamson, and Pegi Deitz Shea. Thank you, all. Two important members of these groups passed on in 2023—Jim Coleman and Mary Elizabeth Lang. Their contributions will be remembered.

A special thanks to Charlie Chase for our weekly writing support calls. I hope I have returned the favor. Thanks also to David Morse for helping me to make the decision to move forward with this novel. A shout out to Jenn Fox & family for fearlessness on roller coasters.

Mentors matter in life and in writing. One of my role models is Baron Wormser. His ability to write compelling essays, fiction, and poetry continues to nudge me to take leaps and consider what is possible. Thanks also to writing friends who impact my life: Geraldine Mills, Lee Desrosiers, Larry Leinoff, Ellen Meeropol, Ted and Annie Deppe, and Alan McMonagle and Four Corners Writers. If I am forgetting anyone, I apologize. The faculty and students I met at Stonecoast MFA and my writing friends in Ireland and the U.S. continue to shape my life as a writer.

Thank you to Alan Hayes and Arlen House for championing my writing for many years. The concept for this novel and its characters came from my story, *Monuments* which first appeared in my short story collection, *Growing a New Tail*, published by Arlen House in 2015. A segment of that story is used with grateful acknowledgement. The epigraph is from my poem, *Brief Clearing* which first appeared in my poetry collection, *Necessary Silence*, also published by Arlen House in 2013.

My longtime love, Russ, makes everything possible. He read and reread this manuscript and was invaluable with edits, spending long hours reviewing every word. Family members, Kira, Andres, Justin and Christina enrich my life. I credit my incredible espresso setup (thanks, kids) for my productivity. Ames has my heart always. He is a remarkable small teacher whose early love of language regularly reminds me that words have power.

Lisa C. Taylor is the author of three poetry collections, most recently *Interrogation of Morning* (2022), two short story collections and two poetry chapbooks. One of her short stories received the Hugo House New Works Fiction Award. Her collaborative poetry collection, *The Other Side of Longing,* with Irish writer, Geraldine Mills was chosen for the Elizabeth Shanley Gerson Lecture for Irish Literature at University of Connecticut. Lisa holds an MFA in Creative Writing from Stonecoast/University of Southern Maine. She is the co-director of the Mesa Verde Writers Conference and the Mesa Verde Literary Festival. She teaches online for writers.com. Her poems, short stories, and creative nonfiction pieces have appeared in numerous literary magazines in the United States and abroad. Lisa also holds an MA in counseling and previously worked as a counselor and therapist in schools, day treatment programs, and on an inpatient adolescent unit. Lisa once held weekly groups for teenagers who had lost parents. She has long been interested in supporting the process of grieving in our society.